FLOWERS OF DYSFUNCTION

PART ONE

BY

CAROLINE SNOW

FLOWERS OF DYSFUNCTION, PART ONE

Flower Press
Copyright © 2014 by Caroline Snow

Published in the United States of America.

Author website: http://www.carolineesnow.com/

ISBN 13: 978-0692215500
ISBN 10: 0692215506

Jacket Design: *Christopher Ensey*

DEDICATED TO

Bob, the love of my life, my best friend, my soul mate and
to my dear family, especially my mom.

CHAPTER 1

ONCE YOU VISIT Natruna—even one time—you will never forget it. It is unique in a surprising way, maybe even humorous. It is known for its isolation and desolation. It is at the western edge of a dry lakebed at the bottom of a valley. It feels unexpectedly flat, solid, and protected. It sits in the middle of rock-strewn mountains, houses cuddled on the sides of rocky, boulder-covered, sandy hills and in the crevices of mountains. It is covered with a combination of fine and coarse desert sand. There isn't really any green, because the searing heat and highly saline soil kills grass. You would be lucky to have a transplanted salt cedar tree in your yard.

The dry temperatures, which can range from 35 chilling degrees in the winter to 120 scorching degrees in the summer, are also distinctive to this one of a kind town. The low humidity and cool night breezes prevail, as Natruna's relatively high elevation of 1,613 feet tempers the desert heat. When the wind blows, it blows hard, frequent, and sandy.

Carha can still remember how it felt when the wind blew and the sand of Natruna hit her exposed skin, like a million insignificant slaps that didn't really hurt, just irritated. She would have to shield her eyes when out in it.

After arriving home from school or playing outside, Carha would have sand in her hair, in her ears, up her nose, and settled in the corners of her eyes. It left her with a fragrance of staleness, salty, baked skin, and a sort of worn-out feeling. You would think that it would prevent the kids from playing outside, but it never did. That's what they did, their pastime, for hours on end. They didn't have fancy toys, ATVs, horses, or anything of that nature to keep them entertained. They had the miles and miles of desert and one another.

Down in the valley that settled in Natruna, their white rock home sat on the wall of a stony, brown, dust-covered mountain. The small, old, yet hardy home was smothered with Dad, Mom, Margaret (Maggie), Dana, Anna, Carha, and little Billy.

Their little hardy home had five rooms altogether. There was the kitchen, living room, one bathroom, and two very small bedrooms. All of the kids slept on one king-size mattress in one room, and their parents slept in the other. The kids had to rotate their bodies to fit, one with her head facing north, one next to her with her head facing south, and so on.

The cement floors were warm in the winter but felt cool and soothing on the bottoms of their feet during the summer months, thanks to the wall heater and swamp cooler.

You couldn't exactly call Mr. Stone a handyman, although he tried. There was a major plumbing problem that occasionally got their dad's attention long enough for him to work on it for hours, only for it to remain in the exact same condition afterward.

Bill Stone was convinced that when time permitted, he

would repair all of the maintenance issues occurring throughout this small, old home but for some reason, there never seemed to be a good time. And call a professional, *forget it!* He could do it and planned on doing it, eventually.

The bathroom was a bit different in that house, compared to their friends' homes. They had to use a large bucket of water to flush the toilet, and the shower had a big, round hole for the drain. At one time or another, the kids all had that nightmare that they were going to be sucked into the hole along with the water and end up being a part of some mysterious and scary underground world. The house definitely wasn't lacking in character or quirks.

Thank goodness that Mrs. Stone never complained or nagged her loving and devoted husband. She went about her days, content for what they had and was so in love with Bill and her children, nothing else mattered. And really, she adored and appreciated that home. It was the first home that she ever had and she was proud of every strange bit of it.

Rocks of all different colors, shapes, and sizes designed their walls from the inside to the outside. These naturally occurring aggregates of minerals molded a solid, protective layer from the outside. The home had its own unique, musty, earthy smell. It wasn't foul; it was calming and outdoorsy. The kids found it entertaining when their voices bounced off the hardened stone enclosure.

Not only was the inside of their home entertaining but there was plenty to do outside as well, especially growing up with an assortment of desert creatures. They never realized how much the mysterious wondrous life all around them meant and fulfilled them with companionship, until they were away from their hometown.

They never thought it unusual to have a sidewinder living under the front steps of their debilitated porch or that they had to walk over it to get to their front door. Every once in a while, they forgot that it was there until they were completely standing inside of their living room when they remembered and experienced a sudden rush of adrenalin inside of them in knowing that they just walked over a poisonous sidewinder. Their parents tried to relocate him several times, but for some reason he would return to his home under their steps.

All of the Stone children loved animals and had grown to need them in their lives.

They spent hours and hours chuckwalla and lizard hunting. The fun of it was who would catch one first—*if* they could catch one—and what would it look like. The larger the better! It was exciting. Some could be as large as 18 inches in length. They could appear big and mean, but they were harmless and had gentle dispositions. The hunts were challenging and competitions fierce as these large lizards retreated into rock crevices and finding them wasn't at all easy. The notable signs were rock crevices that were large enough for them to slide into and out of easy enough with their long flat bodies. Also, looking for their dried disfigured stringy green-bean like feces above and around their habitats is a tell-tale sign.

It seemed that all Natrunans had the same respect for these desert creatures. Carha never witnessed anyone ever harming or keeping these living beings away from their homes and families. These animals were fascinating but after catching and briefly admiring, perhaps even performing some sort of personal ritual, they were placed exactly where they were found.

The Stones were surrounded by lizards of all sorts. They even found lizards inside of their home which never fazed them in the least bit. Common side-blotched lizards, long-tailed brush lizards, desert horned lizards (which they called "horny toads"), fringe-toed lizards, long-nosed leopard lizards, Great Basin collared lizards, zebra-tailed lizards, and the very rare find known as the iguana lived amongst them, to name a few.

Iguana's could be as long as 16 inches and were rounder than chuckwallas. The kids found the wary, diurnal lizard inside of bushes. They burrowed extensively, and their burrows were usually constructed in the mounds of sand that accumulated around the bases of bushes like creosote. They were the hardest to find and catch.

As mentioned, sidewinders were common as were many other snakes. Natruna was home to king snakes and gopher snakes, which they all learned to recognize and respect. "*Red on black, friend of Jack; Red on yellow, kill a fellow*," this is what their father made them memorize at an early age to help distinguish between deadly coral snakes and nonvenomous look-alikes.

The children held these harmless, docile creatures while they swirled and slinked around in their hands and arms until their dad kindly reminded them that it was time to let them be free again. Who needed toys?

They knew without a doubt the sounds of the rattling rattlesnakes which warned them that a mean bite was waiting for them just feet away.

It was part of the children's unconscious carefully listening as they walked, ran, and jumped from one boulder to the next while playing in the desert. All of the children had a collection of rattles and dried snake skin kept somewhere safe. These were just a few of the many of the treasures found in the desert.

They were never uneasy around snakes; it was just the way that it was. They learned almost at the same time that they learned how to walk the sound and look rattlesnakes.

They had unique broad triangular heads and raised

supraocular scales above their eyes. Bill called these scales "horned eye umbrellas". He said that they help shade their eyes and prevented sand from getting in them when they buried themselves in it.

The kids weren't naïve when it came to the dangers of these deadly snakes living with them. It is a wonder that their mother, Patria, ever allowed them to roam the desert as they did but thankfully, she let them go and never put fear into their heads, only awareness and caution.

Even at birth, rattlesnakes have fully functioning fangs and deadly venom. Their heads can see, flick the tongue, and inflict venomous bites for up to an hour after being severed from the body. That's pretty wicked.

One of Bill's co-workers was bitten while hiking and almost lost his entire foot. The venom killed his tissue and interrupted blood clotting within minutes. He immediately couldn't move or feel his foot and then it spread up his leg. He had hard time breathing and said his foot and leg felt as though it was placed in boiling oil. It took months to recover and return to work.

Word got around and preaching wasn't necessary to remind everyone of the dangers. Stories like his were enough to keep everyone on guard.

Snakes weren't the only perilous critters hanging around. While getting ready for work one morning, and pulling up his pants, their father felt something soft, warm, and mushy in between his pants and his thigh. He quickly dropped his pants, and a huge, fuzzy tarantula plopped dazedly to the floor and began wandering about, confused. It was almost as wide as the length his shoe!

Wild horses and burros, coyotes, foxes, mountain lions, mule deer, bobcats, sheep, porcupines, raccoons, squirrels, skunks, badgers, gophers, mice, rats, hawks, owls, and rabbits to were other named mammals that lived in their hometown.

Cottontails hopped across their yard throughout the days as if it were a path used towards a destination. They always appeared to stop at the same spot to check out their surroundings, maybe to think or rest a spell before continuing on their journey, focused and determined to make it home or to a friend's or a relative's den. The kids always imagined that the rabbits had their own families and social lives too. They were so fascinating and fun to watch, especially when they were followed by three or four little ones. They watched their little ones closely and even waited for them, if needed.

The family spent much of their time with the animals that surrounded them but there wasn't anything more important and enjoyable as the time that they spent together.

One of the kids' favorite pastimes was getting into the station wagon to take one of their drives to explore the desert. The kids were born and raised there, and it seemed like they would have become bored of it. But that never happened. They drove approximately thirty miles north on State Route 175, where they could find desert tortoises on the road or alongside of it. No matter how many times they saw one, they still became thrilled and begged their father to pull the car over so that they could kindly examine that one—because that one had to be more unique than the one before—and Bill always did.

When they were out on their explorations, their parents were always calm, relaxed, and never in a hurry. It was their special time. They told stories and listened to their parents talk about simple things, never anything too serious, keeping the atmosphere joyful and comforting.

The kids had furry pets too through the years. They had a jackrabbit named Henry and a white two-horned goat named Penny. She walked alongside them like she was one of them. She often lay in the front yard with her horizontal, slit-shaped pupils focused on the front door just waiting for one of the kids to come out and play. She went everywhere they went and was just part of the gang.

They had chickens cooped up in the small uneven, sloped backyard that was surrounded by wire. It wasn't somewhere to spend time in since it was somewhat dangerous with sharp rocks sticking out and untamed wires poking out and up every which way. The kids didn't really spend much time out there except to feed the chickens.

One day, Anna decided to go exploring up the hill above the coop when she lost her balance and rolled down the hill, hitting every single rock and weed along the way, until she landed on the barbed wire itself.

She was probably only four years old at the time, but she still had the quarter-inch scar right in the middle of her forehead for years to follow. It bled like a river and scared the tar out of everyone.

You had to be tough to grow up in their desert town.

Their mother didn't leave them much but luckily if anything ever did happen, they had friendly and kind neighbors living less than a mile away on either side. They too had homes built into the sides of the mountains.

Mr. and Mrs. Frances were especially fond of the kids and adored their mother. Mrs. Frances babysat the children on occasion, but it was rare, since their mother almost never left them. She was either at home with them or they were with her wherever she went.

Ella Frances gave Patria a baby shower in the Stone's little home when she was expecting Billy. It was a big deal since they didn't have parties and rarely had people over except for family. There just wasn't any room. Many women from their church attended and brought gifts, even people from the church whom Patria didn't know. She felt so special and honored. After Billy was born, the girls were thrilled to have the little baby boy snuggle with them in their big comfy bed every night like a doll. Their mother stayed home taking care of all of them while their dad worked as a postman.

Margaret was the oldest child. She had long, straight, sandy-brown hair that always draped the corners of her eyes and then settled on her shoulders. It was the early '70s, and none of the kids had bangs and seldom had trims to their long hair. Maggie always wore colorful dresses, as all of the kids did, but Maggie wore them like they were a part of who she was. She carried herself dignified and confident. She was more mature and "girly" than the others. She had a rounder face than the other girls too. She had a teeny crease that vertically dented the tip of her freckled, fair-skinned nose. Her oval-shaped, deep-set blue eyes stood out like the desert skies did in the summertime.

Maggie never smelled funny after playing hard outside in the desert heat like all of the other kids; she smelled like she'd just gotten out of the bath, renewed and flowerlike. She seemed to always have a serious and melancholy way about her, sort of like a grown-up but not.

Maggie always took care of Carha and protected her to no end, but wasn't always so nice to Dana and Anna. It was the opposite at times, as siblings closer in age carry on. She carried Billy around like a baby doll, and he never cried or showed bad temper; he just appeared content like a baby monkey dangling every direction from its mother.

Dana was tougher. She had a skein of chestnut hair and adventurous, golden-brown eyes that held a certain tinge of shyness within. She had thin pink lips but a full-on smile with a strong, freckly, Roman-shaped nose, as all of the kids did; however, Anna's stood out a tad bit higher on her face than did those of the others. Dana was a bit duplicitous and at times uncomfortably quiet. She didn't put up with much. Wasn't mean- just wouldn't take rubbish from anyone. She spent much of her time entertaining herself and Anna by teasing Carha. Anna was Dana's shadow, and whatever Dana did, Anna followed suit. For all of her meanness to Carha, Dana was good to Anna, always impressing her, protecting her, and making her happy.

All of the kids had those freckles that darkened over the summer, which they all despised. Carha dreamed of having flawless, porcelain skin like Robin Mathews, who was the exact same age as she was. Robin also had tons of money and lived on some mysterious ranch in Village Gully that no one could see the inside of, only the fancy gates that sealed off a very long driveway. Carha had a jealousy thing going on with her-that was true.

Carha felt like other kids thought that she was dirty, having those brown spots all over her face. The truth of the matter was that Robin was never mean to Carha—an interesting point since they ended up having a pretty strong emotional connection in the years that followed.

Sweet Anna was innocent, insanely shy, and feminine. For some reason, she resembled their mom in many ways, although these traits didn't really describe their mother. Anna also resembled mother physically. She had small features except for her Roman goddess's nose. She had small, enigmatic, chocolate-brown eyes, and a kind, dainty smile that always slightly favored the right. They all had high, defined cheekbones that they inherited from their Cherokee descent. They all were quite short and small in frame, but Anna's features were more ladylike and petite.

They never went to the dentist until they were in their late teens, but thankfully, they all had straight upper teeth and slightly crooked lowers, and their teeth were nice and white. Anna's smile was one of her finest traits. When she smiled, it was gentle and represented who she was. Anna was a little straitlaced, but tender and sensitive at the same time. Anna wasn't perfect, oh no. When she and Dana were together, they were inseparable, and they were desert demons!

Yeah, they lived in the desert, where it was hot, dry, sandy, dirty, and tough. The heat made the sweat and dirt stick to their skin. They always felt like they were carrying around a shield of protection, as if nothing could hurt them. They never wore shoes, and had to run from one shaded area to the next on scorching days. Their feet were brown most of the time, sadly they sometimes were even black from the dirt. It was part of the whole desert amusement or challenge that kept them busy.

Little Billy was the only boy out of five children. Billy had soft, fine, sandy-colored straight hair and small, squinty blue eyes like their dad's. They all were always asked if they had Chinese in them. While they had nothing against the Chinese, they never took this as a compliment. He was of a smaller build too, short and a little stocky off and on growing up—not fat, just not skinny. He was sweet and cute, and the girls adored him.

Carha felt that her little brother was her best friend. He was her buddy. She was boyish much of the time, and he could be girly to fit in with her and her friends. It worked and was comforting to know that they had one another. Carha really felt like a big sister. She felt protective yet controlling at the same time. Billy was a gentleman, even as a little boy. He didn't have a mean bone in his body, just like their father. He was so much like their dad. Billy was so innocent and even as a young boy never had much of an opportunity to be his own person, meaning that he didn't really have a chance to mature at his own pace.

Carha ... well ... she came out looking like their dad too. Her older sisters had bigger—not by much, but bigger—eyes like their mother, darker, lush hair, and darker, attractive skin that didn't turn the color of a tomato when exposed to the sun. Billy and Carha had the smaller, narrower, lighter sapphire-colored eyes. They were quite an intriguing color on which they often received compliments and probably would receive more if people could actually see them.

Carha had fine, dirty-blonde, straggly hair that appeared to have never been trimmed even though it had been. Strangely, for the first three years of her life, it was platinum blonde. The combination of dirt and freckles truly made Carha feel dreadful. Thank goodness their mom made them bathe every night. They played hard and had all the freedom to thoroughly enjoy the outdoors, but their mom and dad didn't allow any slack when they were presenting themselves.

Carha Stone was the skinniest of them all. Her nickname was "Twig" for years, sometimes "Stick," and sometimes just "Toothpick." She was always a bit uninhibited—maybe at times even forceful—when she wanted something, but she was happy and easy to please. She had to be tough in order to put up with the desert demon's brutal, ongoing torture. (This is an exaggeration, of course.)

The kids fought a lot, but they also held hands, played games, enjoyed meals together, laughed, talked, were affectionate toward one another, and came to the others' rescue in a heartbeat.

For years, maybe until Carha was age six or so, she pulled out strands of her fine, thin blonde hair and wrapped it around her right index and middle finger until they were both well insulated, and then she would suck on them for hours. Afterward, she threw that bundle of hair away and the next day repeated the process. Why, you ask? Can't tell you, but she may have had some issues. Possibly she had some anxiety due to her demon sisters endless pestering, she was sure to have bald patches.

Now imagine a steep mountain at least a half a mile long, with a flat clearing wide enough for maybe a jeep to climb. This was known as Tank Hill, because at the very top of it, there sat a huge Smith water tower. The kids would set off on expeditions up the steep mountains, which sat to the left of their home and was basically part of their front yard too.

Now picture three little kids venturing to the very top of that hill with bicycles in tow, two of the kids placing the youngest and skinniest of the three (maybe only four years of age) on one of the bikes—which didn't have any training wheels—and pushing her down the mountain as they yelled, "Pedal! Pedal!"

Yeah, Carha's sisters were good to her. They were always teaching her things. That day, Dana and Anna were kind enough to teach her how to ride a bike for the very first time without dying and at a high, uncontrollable speed—her little eyes pouring fluids, her mouth bloated, her screams only on the inside. Their laughter echoed all the way down Tank Hill and probably back up to every mountain peak in Natruna.

For all of their roughness, luckily they steered clear of the Hospital Emergency Room which was over a thirty minute drive. There were a few occasions that landed them on outpatient visits to the Natruna Clinic, however.

The kids did like the occasional freedom that took place when Mrs. Frances watched over them. There was something freeing about not having a regular guardian present, as usual. One day, while they were rejoicing by jumping up and down on their parents' bed. Carha was singing prettily into a shiny green crochet hook as if it were her microphone. She was a famous singer and talented, too, up until the hook grabbed hold of a part of her that hung in the very back of her throat known as the uvula (the dangly thing in the back of the throat that many mistake for the tonsils) and wouldn't let go. She pulled and pulled at it, but it wouldn't budge—it just bled.

She learned to meditate on that day. She controlled her breaths while Mrs. Frances tracked down all of the kids, ran to get her husband—who had the car—loaded them up, and finally sped off to town, took what seemed like forever... not to mention the waiting at the Natruna Clinic while the only doctor who worked there finished with his stitches in the next room over.

Dr. Clarkson somehow calmly unwrapped the hook. There was more bleeding involved. At that time, Carha looked over at Mrs. Frances's worried face and thought to herself, "She doesn't look too good." She was as white as a ghost. Carha was trying to concentrate on what Mrs. Frances was about to say when she noticed some small sweat beads splattered over the caring woman's forehead. She began twitching and her eyes rolled back in her head. She looked like she was convulsing and bam; she hit the ground like a sack of potatoes. Carha really thought that she was dead, but she had just fainted. Years later, Carha came to witness firsthand many people fainting, but those are stories for a later time.

Carha's mom was notified and came to drive everyone home from the clinic that day.

Natruna Hospital was located right next to the clinic but had closed down years earlier. Carha was one of the lucky few born in that hospital. It was a small, rectangular, blue ranch-style that still stands to this day. She always felt that she may be a miracle.

There may be benefits to having only one doctor in a town and the same two nurses practically your entire life. It makes one wonder how many privacy laws were broken or how many people pretended to be their friends just to find out all of Natruna's secrets.

There were wonderful and amazing memories for this close family while they were growing up. There was so much love and devotion for one another and the home they cherished not for its structure but for what was encased inside of the stone walls. Most of the memories were easily recalled except for a few. Not until Dana became an adult did she remember.

Burying these memories must have been some sort of disassociation from her consciousness. Who would have known? Not even those who were closest to her knew.

It's speculated that repression may be one method used by individuals to cope with traumatic memories, pushing them out of awareness to allow a child to maintain attachment to a person on whom they are dependent for survival, acceptance, love, and nurturing. That's what has been said about it, at least.

Now that you have a clear picture of these sand-mutated children of the desert, they were all actually cute, well mannered, and well adjusted. This family was extremely close and full of life. Their parents were always complimented, and they were proud of their children in their small town of Natruna, California.

Awe...Natruna...their hometown was like no other town in the world, they were certain of it.

CHAPTER 2

NATRUNA WAS A small mining town where everyone knew everyone else. If you grew up there, you knew every bit of it, every feel of it, and every smell of it. You knew each huge rock, each smaller rock, each water tank, and each old railroad track that traced the only highway to and fro. You even knew whose initials were written on the sides of the two biggest boulders ten miles south of town. Then there was Shark Rock. It was exciting to see it on the left side of the two-lane, semi-curvy highway that led to home. It was shaped like a shark's head and protruded forty feet above everyone as they drove toward their hometown. Years ago, someone drew the mouth and eyes, and there you go—Shark Rock came alive and has been alive for Carha's whole life. You knew every curve, when to accelerate, when to decelerate, and which potholes still needed to be fixed.

Once you passed Shark Rock, you drove approximately five miles and hit the corner where seventeen-year-old Sara Marsh ran off the cliff in her light blue Toyota Celica in 1975. Carha saw pictures of her in the yearbook but never knew her. Every time you hit that corner, you remember Sara and see her yearbook photo, imagining her mom and dad and wondering if her younger sister, Lisa, thinks of her every day. Is her room still as it was? How long was she down there before being found? Did she suffer?

You had to drive thirty minutes to get to the "real town" that had an actual Safeway, Mervyn's, Kmart, and so on. That town was considered prosperous, and Natruna was never good enough for the residents there. They didn't care. Natruna used to beat the shit out of them in football. They were studly, without a doubt. It was to their advantage that the other players never played football on a dirt field like the kids in Natruna had. Yeah, they were cool.

Through the years, many people went off of parts of that highway. Some died, some survived intact, and some sustained permanent injuries. The highway that leads to that small town and leaves it is not just a road; it's a memory lane. You can't drive on it without remembering or pondering life.

You veer to the left after the cliff and smell the old, familiar, satisfying aroma of the mineral plant. The Stones' cousins used to tease them and say that they lived in the "fart town," but to the kids it was a comforting smell: it meant security, money, and food.

The town was divided into sections-mini towns-with different names that separated each by stretches of land without homes or neighborhoods. From one end to the other end of all of Natruna, it would only take you about around twenty minutes, that's how small the town was.

The first part of Natruna was called West Point. A teacher lived in the first house on the left; it was surrounded by an old wooden fence and was hidden from sight, as were many of the other homes. There were some more homes lining streets that were perpendicular to the road. A few older homes to the right side gave Natruna the feel of a run-down mining town.

The Stones never seemed to get close to the kids who lived in West Point, for it was too far to walk and therefore too far to really bond with the kids who lived there. There was a swimming pool known as "the tank." It was really a large, rusty Smith tank filled with freshwater. Its use was restricted to the chemical plant employees and their families or invited guests. It always had algae growing on the bottom, sides, and railing. It felt strange slithering in your hands and between your toes. The water burned your nose if you sniffed it. Your eyes felt thick after opening them underwater, trying to avoid your head ending up between someone's bare legs.

There was openness after continuing past West Point, where you could have a few minutes of daydreaming, just peering out past the railroad tracks or to the left side of the road to view the very close gray hillsides.

Carha loved looking out at the dried-up saltwater lake, its white-crusted coat that, when the sun hit it just perfectly, sparkled like little diamonds. There was some water still out there, but it was always mysterious, since no one was allowed to go to it. The railroad always owned it and kept a watchful eye. Still, she wondered if there were some salty alien fish in there.

It was funny, at times, visitors would drive through town with their boat in tow inquiring about the lake and where it is. It was difficult to watch their reactions when they were informed that it's out there, all 640 acres of the dried up lake...has been for years-like centuries.

Passing West Point and across the railroad tracks, on the right, sat the Greys brown and white ranch style home, right across from the trailer park as you first entered the town known as Argos. Argos was more run-down than any other parts of Natruna. Okay, this deserves an explanation ...

Argos was kind of eclectic—a variety of homes, some big with fences, some small and made of rock, some wood and falling apart. There was a gas station on the left side of town and a grocery store on the right, next to a car dealership, auto shop, and hardware store. There was also a shoe store and restaurant on the left side of the road that led to the dump, but the Stones never went to the restaurant, not once. They visited the shoe store about once a year and the dump; well...they were there a lot.

Then you drove over the tracks before the train came, if you were lucky. Sometimes it seemed that everyone in Natruna would be in line waiting while the red safety rails came down, the dinging of the alarm alerting you that the train was coming, and cars on either side of the tracks, waiting. It was almost bonding, all waiting, watching, and really never minding the train.

Continuing, Circle K was on the left, and the low-income apartments were to the right. A hardware store, rest stop, library, clinic, dental office, post office, police station, theater, liquor store, pizza parlor, another grocery store where you knew every aisle, every shelf like your bedroom. Their dad, Bill, eventually worked in this section known as the "Truna." You knew whose dad or mom worked at which plant and who was whose boss. Some of the kids even felt superior to other kids when their parents were higher up in the small-town plant.

Pioneer was the very last section and where the

school bus went at its fullest. It mainly had homes and not much commercial real estate. It did have the Pioneer store, the best cheeseburger joint in the world, known as the Weeds, and many of the best slumber parties. Oh, and the horse corrals. It was the only place that you could keep horses, cows, sheep, mules, or any other livestock around the area.

Two more important places to note: the Vale Springs Pool ... it must have been one of the largest swimming pools in all of California. The memories there! It was about fifteen minutes north of town and sometimes an absolute challenge to get to. At one time or another, all kids had to wheel and deal to catch a ride to the pool.

Approximately ten minutes past Vale Springs Pool was Village Gully, and it only had twenty-five homes or so. To tell the truth, it was a whole other world to the Stone kids. If you drive past Village Gully, it's advised to take extra precautions, since it's days to the nearest town.

That is the Stones' hometown. Their hometown was a huge part in molding who they are and still remains a part of them today. It gave them unforgettable memories that they would cherish forever.

Natruna ... good or bad, right or wrong, at times even difficult and painful, but treasured nonetheless.

CHAPTER 3

BILL AND PATRIA's relationship definitely evolved after having their family. It truly formed even stronger bonds between them that were extremely intimate and admired by many.

When they first met in 1962, they enjoyed each other's company immensely and became best friends. It was less complex, more relaxed, less stressors. It was all fun and exciting.

Bill Stone had been honorably discharged from the air force after giving eight years' time to the United States of America. He returned to San Bernardino, California, to be close to his family.

He quickly became hired by the Smith factory in Grady Dale, California. The commute was a bit of a pain, since it was well over an hour's drive. He would have preferred a position with the police force, but after trying repeatedly, he was denied because he was too short. He was disappointed, since he'd had so much training while in the service as a military policeman. He never thought for a moment that he wouldn't be able to be a policeman once discharged from the air force.

He was saddened, to say the least.

He eventually accepted the circumstances and settled in the area. He began making friends and adapting to his new life with a positive attitude.

Almost three years had passed since Patria had arrived to California at the age of fifteen to stay with her older sister, Wylie and her husband Sidney.

Patria was working in a balloon factory without much of a social life. It wasn't long before Patria began hearing all about her sister's husband's new best friend, Bill. Wylie carried on, "He's such a nice guy. He's fun, and you would really hit it off, but he's a bit of a drinker, Patty."

Patria really didn't have a choice in meeting this man, since they invited him over with the intentions of the two getting together.

Bill arrived in his cool, dented-up white Cadillac, which he was clearly proud of, and he was everything Wylie had said about him and more—nice looking, well groomed, and a perfect gentleman.

Dinner went well, and there definitely was a connection. He was shy, sweet, and yet loved to tell jokes. He made Patria laugh, which obviously made him happy and prideful. He found her to be the most beautiful woman that he had ever seen. He couldn't imagine her wanting to be with him, but that wasn't going to stop his endeavors in any way.

He loved to make and watch her laugh that evening and felt that she needed to be less serious.

He could also tell that she was reserved in many ways and worried much of the evening. He felt that she was too young and beautiful to worry. He wanted to cheer her up, bring light into her life, and make all of that worry disappear, and it had only been one night. That evening, he didn't talk about anything of substance or any personal stuff; it was all fun, and that's just what all of them enjoyed about being around Bill. It was easy.

Bill returned the following week after asking Patria's permission. He was respectful and didn't want to push anything, he knew that she had a daughter. The first time Patria's little girl, Maggie met Bill, she came stumbling out of the room after waking from her nap, rubbing her tired blue eyes while looking around confusedly, noticing the stranger among them. She walked right up to him, looked up, and just gazed. He comfortably stood up from the chair and kneeled down to look at her face-to-face.

He softly touched her nose and said, "I stole your nose."

She whined, "Na-ah."

He insisted, "Yes, I did. You see here, it's in between my fingers. I'm holding it." He had the tip of his thumb between his index finger and middle finger.

Her eyes became big, and she looked in wonder and then puzzlement, reaching her hand up to her face to check that her nose was still on her face. He quickly swooped her up into his arms and laughed, reassuring her that he didn't really have her nose. He and Patria walked to the window together, talking, Maggie in his arms, and that's when it happened. Patria fell in love for the first time in her life.

Soon he was coming over every weekend to see Patria and Maggie. They took drives to Sequoia National Park every weekend. Their relationship really clicked. He was kind and caring, such a gentleman. She was ready to settle down, and he was good to Maggie.

He eventually got an apartment in Grady Dale to be closer to the two. Patria was letting go of fears and guilt from the previous failed marriage (very short one), and she wanted to be with Bill.

She began to trust him and felt that he was sincere. He wasn't like anyone she had ever met. He was responsible, confident, honest, funny, and an easygoing kind of guy. She kept asking herself if it were too good to be true. Could she be this deserving?

One night, it became late, and Patria usually asked that Bill take her and Maggie home, but not that night.

She questioned, "Would you like us to stay over?"

He warily asked, "What do you mean 'stay over'?"

She looked into his eyes and said, "It's okay if you would like me to stay with you. I would like to."

They looked at each other, feeling the warmth and desire burning up inside. He didn't say a word. He took her into his arms, picked her up, and carried her to his bedroom.

He slowly unbuttoned her blouse, enjoying the art of her cleavage. She, feeling no shame, began unbuttoning his Levi's.

She could smell the aftershave on his smooth, soft face. He had never seen such a beautiful body. Her dark skin glistened.

He was tender with every touch, every penetration. Her thighs squeezed both sides of his hips, wanting to never let go. Her pleasure delighted him. They held each other tightly into their dreams. It was nothing like either of them had experienced before.

Bill still remained private about his growing up and much of his personal feelings, which puzzled Patria. She always felt a mystery about him. It was okay, and she respected his privacy. Occasionally, she asked him questions about growing up, but he would make some joke, and she couldn't get anything out of him.

Billy or still sometimes still called Billy didn't talk about his childhood but he thought of his parents often, especially his father. He remembered hearing stories from his father about his own upbringing during World War I.

Billy's father, Erland, who was known as "Curly" was born and raised in Connellsville, Utah, where he lived and worked as dairy farmer. Curly's family members were true-blue Mormons. Curly's grandfather even had seven wives at one time, but surprisingly, Curly only had one brother (called "Brownie") and no sisters.

The Mormon practice really stopped with both Curly and his brother. They never understood it or felt that strong sense of community that they had learned about, for whatever reason.

There wasn't much known about Curly's childhood. Not too many stories passed down, but it is known that—as with many families during that time—the Stones were poor, and times were hard.

World War I was in full swing, and the Stone family like many other American families was feeling the effects of the economy, even though the war took place in Europe. The United States was doing everything that it could to produce the soldiers, food supplies, munitions, and money needed to win the war. It was a strain and felt by all. Of course, it wasn't planned, and things around them were *chaotic and uncertain and Curly's family was witness to this restructuring of Americans.*

Men were drafted and among them, Curly's father. He was sent overseas, like many other men, leaving the women to take their places in the workforce.

As the war progressed, technology advanced, and industry grew, permitting women to spend less time on household chores and more time outside of the home.

Even Curly's mother had to work outside of the home for the first time in her life.

As like many other children, Curly and his brother were affected and didn't have the benefits of the no-worry attitudes and just being kids. There was little time to receive home nurturing. They had to run the farm at a very young age.

Even the curriculum in schools changed as early as the elementary level—patriotic and pro-war lessons were inaugurated in public schools.

Therefore, starting at a very early level, students were taught that the war was a good thing, and they drilled in the importance of patriotism.

Sadly, when Curly's father finally arrived home, he suffered from posttraumatic stress, which greatly changed their family forever.

After the war ended, nationalist movements changed to a larger focus on international peace. There were strong government movements toward peace and antiwar sentiments and the need to avoid further wars.

It was a confusing time, and the world had changed, but for the youth like Curly, this is the only world they knew. This state of anarchy wasn't just a part of the outside world; it was part of his world. It was all he knew, too.

Curly and Brownie spent much time on their own and taking care of one another while their father was fighting in the war and their mother, Emelia, worked in the factory.

At a very young age, Curly learned how to shoot guns and even carried a pistol with him to school every day. His main objective during that time was to protect himself and his brother. There was also a rabies epidemic happening, causing coyotes to go crazy. Walking to and from school was a tense experience for the two.

As a teenager, Curly was still too young for the war, so he helped drive horses from Texas to Oregon. He also made extra cash by breaking them in for the US Cavalry.

Curly was always passionate in his beliefs. Later as a father himself, he reiterated what the schools and his father had taught him and drilled the anti-communism philosophy to his boys.

Billy eventually shared some edited versions of where he came from, a little about his parents and how they met to Patria, but it took almost an entire year. He was always private and secretive. Patria never pushed more than he wanted to share but was curious what Billy wasn't sharing with her and why.

He told Patria of how his mother Dora was born and raised in Roadhouse, Illinois. She had two brothers and a sister, and they had to take care of each other, as well.

Their family moved around a bit, always searching for a better life. They moved to Oklahoma, where they lived on a farm, and then finally to Wyoming, where she graduated high school and moved to Idaho for nursing school.

Dora became a very competent nurse and held well-paying jobs.

She wasn't necessarily a warm, touchy person but was skilled and became in charge of the nursing staff in a small country hospital located in Idaho after only working there for a short time.

One day, while breaking in one of the wild horses for the US Cavalry, Curly was thrown off, landing directly into a wooden fence. He crushed the fence into pieces while cracking a few vertebrae at the same time. This incident landed him on his backside in a hospital in Idaho.

Curly didn't like being down and was noncompliant (to put it mildly), but thankfully, he had a stern nurse to keep him in line daily.

That is how Bill's parents met and fell in love. Curly fell in love with Dora and her stringent, no-nonsense personality, and after recovering without disability, the two were married in a small outside ceremony in April of 1920.

They had planned on having a large family and didn't waste any time in doing so. They relocated to California and continued having children and making a life for themselves. Curly farmed, sold items created from wood, and managed a motel during the summer months. He kept pretty busy with life and was always hardworking and looking for ways to feed six little mouths.

Toby was the eldest, and then Jody came, then Betsy, Natalie, Billy, and then finally baby, Suzanna.

That was about all Billy shared with Patria about his parents and family. It was enough and she felt that they must have done something right since she was totally head over heels in love with their son.

Then it finally happened, one day, out of the blue, Billy surprised Patria. She knew that he was falling in love with her, or maybe even in love but didn't know it was coming.

He said, "Patty, I love you and Maggie. Please be with me forever. Marry me and make me the happiest and luckiest man in the world. Will you?"

She was caught off guard, but she was ecstatic.

There was only one problem: she was still married to Chuck Vaught, Maggie's biological father.

CHAPTER 4

*I*N ORDER TO *get a quick divorce, Patria had to live in Nevada for a minimum of six weeks.*

Bill set her and Maggie up at the Lido Apartments in Las Vegas, Nevada. They didn't get out much because of money. They just stayed inside, read, played and watched TV.

Wylie, Sidney, and Bill carpooled and visited as often as they could.

Finally, after six long weeks and reporting on regular basis to the local attorney, the judge granted the divorce. All four of them were there on that special day and celebrated into the night. Chuck, thankfully, never showed up.

Bill and Patria were married in 1965 in Las Vegas, in a small ceremony with only the four best friends present and little Maggie.

Patria wore a red outfit with a fur collar, black high heels, and of course the red lipstick that she hardly went without. Bill wore a light-blue suit, which brought out his light-blue eyes.

They were a handsome couple!

Months had passed and while Patria and Bill were doing great, Sidney and Wylie weren't. Their marriage was failing. By this time, Wylie was pregnant with their second child. Their oldest, Randy, was only four years old. About a year after Bill and Patria's wedding,

Wylie left Sydney, which was absolutely shocking to everyone. They seemed like such a strong and stable couple. Wylie and Randy needed somewhere to go and moved in with Bill and Patria.

Little Maggie didn't like the way her Aunt Wylie looked at her daddy and even told her mom. She never really cared for Wylie much after witnessing her flirtatious ways, but Patria knew Wylie well and trusted her with her life. She knew that it was innocent and just the way Wylie was. She felt no threat whatsoever; she knew that Bill would never betray her, not in a million years.

Wylie eventually headed back to Texas after her second child, Teah was born after Wylie had a one night stand with some unknown and random stranger and moved in with her momma and her momma's third husband, Mr. Kuykendall. She liked Mr. Kuykendall very much and he was kind and welcoming to her and her children. He never questioned her circumstances, lectured or judge, as far as she could tell. As usual, she didn't stay there very long before meeting a new man and going away with him.

Back in California, life for Patria and Bill was getting better with each passing day.

They moved into Bill's small apartment, it was cozy but Maggie didn't have a yard, Patria made up for it by taking her on daily walks so that she could get some fresh air and rid some of that energy she sometimes didn't know what to do with.

The apartment was so small that Maggie's bed pulled out from the wall, although she found that fun and loved pulling it down.

The family was extraordinarily happy. Bill brought in a steady income from the Mel factory, allowing Patria to remain at home and take care of their daughter and to be ready for his arrival after work. Eventually, he left factory work to become a mailman. It was much better money, and his goal was to get a bigger place with a yard for his family.

Every morning, Bill stopped by the office to sort the mail, and then he walked miles and miles to deliver it to the town of Tujunga. He loved walking and being outside.

Maggie watched the clock daily, asking her mom every five seconds, "Is he coming? Is he coming?" Maggie adored her dad.

Bill wasn't the only one whom loved and adored Patria and Maggie, his entire family took them into their hearts almost immediately. They had a party just for Maggie after the marriage. Bill's mother, Dora, was a quiet, reserved woman, but she was nice enough. Patria felt Dora to also be a private woman who did not discuss personal feelings or events. Patria never knew what she was thinking or how she felt about her, but she was relaxed nonetheless with his family. They had fun get-togethers. Patria and Bill's sisters cooked together, sipped wine, and got along very well.

Bill and Patria faithfully saved money until they finally had enough to move into a larger house with a big yard.

Patria and Bill were happy and focused on their family without any real interference from Maggie's father, Chuck Vaught, until many years later when his violent and psychotic behaviors finally lead to murder. That part of this story will have to wait until later.

Back to Bill and Patria...it wasn't long before Patria was expecting and they were completely delighted! It was an easy pregnancy and Bill and Patria were more in love than ever. Bill used to lay his head over his beautiful wife's belly and talk to his growing baby. He would tell the baby funny stories and make Patria laugh. He had a way in doing that. They laughed a lot.

Dana came and unfortunately, Bill and Patria weren't laughing as much. Dana was the fussiest, most exhausting baby ever. She constantly had projectile vomiting and cried all of the time. She slept close to her mom and dad so that they could make sure she didn't choke during the night. Her pediatrician, Dr. Nuttingcomb, reassured Patria and Bill, saying, "Rest assured, Dana won't be throwing up on her wedding day."

A year later, Patria was pregnant again with yet another girl, Anna. She was just an angel compared to Dana. She hardly cried and was easily entertained.

They were hoping for a boy, but it was the way it was and they *loved having a family and Maggie kept busy being the other mother to her little sisters.*

Like Billy's large family, he looked forward to having many children.

Bill wanted out of the big city. He had heard of work in a small town in the middle of nowhere. It was booming and had a future. It was known as a modern industrial village in the desert, the home of a highly successful chemical corporation. It was said to be a unique community—a self-contained town operated on a cost basis by the company for the benefit of its employees. It had all the advantages found in larger communities, including modern stores, a public library, an elementary and high school, a theater, a clubhouse, bowling alleys, billiard parlors, tennis courts, a golf course, baseball fields, and a spacious swimming pool. Desert and mountains within driving distance afforded good hunting and fishing.

This plant produced chemicals and operated seven days a week, twenty-four hours a day, year in and year out. In peace, the products went to all parts of the globe, and in World War I and World War II, it ultimately made chemicals for victory.

Off they went, trailer in tow, on a new adventure with their joyful and excited growing family to the town of Natruna.

Little Carha would come into the world in the tough little town of Natruna, as would her little brother-the only boy in the entire Stone clan and that completed their happy and loving family as their adventures would continue in their new town!

Chapter 5

PETE GOMEZ WAS born in Los Angeles, California, and moved to Natruna in the 1940s. His father moved there to work at the plant, as well. They had a big family and lots of mouths to feed. For years, they actually lived in a tent in Argos without electricity, running water, or plumbing. It was challenging, but they made do.

Pete wasn't close to his father, he worked all of the time and really wasn't ever home. His mother was an amazing, loving, charismatic woman whom everyone adored. They were pretty strong into the Catholic faith and tried to respect their religion growing up.

Audrey grew up not too far from Natruna. Her family owned a small business and had a long family history in the area. She moved to Natruna in the '50s to also work at the plant.

It was there that the two met, fell in love, and started their family.

Their oldest boy, William, or Willie as everyone called him, was a year or so older than Maggie. Then came Sylvia, who was Maggie's age, and then Tabitha, who was a few years younger.

Willie was born colicky; he was fussy and irritable from the start, and his parents felt frustration from the beginning. The two young lovers were even hesitant to have more children due to the hardship of raising such a fussy boy, but they did. Thankfully, the girls were much easier.

The Gomez siblings and cousins were close and spent much of their time playing with one another while the adults passed time working and visiting in the kitchen. The adults usually made the children play outside and out of sight. They didn't want to hear them and didn't really want to spend much time with them, either, especially when they played their card games.

As the kids began getting older, the sibling rivalry was obvious and became problematic.

Willie seemed to always be in trouble, causing trouble or getting in trouble for something he never even did in the first place. After a while, he accepted his fate and just anticipated the next mishap he would find himself in. Taking all blame, deserved or not.

When Willie was just five years of age, his parents bought a Doughboy pool and set it up in the backyard. They worked diligently, ensuring that it was put together correctly. It took them three days to level the ground, place blocks, fill it with silica sand, and follow the hundred steps involved in assembling the hundred parts until it was finally up.

Filling the pool with water was exciting for the entire family, and it was evident that Pete and Audrey were more than proud. They were looking forward to having an area close by for the kids to cool off and play safely.

Willie became angry within days of the erection of this water-filled paradise. He soon forgot what he was actually angry about following the incident, but no matter the reason, he took a shovel to the inside of the pool and poked it, piercing through the plastic bottom and sides of the plastic pool repeatedly.

His father whipped him over and over with a thin belt; they called a razor belt, which wasn't unfamiliar to him at all. There wasn't a time when he didn't feel that he deserved the whip, but he still disagreed that it was the answer or that it would cure him of his anger. It only made him angrier.

Oh, and his sisters knew how to tease him and get him heated. They taunted, they screamed, and out came the whip. Sometimes Willie didn't do anything, but sometimes he did.

The older they became, the more he resented them and his parents for the trouble he seemed to constantly be in.

Once, while the girls were taking a bath, Willie caused them to scream out for help.

"Dad! Dad!" (They always screamed for their father.) "Willie's hitting us! Willie won't leave us alone."

The two brown-eyed girls clung dramatically to one side of the tub. By that time, Willie had decided that he was already going to get into trouble, so he might as well make it worth it. He began tossing cold water from the sink toward them, making a mess of water puddles in the process. The more the innocent little girls—who never got whipped—cried out, the more Willie splashed them pleasurably.

All of a sudden but yet still unexpectedly, Willie was grabbed by his upper arm and immediately yanked from the situation by his annoyed father and all Willie could think was, "Oh, here it comes again."

Usually, Pete grabbed whatever was convenient. This time, he flung Willie's skinny body out the back door. "Stay put, God dammit!" He always yelled when he was mad. Pete grabbed a tree branch—a salt cedar branch, to be exact.

Willie was fully aware of the dreadful way the branches

of salt cedar trees burned the skin, especially once irritation began. It felt like a fire-hot wire nightmarishly hitting the skin over and over again, as he did not have time between the whippings to breathe. It was both shocking and disturbing at the same time.

His dad had little patience with Willie by the time he was in elementary school. He was helplessly frustrated and did the only thing he knew how to do: try to beat some sense into this hardheaded child.

When Willie was around ten years old, he watched a show on electricity and thought it was the coolest. He took a short black comb and wrapped tinfoil around it, thinking that he would form an experiment of his own. He stuck the homemade electrical tool directly into the electrical outlet.

It popped, sparked, and then smoked. He thought it was too cool and decided to move to the next socket and do it again.

After the loud poof, black soot shot out of the holes. Willie thought it was the coolest thing he had ever seen. He was quite proud of his experiment and was curious how the next outlet would react. He tried that, which wasn't as exciting, so he tried another one, which reacted louder the first one and even poofed out twice the amount of soot. Before he knew it, he had inserted that comb into all of the sockets in the living room and had begun hitting the ones in the kitchen.

He was deep into his thoughts and experiment when he was awakened from his state by his father's deep voice. "What the hell is going on, dammit?! Willie, what the fuck are you doing now?"

Pete again picked his mischievous son up by his arm and flung him into his workshop, this time to whip him with a cut-up green watering hose.

Pete couldn't understand his son's behavior ever, and

Willie really couldn't, either. He did things without realizing why he was doing them. He never tried to defend his stupidity or get out of the whippings. He just took them as he felt he deserved. This vicious cycle continued for most of Willie's childhood. Some beatings were worse than others. They always hurt, but it was the way it was.

Pete made Willie make a wooden whipping board for himself, and Pete spanked him with that for quite a while. That brought a whole new meaning to the word "pain" because it was such a hard, solid, raw stimulus that took air right out of his lungs and caused discomfort for days that followed.

The last time that he was whipped, he was around thirteen years old, but it wasn't just him acting out this time—it was his sisters too. They were told to all line up and get ready for spankings. Tabitha cried, and Sylvia ran around in circles to avoid the belt—not that their father really tried that hard to get her—and by the time it was said and done, Willie was the one to get it for all three, with Pete's paddle.

Pete never really physically disciplined the girls. They were girls, he said.

Tabitha was closest to her mom, and well, Sylvia was Pete's favorite, it was clear. Willie, on the other hand, did not feel that he was either one's.

Willie's family, like most Natrunan's, was prideful when it came to their desolate hometown.

This town with the dry heat, sand blown wind, brown weeds, salt cedar trees, tough rugged surrounding mountains, dried up lake bed and stinky smell was a very close-net proud unique community.

It was officially established in the early 1900s as a self-contained company town, wholly operated by its resident mining company to house employees.

Employees were even paid in company scrip instead of cash. The mining company also built a library, a scrip-accepting for-profit grocery store, a school, basic housing, and minimal recreation facilities. The Natruna Railway was built to provide the town with a rail connection.

Bill Stone, like Pete Gomez, became one of the many lucky contributors of the main economic growth of the little town.

Once the Stone family arrived in Natruna, they moved into some older, run-down apartments for a while before moving into the little house embedded on the side of the mountain located in Pioneer.

The chemical company built housing for employees with families, but they were limited and assigned on a basis of earnings and seniority. The company built forty-seven modern homes altogether and sold them at cost to employees.

The Gomez family already had the comfortable ranch home that they built across from the horse corrals in 1965.

However, for the Stone family they were in need of a larger home after the birth of Carha and then Billy and fortunately, there were some company homes left to buy.

The search for the perfect home was on. Patria Stone was reluctant in that she was comfortable where they were because it was the first real home she had ever had, but it was too small. Carha tagged along on one of the house-hunting trips but only remembered one house, the house that became their home.

Carha felt special because she was the one to go with her parents to pick out the house. She remembered that day like it was yesterday. She was standing in what would later become Maggie's room with one arm wrapped around her mom's leg, her mom and dad had finished their conversation with the realtor, and then both of them turned to look down at Carha at the same time. They looked serious as they both made eye contact with Carha, which made her nervous. She felt that she was doing something wrong. Nobody else was there.

Her dad asked, "Well, Carha, what do you think? Do you think that we should buy this home?"

She felt very shy and surprised that they asked her opinion. She grinned, her eyes enlarged, and she excitedly nodded her head and exclaimed, "Yes!"

Her parents looked at one another with big smiles, and then her dad said, "Well, then, it's a done deal!"

It was located in the section of town known as Truna. It was sort of the middle section of the town and within walking distance to the schools, stores, theater, and post office.

The home was spectacular. It was grand, and it was green—not just one color of green but many shades of green. The base was light green; the trim was dark green. The mailbox post was green. Okay, the fence was kept wooden and natural colored, which was probably a good thing! The home was roofed with Spanish tile, which added even more character. It was a one-story home with four bedrooms and two bathrooms and plenty of space. It was located almost at the very top of Flower Street.

The upper part of Flower Street was fenced off by the chemical plant—and the fence was probably twenty feet tall with barbed wire sticking out from every which way at the top of the enormous barrier. Nobody in his right mind would climb that baby.

The train tracks sat perched on mountains of dirt just on the other side of the huge fence.

From their front yard, they could watch as the loaded train powerfully roared along the curved, rusted tracks. The engine led a variety of cars with its beautiful yellow lights, almost like eyes except that one was on top of the other. This diesel-driven locomotive seemed as if it were an intimidating entity of its own. You could hear its grumble and pounding before you could see it, as if it were warning you of its coming.

In the backdrop, and not in the too far distance, stood the beautiful rugged mountain ranges.

Between the tracks and mountain peaks, the plant stood solidly with its smokestacks ranging in all different sizes, releasing puffs and shimmers of smoke throughout the day and night. They never really knew what was in the smoke.

There were flickering lights that melted from these industrial plants that magnificently lit up at night and many different mysterious sounds which created much curiosity.

Looking up to the night skies, there was such desert clarity of the stars in between the power lines, cables, rooftops, and corner streetlights that it made Carha feel small yet significant to be a part of the glorious universe.

The night air was cool and crisp in the winter and warm and dry in the summer.

Natruna smelled like a combination of wildflowers, asphalt, earth, and minerals, with a touch of sagebrush; the sulfur smell vanished from your senses the longer that you were there.

Usually, it was warm when it rained, and the ground seemed to come alive in all different comforting aromas. There wasn't another place on earth that created these unique smells, and there wasn't any place on earth with such amazing, special people. There were trails and alleys in between homes, behind homes, and on the sides of homes. It was liberating for the children, since they were allowed to roam freely. They weren't afraid to go anywhere. They felt it all belonged to them. They usually ran so fast that no one saw them, or so they felt. Occasionally, Mr.

Anderson's caretaker would yell "Hey!" if they got too uninhibited.

Their home sat on a half-acre lot and was located smack in a neighborhood. It had one of the nicest and largest dirt front yards in all of Natruna.

The front yard was split in half by a four-foot-wide walkway of pink cement that began at the mailbox and ended at the front door. It led to three eight-feet-wide matching concrete front steps. Once you were up the steps, you stood on a wraparound gray cement porch. The kids knew every crack, hole, and inch of their porch.

This wraparound porch ended at the glass doors to the far right. These doors were entries into a back bedroom behind Patria and Bill's bedroom. They were never used.

Following the porch in the other direction, it cut a corner, wrapping around the house, passing through the wooden gate, wrapping around another corner, continuing past the back door, and ending again at yet another set of glass doors, which led to the girls' bedrooms. They didn't use these doors either.

It had a striking solid-wood front door that was a different shade of green. There were a number of salt cedar trees in the front yard and planter boxes that lined the front porch.

Patria eventually planted what the kids always called "green bean plants." They didn't taste like green beans at all. They were firmer, sour, and weren't good to eat, but they were fun to squish between their fingers.

The kids were proud when their mother raked the front yard and then sprayed it down with water. She kept it well manicured for a dirt yard, and this kept the dirt from blowing as much on many of their windy days.

After drying, it formed these dark-colored crusted tips and lines that gave it the finishing touch. It had to have taken her all day to do that. The kids never thought about that. They just appreciated the way that it looked. It smelled similar to fresh rain, which rarely happened, but when it did, it was lovely.

They also had a few light-brown brushes scattered around in the front yard and backyard. They were really weeds, but they added to the desert decor, and the kids liked them.

Their mom could bring anything to life. That was what she did best—bringing things and people to life.

The inside of the house was spacious compared to their other home. Once stepping through that front door, you were standing in huge living room where a beautiful emerald glass Spanish chandelier hung; it magically sparkled as it appeared to gently sway at times. The room was bright and had lots of small white paned windows, white concrete walls, and a cozy, multicolored-brown shag carpet.

The formal dining room was to the left and led to the kitchen, which led to the laundry room to its right, which led to the back door.

The dining room had one large table full of many chairs and two china hutches, one built in and one purchased.

These hutches were full of collectables, nic nacs, tea pots, ceramic pieces, old bottles found throughout the desert and miscellaneous dinnerware that Patria had collected through the years.

Patria usually draped the table with a variety of table clothes depending on the time of the year and always a small vase of flowers. This table, along with the black rod iron rectangular chandelier dangling from the ceiling was the center of many cherished family dinners and celebrations.

The kitchen was cozy and had many white cabinets that housed all of their ecliptic serving items that were used meal after meal and year after year. Each item was particularly placed in its particular cabinet on its particular shelf.

To the right of the living room was the main corridor that led to the central main bathroom and all of the bedrooms. The small corridor contained a linen closet and yellow rotary telephone that hung on the wall and a closet that contained the heater. This area was the busiest area of the entire house. The family members all bumped into one another there, visited there, and most commonly fought over the phone there.

The doorway on the right of the heater closet was the entrance into a large square room with one large window centered along the wall, looking out to the front yard; this one became their parents' bedroom. Their room led to a back small bedroom that ended up belonging to little Billy; it had a small bathroom in it. The kids never used that bathroom; it was solely their mom and dad's personal space.

The doorway on the left side of the corridor—after the linen closet—led to another large square room with white walls, almost one entire wall had the same white paned small windows creating a visual opening this room to the back room. It also had beautiful shiny wooden floors. This became Maggie's room. It had one closet that was narrow but tall. It had two shelves on either side of it about three feet from the ceiling. It ended up being one of the best hiding spots in the entire house.

After leaving Maggie's room, there was an L-shaped bedroom with cement floors and lots of windows. It also had two glass doors, which they had to keep locked and weren't permitted to use. There was a small closet in the very back of the room that was always crammed yet organized with the girl's clothing.

This L-shaped room belonged to Anna, Carha, and Dana. It was partitioned three ways with dressers, headboards, and whatever else they could use. They weren't ever bothered about the size or sharing. They didn't know any differently and loved their room and one another.

In this room is where the wall heater was that etched the cross pattern burn into little Billie's left buttock.

Many fond memories took place in that back room. When the girls became bored, they all worked together, music blaring through the cassette player, and off they went cleaning the entire room from ceiling to floor. They wiped everything down with cloths dipped in buckets of Pine Sol. They laughed and told stories, having to raise their voices to be heard over the Eagles, the Beatles or Kansas. They played all different types of music. They enjoyed work just like their mother and looked forward to the refreshing change in their living quarters and end results. They worked together to craft new partitions, sometimes exchanging dressers or creating new angles for a partition. During those times, they didn't fight or argue; they just worked together forming stronger bonds between sisters.

They had a huge fenced-in backyard. It had a concrete basketball court that connected with a strip of the concrete porch. They had a basketball hoop smack-dab in the middle of it with a large floodlight attached to a wooden pole.

On either side of the concrete patio was a dirt yard landscape. One side pretty much belonged to their father, and the other side was their play area. They had a tetherball, old wagons, play cars, and all sorts of toys.

The very back of the yard was lined with a row of salt cedar trees which stood taller than the fence. In the back of the garage and behind their dad's work area were the chicken and rabbit coops.

Having chicken coops always reminded Bill of his

childhood. Since Bill hardly spoke of his childhood, when he did, it was forever recorded in someone's brain. He would really have to be three sheets to the wind to share anything private. Who knew what made him decide to, they just knew to listen and remember.

One of Bill's favorite activities growing up involved spending hours and hours helping his dad build chicken coops out on their property.

As a young boy, Bill adored his father and was always aching to know him better. He felt that he couldn't ever have enough conversations with his father to curve his longing to know him better for his father was a man of few words-sounds similar to the way his own family felt about him.

He felt that he worked harder than any other boy his age could possibly work, he would eventually impress his father. He didn't know if he did or didn't, he just wanted more, more pats on the back to make his day and make him feel better about himself. He wanted to be just like his father. He attempted to mimic the way he spoke, the way he held his shoulders up high, what he wore to how he laughed.

As a child, his most valued memories were building things out of wood with his father, not just chicken coops. He the freedom to build anything that he wanted with what they had lying around their property and Bill permitted his own children the same freedom.

Anna, Dana, Cara and Billy built the most imaginative playhouses and tree houses in that backyard. They were allowed to take items from out of the home to create the makeshift homes and make them comfy.

Maggie never really cared to make forts. She preferred to not get dirty.

The kids lived outside, winter, spring, summer, and fall. They loved it.

Their home on Flower Street was dreamy and strong. It was solid and spacious. The things that happened inside of the home transformed its structure, its being.

Patria, Bill, Maggie, Dana, Anna, Carha, Billy, dogs,

cats, their granny, relatives, were all part of the new family home for a long time, until it all fell apart.

What was once this amazing place with cherished memories became overridden by the pain of what was, how it fell apart, and how it ended with only scattered debris laying on the surface and faint memories entrenched in its soil.

CHAPTER 6

PATRIA WAS A regular at the only salon in town, called Mel's Styles. She never went anywhere else. It was always the same two women who owned it, ran it, and worked it. Getting your hair done was like reading the *Natruna Enquirer* without ever having to pick up a paper.

Patria never wore much makeup—maybe a small amount of mascara and of course her red lipstick. Between her mother's Indian background and her father's Mexican and Indian genetics, she was striking and naturally beautiful.

She had dark thick hair that she wore shorter and permed most of the time. Patria's mom, Ethel said that Patria looked very much like her own mother, Azlee in many ways.

Ethel spoke of her mother with fondness and admiration.

She bragged that her mom was the most beautiful woman she had ever seen. She had long, thick, pretty, coal-black hair, which she kept in a long braid, and she had matching deep, dark coal eyes. She was always a bit bony.

When Ethel was growing up she remembers that her mother, Azlee never wore anything other than dresses and flat shoes. Azlee never differed from a true ladylike disposition and was sensually soft spoken. Her easy nature allowed her to be a dutiful wife and mother. She gracefully served her family and guests and this was her life, a lot like Patria felt about her family.

Azlee was a beauty and mysterious. She was one hundred percent Cherokee, raised in a tribe and traditional in her values. She struggled with what she knew and what she felt had to change to fit into her new world after having her own family and moving off from the reservation.

Many times, Ethel spoke of her mother with sadness and regret that she didn't have more time with her. When raising her own children, she often reminded them to appreciate their time with her and the importance of not taking the time with loved ones for granted.

Patria didn't have to verbally remind her children of this while she was raising them, but somehow she must have subliminally got the message through. The kids loved life, as their mother loved and appreciated life. They loved one another, their home, their hometown, their friends and their selves. There weren't many bad days, just days to look forward to, to be excited about and to wonder what fun was coming their way!

Patria demonstrated her love for life in always staying active and taking advantage of each day. She treasured the outdoors and usually after chores were completed, found something to do outside with her children.

She took the kids to the pool on a regular basis and rode bikes, which was usually every day if the weather allowed. They rode everywhere, from one end of town to the other end. Natruna had bike paths from West Point all the way to Pioneer. She also went for walks with the kids, enjoyed fishing and camping, and was a hard worker. She wasn't one to sit around.

She took pride in a well-kept home and took great care of the kids and their father.

She could do just about anything, from sewing the

family's clothes, repairing damaged toys, fixing the plumbing, doing yard work, to dancing in the living room with family and friends. She wasn't much help with homework, but then again, the kids never really needed help. She was a school volunteer and never missed their parent-teacher conference, play, or sports activity.

Carha remembered waking up some mornings to light shining underneath her bedroom door, trailing as if it were magical and calling her name. It felt as if she were dreaming as she followed it. The light led to her mother, who was sewing at the head of the dining room table. Patria would stop momentarily to give Carha a morning hug, say hello, and then she resumed her sewing dance.

Carha could watch for what seemed like hours but were most likely only minutes. She loved to watch and admire her mother. She felt proud and pretty that she came from her.

Her mother worked with love. Every stroke, her intense concentration, and her focus seemed as if she was in some kind of relaxed trance. She wore a tranquil smile on her face. She didn't have to say anything, but young Carha knew that her mom liked her there, watching and being with her. Carha never felt like an intruder. She wouldn't say anything, just watch and listen to the sound of the sewing machine's motor roar. It was like music.

Patria glided her hands and arms up and down, back and forth, while accelerating and decelerating the foot pedal. Her back swayed forward and then gently back, barely touching the chair. Carha never really understood what she was doing, but she was still intensely intrigued with this ritual.

The house was warm and cozy. Patria made it a home, filled with love, fun, laughter, and security. She put her heart and soul into her family. She naturally thought of them without hurry and without frustration. She gave them love and acceptance from her whole being. Carha dreamed to be like that one day. How did she do this?

Cooking, on the other hand, wasn't one of Patria's greatest strengths.

The kids usually had a simple breakfast, typically cereal, but they had a wide assortment to choose from. They crunched on their cereal while reading the backs of the cereal boxes, talking, sometimes fighting over who got to read which box and they generally ate sandwiches for lunch.

A saving grace to all Natruna kids had to be the School cafeteria. No matter how bad breakfast may have been, or how horrible dinner would be, they could always count on the good ole school lunches.

School lunches were the best. They loved the variety and surprise of not knowing what they were eating each day. Part of the fun was standing in the lunch line while holding one of their beige, rectangular-compartment lunch trays, anxiously awaiting the food to be placed on their trays by one of the familiar cafeteria staff or one of the student volunteers.

Students felt honored to be in the rotation for a cafeteria helper. They felt proud, almost heroic, being allowed to serve their fellow classmates.

To finish off their delicious lunch trays, they picked up a small carton of milk from the top of a cold double-decker serving cart.

On rare occasions, they were lucky enough to get one of Natruna's famous peanut butter balls placed on their trays. That was a treat! They were grainy, firm, and not too sweet—just perfect.

The children exited the kitchen and looked around, scoping out the large open cafeteria, appearing as if they had no idea where they were going to sit when they really did know exactly where. It was the same place almost every time—next to one of their friends.

They slid into the built-in benches and placed their trays on the long, sturdy cafeteria tables.

Milk always tasted better from the small carton and with a straw. The kids always reminded themselves to be extra gentle while pushing the flimsy straw in the hole; they didn't want to waste a drop of the delicious nutritional goodness or get embarrassed from it shooting right out from the top and making a mess.

Once, while eating lunch, Carha was laughing so hard at her goofy friend Darcie that milk shot out from both nostrils and landed directly into Darcie's lunch tray that was still full of food. That was one of the most humiliating moments of Carha's elementary school days.

Elementary age was both fun and challenging for the Stone children. Each and every one of the children had the misfortune of having slight speech impediments. The school called it a "speech delay," but their delays lasted years. They had to leave their regular class to attend speech therapy on scheduled days of the week. All of the other students knew that they were going but never mentioned it or teased the Stones.

Carha dreaded having to say her name in front of other students. The teacher would say, "Okay, everyone, say your name to the class." Carha automatically became red in the face, and her breathing became labored just knowing that she would eventually have to say her name in front of the class.

By the time it was her turn, her eyes nervously began watering like she was having a huge allergic reaction. No, she didn't have allergies—unless the allergies were having eyes on her.

She would courageously and quietly state, "Ca-a." The

teacher boldly instructed Carha to repeat it. She did after practicing repeatedly how to say it in her head, only for it to come out the same. The teacher then would realize that the scared little girl had speech problems for sure and help her out by saying, "Oh … Car-ha. That's a very nice name." Reading aloud was the worst. It was so horrible that staying home would have been much easier, but that wasn't going to happen.

For all the embarrassment of their speech delay, both Carha and Billy loved school, and as stated loved school food! This is not to say Patria didn't try, it's just that the simplest things can become hard if you don't have the right tools.

Patria always cooked a full-blown dinner and sitting at the table was a ritual that took place perfectly at the same time every evening. Everyone had his or her own place to sit. These were times when interruptions weren't allowed. If the phone rang, they all looked quietly and curiously at one another, biting at the bit wondering who was calling. Their minds quickly returned to their family time, which united them, and they cherished it dearly.

The dinner menu was somewhat limited. They usually had spaghetti, fried chicken, chicken and dumplings, or tacos.

Tacos were the family tradition in the Stone home. It was a production. All of the kids had a task—chopping tomatoes, lettuce, and onions or grating mounds of cheese. The kids stood in the single line waiting to fry up their corn tortillas in the cast-iron skillet full of vegetable oil. They scooped the flavored ground beef on the top of that. They then proceeded to the table where all of the cut-up toppings were waiting in bowls. The race would begin when they all had their tacos and were ready. Who would finish the greatest amount of tacos in the least amount of time?

The main competitor was their father. He was the one to beat. He ate thirteen tacos in one night. Everyone cheered everyone on; this was the only time that their father permitted them to be wild at the dining room table.

Steak was a rare commodity, and the only way Patria knew to cook it was to fry it for a long period of time in hot oil. The kids had difficulties chewing it because it was so tough. They chewed and chewed but could never break through the leathery, dried-up meat.

Carha resigned to sucking all the juices from it, which wasn't that much, and then wrapping the destroyed, used-up piece of meat in her napkin to throw away.

Their dad was always a stickler for manners, especially at the table. The children had to sit up straight, have polite and civilized discussions, chew with their mouths closed, and eat all of the food on their plates.

Bill's own mother, Dora must have instilled these codes of etiquette in her children to be passed down to their children. She could be extremely unsympathetic and strict during meal time when her children were growing up. All of the dinner utensils had to be perfectly polished and reflect the light. In preparation for their meals, they had to be in correct presentation, as well.

She was definitely a woman set in her ways and wouldn't budge. She even refused to use a mop on the floor, only a sponge while on her hands and knees. She said that this is the way that she was taught to clean a floor and this is the way to do it right. Billy said, "My mother was strict, but she was a good mother and wasn't partial to any of the kids."

Billy claims that there wasn't ever a bad word that came out of her mouth, and she always spoke in proper English and expected nothing less from her children. It didn't matter their age. Bill's father Curly, on the other hand could curse like a sailor.

Bill would not allow his children to use any profanity, or say any words that he deemed negative or bad. He too was stern and stubborn. It would be his way around the house. The kids and Patria would obey his rules, guidelines and philosophy. It wasn't much of a big deal because when he left to go to work, the kids and Patria could relax and feel freer to speak without being remanded for not speaking correctly.

When their father wasn't around, they were able to watch TV, run in the house, play their music louder than usual and things like that. It wasn't that he would beat them, he never did anything like that, nor was he verbally abusive, it was just that "disapproving look". That was all it took.

At times, one of the kids would still be sitting at the dinner table when the rest of the family was getting ready for bed. It was horrible. Why did they serve themselves up with so much dang food? They never really seemed to get it, even after the kind reminder from their father. Bill would say, "Remember that you will have to eat whatever you place on your plate". And if they piled food onto their plate, it never failed that their father was paying mindful attention and they knew it. They justified all that food with —"*This time is different. I have room in my stomach for all of this tonight*".

Then they could kick themselves in the rear for not listening to their conscious…to their father's disapproving eyes.

Thank goodness their mom would sneak back into the kitchen, scrape their plates into a big napkin, and give it to the dogs. Otherwise, they would have still been sitting there in the morning.

From time to time, Patria placed a plate of fried meat in the center of the table as the main course and never really admitted to what it was. The kids never said much or pushed the matter, but they knew that it wasn't something from the grocery store. There were rumors that it was a wild donkey from the desert. Hey, anything fried and coated with flour and a seasoning wasn't something to complain about.

Bill wasn't much for spending money. One of the ways to decrease the family budget of seven was to raise and butcher rabbits for the protein. He had big hooks hanging down from the wooden rafters in the garage. After gutting the rabbits, he hung them from the large hooks, and their skinny, shiny pink bodies dangled from high above. It was a disturbing sight for the kids. They tried not to visit their dad in the garage while he was cleaning a rabbit. They did however eat the rabbits without any hesitation. Patria could make any meat taste delicious with her famous flour coating which was passed down by her own mother and anything fried in oil was enough to make the kids eat the juicy, greasy pieces of meat with sincere pleasure.

To aid in their appetites, the kids weren't allowed to spend too much time with the rabbits to prevent attachment. Carha snuck one of the bunnies from the rabbit cages into the house one night. It was her favorite white, furry baby bunny, and she had been fantasizing about sleeping with the sweet little fur ball. She cuddled and loved on the sweet baby rabbit throughout the night, but in the morning, she discovered that she had smashed and suffocated the poor bunny. She cried and took it to her mother. The demon sisters found out about the incident and for the next couple of years, they replaced her nickname of "Twig" with "Rabbit Killer."

As stated Bill was very firm with the children and didn't let them get away with anything and didn't permit Patria to let them get away with anything either- if he knew of it. He stuck to his word, so when he said something, you knew that he meant it.

The kids weren't permitted to say, "pee," "poo," or "poop." It had to be "number one" or "number two." Topics like elimination had to be private matters.

When their dad had to go to the bathroom, he would say, "I have to see a man about a horse." Away he went. They kids never understood what this had to do with going to the restroom. Why didn't he just say that he had to use the restroom?

Bill was a modest man and never hardly took off his shirt in front of the children and wasn't much on wearing shorts, either. They never really knew if it was that he didn't feel it respectful or he was embarrassed or maybe shy.

Cursing and treating others disrespectfully also wasn't allowed.

Time in front of the television was limited. They could watch cartoons in the morning but only on the weekends, and that was about it, but when their dad was working, Patria let them watch night shows. Bill only watched the news and boxing. Everything else was nonsense and mind-numbing nothing.

Patria strove to always make the kids happy. She never wanted them to be angry or upset with her, and she always protected them from their father's discontent, even when she really shouldn't have.

Sometimes, she acted more like a big protective sister than a mother. She just loved them so much. It was definitely more relaxing and fun for them to be around their mother.

It was a good combination to grow up with. They had the best of both worlds and were healthy and happy kids.

It wasn't that their father spanked them. As a matter of fact, he hardly did. Each one of the kids could actually count the number of times he or she received the belt. It wasn't even the spankings that they were afraid of; it was the emotional disappointment that transferred from their dad deep into their souls. They quickly went from feeling good about themselves to feeling like they belonged in the bottom of a mud puddle.

Their father just looked at them a certain way, and they knew to watch their step. They did anything to avoid "the look." His eyes would slightly squint, his lips immediately became smaller and tighter, lines became more predominant on his forehead, and he became stiffer.

Yeah, the looks were brief but deadly.

All of the kids sought their dad's respect, for they had so much respect for him. He did what was best for them, not what made him feel the best.

Once Bill shared a story with Carha about how his father never spanked him or any of his siblings. As previously stated, it was a memorable event when their father talked about personal stuff.

He said that one day when he was in elementary school; he decided to ditch school just because he didn't feel like going. His father scolded him and sternly called to him, "Billy, come here now!" Billy ran from him, and Erland (Curly) chased him around the car, trying to get hold on him. Billy ran and ran until Curly finally became too weak and just gave up. He said softly to Billy, "Okay, come here, and you won't get into trouble." Billy went to him but received the worst lecture with accompanying disappointment that he had ever received from his father. He felt that it was far worse than being spanked. He said that was the very last lecture that he ever received from his father and he never forgot it.

Bill was stern with his own children but he could often be very fun too. He smiled, joked, teased, and shared more of his time with them when he felt that they were being good. It was his way to reward them. When he wasn't happy with their behavior, he reserved his attention. This was hurtful, and that's why it didn't happen very often.

He was affectionate and loving to the kids. He was timeless when hugging and holding them. He was soothing in the way that he rubbed their backs while he said kind things to them. They could have stayed in his arms forever. There wasn't another place on earth that made them feel safer than in their father's arms.

Their parents were quite contrary when it came to raising the children. Bill was unquestionably the disciplinarian, and Patria was not.

Bill was a strong, yet lean man who stood about five feet eight inches. He still had the fit boxer's physique that he maintained even after the air force. He had sandy-brown hair that receded into a sort of spider's web in the front and curled all different crazy directions in the back. He went gray fairly young. His nose was slightly convex and then thin and sharp, fitting his face impeccably. He was a distinguished and handsome man. He had light sapphire-blue small eyes; his skin was fair and easily burned in the sun. The hair follicles on his neck were noticeable, and sometimes he rubbed his coarse stubble against the kids' cheeks when he kissed them, which made them laugh. He carried himself confidently and gentlemanly. He was always well groomed, and he always smelled good. He wore nice jeans and usually a button up collared shirt unless on his days off, he just wore a white t-shirt with his jeans. There wasn't one person who did not like Bill Stone.

Their parents woke early every morning.

Patria made Bill's breakfast, filled and refilled his coffee cup, made quiet small talk, letting him adjust to the day ahead, and then she kissed him gently at the back door, the same place day after day and year after year. Off he went, smiling with his old tin lunch box in his hand.

After the door closed, she proceeded to the kitchen sink to wash dishes as if she were in a peaceful bliss. They were always cheerful and considerate to one another. It was calming to witness. This too was a familiar routine that never detoured. It would be something to witness one of those mornings again, just one more time.

Their mother began her day getting the kids up for school, feeding them and sending some of them off to school one at a time and then continuing to perform the abundance of daily chores. She moved quickly about cleaning the house, yard, toys, and vehicles, doing bills, grocery shopping, cooking, and so on. She was always doing something and was never bored. She enjoyed everything that she did and didn't complain, not to the children and not to their dad.

She carried herself with contentment and calmness. Patria was thankful that her children were allowed to simply be children for the majority of the time and appreciated their father's input and installation of morals, manners and ethics. Quite different than her childhood, she would fully recollect and note.

The children thoroughly felt secure and happy. It was an absolutely incredible childhood.

Bill's own father, Curly was known as an unobtrusive man who kept to himself and didn't have too much to say, as previously stated. He was never loud or belligerent. Dora didn't really laugh, play, or celebrate much as the children were growing. They both struggled to place a roof over their heads, put food on the table, and deal with the overwhelming sorrow that eventually intruded their home. Billy thought back, "It probably wasn't always like that, always sad but it's all that I can really remember."

Matter of fact, there wasn't much laughter at all in his childhood home. There was a sort of dark gloom which filled the air. He didn't really understand, for he was so young.

It wasn't until he was around nine years of age, when he became aware of his father's illness which claimed more and more of not only his own well-being but the happiness of his family more and more as time went on.

They said that it was cancer, and over time Curly gave up any hope of ever getting better. They didn't have the means. He didn't have the money for the medical bills and his family too. He chose to work instead of continuing to be in and out of hospitals. He felt that the expensive medications were wasteful and that alcohol was more affordable in assisting with the pain. The more that the poison began consuming his body, the more that he drank and separated from his family emotionally.

Rumor had it that Curly was unkind at times to Bill, but Bill always denied this. He claimed to only have good memories, but that's Bill. If it isn't positive, don't say it.

Maybe this is why he never discussed his childhood.

Bill and Patria didn't have fancy things or even many brand-new things but they weren't poor either. They never went without and Patria felt rich and full most of the time.

Their house was stocked with used and eclectic items, from dishes to furniture to clothes and even knickknacks. It never mattered to them, for they had the best of everything and loved it all. It was a happy home and somewhat routine and organized.

All of the kids had their chores and knew their responsibilities. They even had a chore list taped to the inside of a kitchen cupboard allowing the kids to know exactly what they had to do on a daily basis.

Maggie and Carha were usually partners, and Dana and Anna were a team. When Maggie and Carha had kitchen duty, Maggie washed and Carha rinsed, dried, and put the dishes away. The next night, Dana and Anna would do them, and then Maggie and Carha switched positions and repeated the sequence.

Cleaning the kitchen at night wasn't just doing dishes; it was putting away food and dishes until they were back where they belonged. The girls had to wipe down counters, sweep, and even mop if needed. They worked hard and never minded. It taught them to work together, and they actually found pride after the chores were completed when they looked back on their work. Counters were shiny, floors were spotless, everything smelled clean, and it was ready for another family gathering because of them. The teams secretly contended against one another as to which would do the better job—not to impress their parents but themselves.

Billy never really had chores. He was Patria's "Little Bugs." She spoiled him like crazy!

The house ran smoothly. They were well-mannered, well-adjusted, and well-liked kids. They were always happy, truly. They played as a family, ate as a family, dealt with difficult times as a family, and were extremely close. Above all, they felt so much love and warmth in their green home and for one another; little did they know how suddenly it would change. It was gone, just like that. No matter how badly they wanted it all back, they couldn't ... life lesson number one.

CHAPTER 7

JUST AS BILL was busy with his family and life, so was the rest of his family. They were doing well, raising children, and working toward their goals.

Bill's big brother, Toby, had spent eight and a half years working for a police department. While on the police department, he attended three years of junior college to earn an AA degree with a focus in mental health. He continued his education in Los Angeles, California, full time and received his bachelor's degree in Psychology. He resigned from the police department to attend college and work towards a doctorate in chiropractic medicine while working for a private patrol business in Beverly Hills. He completed his degree in three years instead of four. He married an elementary schoolteacher, Joan, and then they adopted two boys. After acing his state test, he began his private practice as a chiropractor.

Toby and Joan made frequent trips to Natruna to visit the family, and occasionally Bill, Patria, and the kids visited them too.

They also had many family reunions at their aunt Natalie's in Bakersfield, CA. Their grandmother Dora was always there, as well as all of Bill's other siblings and their growing families.

Bill's families were all genuinely hospitable and sincerely adored Patria and the children, but they too were very private, not sharing anything too personal or undesirable to society. There were many kept secrets within that family. They had strong morals and never cursed. Most didn't smoke, but a few drank behind closed doors, just like Bill. They all seemed to begin driving recreational vehicles around the country at early ages. They all generated moderate incomes; no one was rich, but they all seemed comfortable and seemed like model US citizens.

Patria's relatives, on the other hand, could be uninhibited at times but always full of warmth and love!

Patria's mom, Ethel soon came to live with the Stone family in Natruna after Tully couldn't help her out anymore. Ethel was able to take care of herself in her environment okay but didn't seem to comprehend finances, and she never learned how to drive. She enjoyed living there and having all of the children to talk to, and Patria felt better having her close, knowing that she was being taken care of. Ethel was especially fond of Bill. She never really expressed her feelings, but her pride showed, and Bill felt the same toward his mother-in-law. Bill admittedly lost his patience at times with her talking so much, but he loved her and was always kind to her.

Ethel wore long dresses with slips underneath, aprons, and interchangeable, colorful handkerchiefs which dangled from her front apron pocket at all times. She wore a money sachet pinned to the inside of her slip, right next to her chest. She kept her bony legs covered in tan stockings. Ethel had black, straight, thick long hair, which she always kept braided, just like her mom. She was tiny and delicate, even when she was young. Full breasts were not gifted to her; she was unquestionably flat chested. She also had high cheekbones, just like her mother, but Ethel was different. Ethel was plain and didn't fix herself up. She didn't believe in makeup but sometimes wore a little face powder. She didn't pluck her eyebrows or even shave her legs or underarms because they weren't hairy. At night, she always wore a nightgown, a nightcap on her head, and slippers. Ethel may not have stood out in looks, but she did in goodness. She was envied and respected in nature.

It seemed that the older that Ethel became the more important sharing her past became. She shared story after story. They never really went in chronological order, but after years of hearing them, her life began to piece together like a multifarious jigsaw puzzle.

She and Patria's father, Fred must have been destined to be together in some strange way. Their story was a sweet love story in the beginning but like many, it didn't necessarily have a happy ending.

Ethel knew of Fred's past. She knew of his escape from Mexico and the family that he left behind and she always accepted and supported him. She also knew that he didn't like to talk of it too often and respected that as well.

Fred knew of Ethel's past. He knew of the loss of her mother at a young age, her dad abandoning her, the abuse she suffered by the hand of her first husband, Roy and all of the goodness which was inside of her. He always knew that she was a treasure but somehow over time, it must have slipped his mind or become distorted from alcohol.

It all began in 1940, Fred proposed, and Ethel accepted. They were off to the justice of the peace where they said "I do" in Gunner, Texas, three-year-old Ruby at their side. Their marriage ceremony cost them a whole seven bucks. Ethel said that it was the best seven dollars that they had ever spent. Ethel was twenty-two years old, and Fred claimed to be a young forty-three. Ethel knew he wasn't completely honest about his age, but she never said a word. According to his registration card she discovered one day, he would have been forty-seven years old at the time.

For their unforgettable, romantic honeymoon, they ate a good supper at a café down the road from the justice of the peace, and then all three of them caught a picture show and chowed down on popcorn. After the movie, they stayed the night in a cheap hotel, which was a big deal for Ethel, since it was her first time she ever slept in one. In the morning, they went back to that same café and had a lovely breakfast. This too was adventurous and exciting to Ethel, since she rarely ate at restaurants. Ethel felt this all to be a sensational beginning for her new family.

Fred took care of Ruby like she was his own. Once, a man in town referred to her as Fred's stepdaughter, and it offended Fred. He sternly replied to the gentleman, "She is not my stepdaughter; she is my real daughter."

They were pretty underprivileged, and it was challenging from the start. Fred worked odd jobs doing whatever he could do. He began working more and more for a man named Mr. Robert Black, also known as R. J. R. J. had money, numerous properties, and work that needed to be done. Fred wasn't an indolent man by any means, and Mr. Black respected his work ethic. Mr. Black also took a liking to Ethel and young Ruby.

Mr. Black rented the newlyweds a very small house. By small, the entire house only had two rooms, and the house sat in the center of a moist pasture outside of Shaward, Texas. They were delighted. They had nothing to their names, not even a bed. One day, Fred discovered an old rusted boxed bedspring lying next to one of the homes which Mr. Black owned. He asked if they could have it, took it home, and placed it smack-dab in the middle of the living room floor. The box bedspring sat there for quite some time until they stuffed it full of corn husks, wrapped each metal piece with duckling fabric, and finally sewed the whole thing up. They didn't have any pillows to place under their heads, so they used coats. Fred had some old army blankets, and that's what they used to cover themselves. Ethel said, "It was a special bed, our very first bed together, and it was a comfortable one!" She added that they slept well every night.

They were a happy family. She recollects cooking their breakfast in their front yard over a campfire because they didn't have a kitchen of any sort. There was a stone-lined, hand-dug water well on the property, but it was forty yards from the house. They had to use buckets to raise the water up out of the well and carry it all the way to their home. They didn't complain and appreciated having water, but they had a constant battle with rabbits falling into it and causing horrible rot.

One day Fred needed to look nice for a trip that he was taking into Shaward for some type of business deal, but he was disappointed and unconfident because his clothes were all wrinkled. As a matter of fact, he had never had his slacks ironed before in his entire life, and of course they didn't even own an iron. Ethel, feeling like the gallant, devoted wife, knew the importance of this to Fred, so she created a plan. She placed four bricks around the campfire, sat two wooden planks on them, and used a hot brick as an iron. She felt brilliant and even bragged, which said a lot since she never boasted about herself.

Mr. Black also owned a much larger home, which became vacant after some time. He offered Fred and the family to move into it in trade for labor. Ethel agreed to milk the cows, clean out the chicken coops, and take care of the sheep and turkeys and Fred continued to be Mr. Black's assistant and handyman. It was a sweet deal, and they were ecstatic. This house was located seventeen miles outside of Shaward, further out in the country, and about four and a half miles from the small town of Gunner, Texas. Although it was challenging for them to make it to town, they enjoyed the tranquility of living in the country. They farmed, worked for the Blacks, and were happy living in this four-room country home that had a large, wraparound front porch. Ethel loved to sit in her rocking chair on that front porch.

This big lovely home had its trials and tribulations, as well. For one, it didn't have any electricity. They only had one oil lamp to travel through the entire home, and the home didn't have a well anywhere in sight. Fred eventually invented a trough to collect rainwater. Ethel said that it worked sometimes. In due course, Robert Black installed electricity, and it was heavenly, but they found water to remain an issue.

The Blacks were also proud owners of four huge gray hound dogs. One day, they ran loose and killed fifteen chickens. Ethel said she didn't know that Mrs. Black had such venom in her as she demonstrated on that day, all directed toward R. J. for not latching the gate properly. She yelled like Ethel and Fred had never heard. She also tried to hit RJ with one of the dead chickens but luckily for RJ, it barely missed him. It was quite the scene. Fred and Ethel didn't worry themselves over the couple's feud, for they saw the perfect opportunity: a food supply that could last for several weeks. So they enthusiastically brought home each and every dead chicken.

Fred and Ethel worked hard, remained focused, and moved quickly.

There are many steps and items to gather to prep the chickens. One chicken is a lot of work; fifteen chickens is a humongous amount of work.

They started by gathering the dead chickens and cutting the arteries in their necks to allow the birds to bleed out. They then dunked each bird one by one in boiling water for easier feather removal. Then they dunked them in cold water to prevent skin tearing, and then they pulled feathers, pluck and pluck to what seemed to have no end! Next, they cut their heads off with a pair of shears. Then tended to necks, pulling the skin down tightly, slitting the skin on top of the neck from the backbone, they had to separate the necks from the windpipes and crop, and then proceed to pull the crops and windpipes completely away from bird. Then cutting the feet off at the leg joint, carefully they slit body cavities and removed the vents, then removed innards, took out the livers and pulled off bile ducts, removed all the lungs, removed the gizzards and butterflied them open and peeled, took their socks off their feet, if they didn't come off easily, they had to re-

scald them. They proceeded by scraping the bird's body cavities for any leftovers, removed glands, removed wings, cut legs, hip joints, shoulders, backbones from breasts, separated thighs from legs at knee joints, halved the backs. Finally, they cleaned all of the backbones, necks, feet, heads, gizzards and hearts for the best chicken stock ever.

They were wore to the core after working all day, and all night and half of the following day. They had feathers stuck to their legs, arms, and other body parts too. You would have thought it was Christmas, they were so ecstatic to have chicken to eat for three entire weeks! During the process, they worked as a team, husband and wife. They laughed, joked, smiled, kissed between the work and felt proud of themselves.

There were always chores that needed to be done, and there was not much downtime. On the rare occasion that the couple were able to get away and do something fun, one of Ethel's favorite things to do was to go to the movies and watch old Westerns. She called them "picture shows."

Ethel began dipping moist snuff, also known as dipping tobacco with her father at an early age. Her crooked teeth were stained with it, especially in between the bigger cracks—the bigger the crack, the darker implantation of the snuff. Even her lip lines were stained brown.

Ethel was a talker, even as a young girl. She hardly took a breath. She always carried a small paper-towel-lined Folgers coffee can around with her to spit in. She seemed to talk, spit, breathe, talk, spit, and breathe. When she spit, it went "ding."

She never complained and never spoke an ill word of anyone. She saw the good in everything this world had to offer. She got excited over the simple things in life and didn't dwell on anything else. She was maybe emotionally disconnected or appeared to be, almost shut down and distant but content at the same time—at times maybe too content.

Wylie came along and had a great resemblance to Ethel's mom, Azlee Dawes. She was beautiful even as a baby. As a young girl, she was confident and strong. Wylie was petite and feminine and took after Fred in her cleanliness.

It seemed that things could not get any better when Mr. Black became ill and lost his business and homes. He couldn't employ Fred any longer. When Wylie was only six months old, the Traughters had to move into a one-room home, if that's what you could call it. It didn't have any electricity, running water, or even a kitchen. This home was located on the other side of the tracks, literally. Thankfully, their landlord was a pleasant, generous, old black woman named Deb Woods, and the Traughters hardly had to pay anything.

This timeworn house was roofed with a rusty-colored sheet of iron. It had all-dirt floors, but eventually Fred bought a large carpet remnant to lie right on top of it in the living area, which Ethel greatly appreciated. They also purchased a small table and a camp cookstove, which made Ethel's life much easier. Ethel stated, "It was a pretty good house. When it rained, our one-room house never did leak." They still only owned the one kerosene lamp but it was enough to light the small, decrepit, cold house. Unfortunately, they had to leave their homemade bed behind and just slept on the floor.

In June of 1944, Patria Ann was born. She was delivered by a midwife named Ilene Matron who later became a role model for Patria. Fred meant to say "Patty," but because he couldn't write or speak English very well, the midwife misunderstood and wrote "Patria." Fred always called her "Pat-ty." Ethel couldn't read or write much better.

Even at a very young age, Wylie took care of her little sister as if she were her mother.

One night, Ethel went out to tend to the chickens and instructed little Wylie to look over her baby sister. Patria was probably around five months old at the time. When Ethel returned from outside, she noticed that nearly the entire bottle of castor oil that was sitting on the end table was completely empty.

She questioned Wylie, "What happen to the bottle of castor oil?"

Wylie replied, "Momma, Patty was crying, and I fixed her. She ain't crying no more."

Barely a year later came Annie Marie. Annie looked more like Ethel, with fairer skin and lighter eyes. She was an extremely easy baby and hardly fussed.

For an unknown reason, Ethel became sick and weak after Annie's birth. She couldn't seem to regain her strength, felt extreme fatigue, muscle pain and even experienced some hair loss. She couldn't produce breast milk and hardly had the energy to care for the other kids even after several months.

The doctor didn't know what was wrong. Ethel was instructed to just rest as much as possible but it seemed with each passing day, she couldn't function. Eventually, her Doctor and Fred talked her into asking her first husband's sister, June, and her family to take Annie Marie for a while until she felt better. She had always kept in touch with June and she had become her closest and most trusted friend through the years.

Annie was six months old when she passed in her sleep while in the care of June and her family.

Ethel swore that it was due to Annie being fed cold milk. Ethel took this hard, which didn't aid in her recovery. She kept Annie's white lace sweater, little cap, matching booties, and perfectly folded white blanket all stored inside of a wooden box, which she protected and treasured for all the years of her life.

She had what the Doctor called a breakdown. The kids called her numb... nonexistent. She would stare off into nowhere. She didn't talk and tell her stories any more. She looked sad and sometimes didn't get out of bed in the morning. Fred just yelled at her. He told her that enough was enough and to get up and take care of the other children, clean his house and make their supper.

Ethel felt guilt and shame, like she killed her baby and felt like she didn't have anyone to talk to. She didn't want to talk to God anymore. She was angry at him. She lost her baby, felt removed from her family, church and from God for the first time in her life.

The Doctor couldn't help her, no one could. She didn't cry. She never cried. She didn't eat for days...weeks. One day, Patria went to *her bedside and softly rubbed her arm, pleading with her to get up and told her that she missed her. There wasn't any response, just a blank stare. Patria said, "Momma, God took our baby Annie to heaven, she is happy and okay there. Can't you please pray to God and he will make it all better, so he will help you come back to us? We need you back momma, please" Ethel turned her eyes to her young daughter and faintly and robotically replied; "I am not talking to God right now Patria, he stole my baby." She then turned and looked back towards the window, staring. Patria couldn't understand why her mother wouldn't just talk it over to God because he always fixed things. Her mom always told her that.*

Each breath felt like an effort for Ethel. She thought, "I will never hear Annie laugh, see her smile, smell her, and feel her heart beating in my arms again.

She dwelled on it and dwelled hard. She had to. She didn't move on, she moved forward- carrying the pain but slowly began functioning again. People didn't talk about it. They didn't bring up Annie's name. They figured that it would just hurt her more to remind her of her loss. Fred just treated it like it was unfortunate but happened, that's life and she needed to get over it. He told her they could have more.

These things didn't make her feel better. If only someone would say her name, talk about her, who she was and tell her that it was okay to hurt, it was normal to "dwell". This is the grieving process and everyone grieves in their own way at their own pace. And Fred telling her that they could have more children only made her feel worse and made her feel that he belittled who Annie was.

The grief came in waves and never when she expected it. It was the most emotionally painful experience Ethel had ever gone through. The pain was bewildering and at times she wanted to die but couldn't leave her children and even though she was angry at God, she couldn't go to hell, as she knew she would by taking her own life.

She slowly got out of bed, regained some of her strength, but there wasn't a day that went by when she didn't think of Annie, talk to

Annie or feel guilt for not being able to save her daughter. Was she angry at June? Yes-hell yes! And this didn't make Ethel feel any better about it all. This was the first time she was angry at anyone and first time to be angry with God.

With each passing day, she thought of what Annie would be like, what she would be doing, how old she would be and broke her heart all over again. What was worse, was the aloneness she felt. It seemed that if she ever wanted to talk about it to someone, they just upset her by saying stupid things. She would spend hours or even days afterwards more upset because someone she thought was a friend didn't understand what she was going through. It just hurt worse until she didn't care to be around anyone at all.

It took a very long time and eventually a lot of prayers for her to feel happy again. And looking into her children's eyes, hearing them laugh, knowing she was still needed and loved, made her slowly heal.

She was glad that she didn't give up and that she came alive again but she always knew that she would never forget Annie and over time, she openly and lovingly talked about her and shared who she was so that she would never be forgotten.

A few years later, Alfie came into the world and was pure boy, and the twins followed a few years later. Ardon and Arne were inseparable. All of the kids were extraordinarily good looking with thick, lustrous, wavy black hair, big dark brown eyes, perfectly etched noses, high cheekbones, and beautifully crafted lips.

Fred got a job at the King Railroad Company which was a wonderful blessing! It was certainly the best job that Fred ever had.

The family was rapidly growing, but they still lived in the one-room home and remained dirt poor. For years to follow, they still didn't have water to bathe or wash in, and this was unacceptable to Fred. They might have been poor, dirt poor, some would call it, but they weren't going to be dirty, ever. He drove miles in the wagon with rain barrels in the back, buying their water. They usually took a few of the kids along to hold on to the barrels to prevent the water from spilling out. This was costly for the family to spend money on, but

Fred felt it a necessity. They weren't able to do this on a regular basis but as often as possible. They gradually upgraded from one small round washtub to a medium-size tub and then two medium-size tubs. Then it became doable.

They had a wooden icebox that they kept cold by placing blocks of ice inside of it. They picked up their ice from one of the many trains they that frequented their little town. They would wait until the train stopped, and Fred would crawl up inside of it using one of his homemade contraptions and fling the ice up and over the sides of the railcar. The kids would run down the hillside to fetch it. They all knew what to do without getting caught. The railroad men really knew that they were being robbed of the ice, but kindheartedly ignored the family's routine. The kids all moved quickly and frantically retrieving the ice, never really knowing what could happen.

In 1952, Ethel was pregnant again. As with each pregnancy, Fred and Ethel were delighted. They felt that their babies were God's gifts and he would provide.

The pregnancy was uneventful and she never noticed anything different about it.

It was early spring when her labor began and Fred called Ilene, the Midwife to the house. She had delivered all of their babies and wonderfully enough lived on the same street.

After twelve hours of labor, the baby was finally coming. Ethel heard the cries and felt instant relief. It was a girl. Ethel was delighted. She was pink, plump and healthy.

Almost twenty minutes had past when Ilene became concerned that the placenta wasn't coming out. It wasn't normal for Ethel. It wasn't but a few minutes after that when Ethel began feeling excruciating pain and cramping. This didn't feel normal. "What is happening?" She screamed out to Ilene.

Ilene yelled back, "Ethel, there is another one coming, you have twins for Christ sake! Push Ethel, Push!"

Ethel was exhausted, astonished and excited at the same time.

Her eyes were big, her heart pounding, her blue engorged veins *bulging in her bony pale hands. Her legs were trembling and she had small beads of sweat noticeable to her forehead but now her adrenaline kicked into to overdrive…another one, she can do this, she thought.*

Finally, the baby came. It felt different. It felt quite smaller and less painful coming through her canal.

"Is my baby okay?"

She heard a great big inhale from Ilene and no cry. Nothing.

"Tell me!"

Ilene was frantically fidgeting down there and not saying a word, finally she replied, "I am sorry dear Ethel, she didn't make it. It appears that she has been dead for some time now. I am sorry."

Ethel was already frail, emotionally scarred from the loss of Annie and now another baby dead that she grew from her body. "Why?" She asked herself. She felt like a failure. She felt ashamed.

Ilene asked if she wanted to see her but Ethel couldn't. All the while, her new alive warm baby girl was making small noises and suckling her breast.

She again felt numb. She looked down at her warm baby and then would look over at her dead baby who lied wrapped inside of a light blue torn up towel which Ilene placed on the dresser as if she were a package of some sort going somewhere other than there. She could make out the impression of her baby's arms, her head, see the depression of her eyes and then she noticed her little blue foot and little toes poking out of the towel. Ethel couldn't breathe.

It was a cruel and surreal and that day changed her forever. Why did one baby live and that one die? Why? Did she do something wrong? Does she deserve to be a mother at all?

Everything hurt. Literally everything. She felt like she was losing her mind. It was awful but this time she looked to God from the beginning. She knew that she couldn't make it through this sorrow without him. She prayed and prayed for strength from God. And eventually, she saw light again and sincerely felt that he took her sweet baby to be with the angels, to be with Annie, her father, her mother and she would see her again. This time, she had more clarity and let go. If it weren't for God, she knew she wouldn't have made it.

Fred encouraged his wife to remain strong and take care of all her living children. "It wasn't meant to be," he rehearsed.

They didn't have a burial or say good-byes, they couldn't handle the pain.

Ilene just took care of it.

Their new baby girl, Tully was growing and healthy physically but between Ethel's frailness and the other girls being so much older, bonding amongst her and her siblings was almost nonexistent.

Ethel again took ill after this birth as well and struggled for years afterwards. The Doctor still couldn't figure out what was wrong. He called it a curse during one visit. "An unlucky curse of misfortune." He casually informed the couple.

While Tully spent much of her time on her own, Wylie and Patria were extremely close.

Wylie was always so nurturing to her little sister Patria, though Patria could never understand why since she wasn't always the nicest and most appreciative sister.

When Patria was around seven years old, she and Wylie had to go across the railroad tracks to get some buttermilk. Patria wanted to carry the milk, but Wylie wouldn't let her, so while walking next to a well, Patria pushed her in. Wylie fell down the well, so far down that Patria couldn't see or hear her. She didn't realize that the well was so deep. She quickly looked around for help and saw an elderly man down by the railroad tracks. Patria began panicking, shouting for help and finally the man heard her and came running.

Patria could hear her sister's screams but couldn't see her. Wylie cried, "Get me out of here, please, get me out of here!" She repeated these cries over and over again. Patria's head was spinning. Even if they could rescue her sister, her father was going to kill her.

Rescuing Wylie wasn't easy, and the man ended up having to get fellow co-workers to help, they threw a rope down to her, and instructed her to wrap it around her waist. Just as they began to get visual, she began falling back down, one worker miraculously reached down and grabbed a hold of her shirt and pulled her up but the shirt began to lift up over her head and out of desperation, he grabbed a hold of her hair and pulled. He pulled hard and firmly.

Wylie's faint screams were now mind-blowing loud screams as he pulled her up and out. She was intact with the exception of her hair, which was missing huge chunks.

Patria and the three men were crying by this time, very scared and shaken up.

Patria regretted what she had done right afterwards but couldn't take it back. She really didn't think that the well was that deep. She didn't think at all, she just became angry and reacted.

Of course, Wylie refused to speak to Patria for many days that followed. She was obviously shook up and maybe even traumatized by the experience.

The railroad men never called the authorities but did drive the girl's home and told their mother the entire events.

Ethel had to re-tell the story to Fred when he arrived home but of course; it was down played in order to save Patria's life. That's exaggerated, but maybe not.

Patria never really said sorry, but she was. She was puzzled by the fact that she became so angry over who was going to carry the buttermilk home. They just eventually acted as if it hadn't happened and other than a lecture from both her mother and father, she didn't get a punishment. Honestly, her punishment was regret and daily guilt for a long, long time.

Ethel's eldest, Ruby was sweet and kind natured even as she was moving into her pre-teen years. She spent much of her time divided between her Aunt June's and Ethel's. Patria enjoyed her company very much when she stayed over. They played like best friends and spent hours cutting out paper dolls and designing colorful paper dresses for them. It seemed like she was more of a visitor than a family member.

Fred did yard work on the weekends for an attorney, Mr. Gullet, and his schoolteacher wife, whom they called "Smiley." The Gullets were fond of Fred and wanted to help the family out. They helped *them move into a brand-new home on Sheep Street in the town of Denizen, Texas. The house was not entirely completed, though. Some of its gray-colored wood shingles were never put on, and a portion of the roof was missing. It was about the same size as the other small home, but this one had one additional room. There was the living room, one bedroom, and a kitchen. All Fred had to do was make the house payments. It was unbelievable, and they couldn't get over the fact that it was actually theirs.*

Patria remembered the stony cement floors. She said that it always felt cold in the house. They only had one wood heater, and it was in the living room. The house was always cold, caringly her father had a nice fire going almost around the clock and always when they woke up, to help ease the chill.

They luckily had a creek down the hill, and the kids were sent daily to fetch water with buckets. This was their only means of water.

They had a one-seater outhouse that was a ways up a hill. There was usually a stack of newspaper or whatever kind of paper they were able to get hold of to wipe with. There was never a light. Patria can't remember ever needing one. This was all she knew.

Patria soon realized that they lived differently from her friends, and even the school had accommodations that she never knew. The kids never felt sorry for themselves or complained. It was just the way that it was.

They eventually got water into their home that entered into their kitchen via a spigot. It was cold, not hot, but it was right there in their kitchen. They had a cookstove in the kitchen too. They were very appreciative and cheerful with their new home and couldn't believe that they had water accessible inside of their home.

Bathing was still a challenge, since they didn't have an inside bathroom. They sat a water filled round galvanized tub out in the sun until it became warm enough to enjoy. If it didn't get warm enough, they didn't bathe. They would towel off to freshen up.

Patria said that she wished that she had a picture of herself when she was young. She stated that she was probably the skinniest, ugliest, and puniest girl in school and she never even combed her hair.

Their neighborhood was predominantly black, and it was a safe, familiar place to live. There was one white family way up on the hill. The family had a daughter a few years younger than Patria. Her name was Elizabeth. She was kind of shy but seemed sweet. Sometimes the two walked to school together. They didn't chat too much, but it was nice for the two to not have to walk alone. They weren't ever fearful in their neighborhood, but it was still comforting.

One day, Elizabeth didn't arrive home from school. Her parents began to frantically look for her, contacting everyone that they could think of to see if they knew where she was but to no avail. The families filed a missing persons report and continued to look for her on their own.

The news of the missing girl was all over the town, with many prayers in hopes of finding her. Everyone became afraid to be alone, especially the young girls. This changed the neighborhood for the Traughters. They were the only other white family on the street.

More than two years later, a couple of teenage boys were walking in the woods several miles from town when their yellow lab led them to a disturbing sight. There, lying in the woods, they found a skeleton with a blonde hair strands still intact and Elizabeth's decomposing shoes at the bottoms of her small feet.

The coroner's report stated that Elizabeth's two front teeth were knocked out and that two of her ribs had been broken in the brutal attack that left her dead. They never found her murderer.

The events surrounding their home were tragic and terrifying, but the Traughters still loved their neighborhood and slowly placed the murder of Elizabeth in the rear of their minds.

Mrs. Acosta was their closest and most favorite neighbor. If they ever needed sugar or anything else that she could loan them, she kindly helped out. All of her children were about the same ages as the Traughters' children.

She had one son that had a disturbingly big head. He also had long fingernails, and he laid in a crib most of the time. He scared

Patria and the other kids, but Mrs. Acosta adored the deformed child and took good care of him.

As time went on, Fred's health began to decline, and he ended up being hospitalized. When he finally was released from the hospital, he couldn't urinate on his own any longer. Ethel had to use a use a skinny tube that she inserted into his penis, and then she sucked the urine out with a syringe.

One thing led to another, and he began having heart problems and then problems with his stomach. He had to take numerous medications and finally lost his job on the railroad. They had to get financial support from the state and were all terribly ashamed.

Ethel struggled to care for the children, Fred, cook dinners, and clean the house. They didn't have much money, but Fred hired a hobo named Lizza Croner to help out at times in exchange for a cot to sleep on in the shed and some food.

Lizza had thin, straggly, uninhibited, out-of-control gray hair. She was pale and skinny and had long arms and long hands and elongated, skinny legs. She seemed to always wear the same quilted, colorful, patterned skirt and raggedy light-brown shirt. She also always wore ankle high brown, worn, leather boots with the same tan muted socks which would barely show just above her boots.

She was quiet yet always passionately full of life. She had a great big thinned-lip smile showing off her slightly grayish, crooked teeth. Her wrinkles, going every which way across her face, made her unique and maybe even a little distinguished. She wore not an ounce of jewelry and no makeup, and she was soft in her mannerisms. Her eyes were a light, friendly, gentle blue.

Lizza loved the family and was good to Ethel. She spoke to her and Fred with utmost respect. She referred to them as "Ma'am" and "Sir." She was good at throwing meals together when there wasn't anything really to throw together. She created flavors and aromas that were delightful and new. Additionally, while there for her short stints, she quickly decluttered the home.

She never spoke of family or even of friends. She was a bit of a *loner in spite of her hobo life. When asked by one of the kids about her family, she gave a great big smile and replied, "Y'all's my family and all this woman need!" Then she would delicately laugh.*

Lizza traveled back and forth from the hobo jungles. She often disappeared and then reappeared out of nowhere. Like many of the hobos, she hopped freight trains as a way of travel.

The hobo jungles sat right on the other side of the train tracks behind Sheep Street, not too far from their home. These camps were established when people lost their jobs during the Great Depression and took to the roads and railroads, becoming vagabonds or hobos. They lived in makeshift shelters and cooked beans and bacon in tin cans over campfires. They didn't beg but wanted to be readily available for any work that would come. Most often, men became hobos, but there were women too and sometimes even children looking for refuge. They traveled from town to town, working where and when they could. Sometimes they stowed away in railroad cars, hiding from railroad workers in boxcars and even under the trains. It was a dangerous way to travel, but men had been doing it for many years. Because they carried their belongings rolled in blankets tied on sticks, some railroad workers called them "blanket stiffs." The hobos were always kind to passersby, stayed out of the public eye, and minded their own business.

The Traughters knew all of the local hobos and were well liked by them. Fred and Ethel often bigheartedly gave them old biscuits to eat whenever they could.

Hobos shared an ethical code and Patria knew most of the code by heart...

The code stated that you should be in charge of your own life, to always respect the law, to not take advantage of anybody in a vulnerable situation, always try and find work of some kind...paid or unpaid, don't be a stupid drunk, gracefully accept handouts, respect nature, be a team player, be clean, ride the trains respectfully, don't cause problems in a train yard, don't allow other hobos to molest children, help runaway children, help your fellow hobos, your voice counts in hobo court!

Times could be trying and difficult for the Traughters but they loved each other through it all and looked out for one another. The number one thing that the kids all had in common was laughter. They laughed at the toughest and roughest of situations. They laughed alone, they laughed at each other and they laughed at themselves.

CHAPTER 8

BY 1968, PATRIA'S oldest sister, Wylie, had just had her third child, Grady Smith. His father wasn't much of a breadwinner and was inebriated much of the time, but she seemed happy.

Patria's little sister, Tully, married Jerry and had a son named Joseph. Carha, Grady, and Joseph were all born around the same year and were pretty close for cousins.

The twins, Arne and Ardon, continued to be part of the family and almost as close as their immediate family. When they visited, they usually stayed for a while.

The whole house would rock and roll when Patria's siblings visited. The four siblings were extremely close. Maybe all of those hard times on Sheep Street back in Texas bonded them together a little like glue.

Freddie Fender and Johnny Cash blared from the record player and the living room became a dance floor. The kids loved it and adored their aunts and uncles. Patria lit up around her brothers, and they had a way of turning Bill into a teenager.

Nights when Bill wasn't working, the backyard lit up with a huge floodlight. They played basketball or roller-skated to loud music and played outside into what seemed like the morning hours.

Sometimes, one of the uncles and Bill put on the old boxing gloves, and all of the family gathered around that concrete slab and watched as long as they could tolerate. They had bells and a timer, and they pretended that it was a real boxing match. Once the blood started slinging, that's when Patria would put a halt to their match. It was all in good fun and never resulted in hard feelings. Sometimes, the next day they had bruises on their faces and even black eyes. They laughed as they recalled the match around the breakfast table.

Neither Arne nor Ardon ever seemed to make one smart decision in regards to their own well-being, but they were nothing short of perfection when it came to taking care of the ones that they loved. Arne and Ardon usually came to visit at different times, seldom together, and were something of drifters. They'd stay for a while and then seemed to vanish in the night. Months would pass by, and the family wouldn't hear from them, and then one day, one of them would magically appear all full of life, as if he always had been there. They usually caught—meaning jumped—the train from Texas. They never kept real jobs for very long. They didn't like commitments or being held down. They hardly broke the law. They preferred just to be free in this world.

The children's mom, Patria, was so close to her brothers, with the exception of Alfie. The Stone family enjoyed their family visits. It always seemed that when they were around, the whole house lit up as if it were some sort of celebration or holiday.

Ardon and Arne had many women, but not many of them actually tied them down. This didn't mean that they didn't tie the knot—they did several times throughout the years and loved their ladies—but too often, the freight trains called out to them.

After Ardon married Bella and they had a baby girl, he did settle a bit. His daughter was beautiful, just like Bella, with long red locks by the age of three and big, penetrating dark brown eyes, and full lips like Ardon's. He and Bella fought regularly, and it became a love-hate relationship. She tried to keep him home, but as much as he loved her, it wasn't in him. After the birth of their second child, the home with Bella in Texas became his home base, but everywhere else in the world was his true home.

The children's dad, Bill, was exceptionally close to Arne. He and Arne were like little boys anxiously waiting to go out on another one of their sidewinder rattlesnake hunts. They gathered their supplies and headed out toward the big, empty desert without boots and without gloves. They knew exactly how to spot a snake den. These fanged creatures often congregated inside caves, on ledges of large rock formations, and even in rock crevices. Plus, these snakes left a pretty recognizable trail.

Bill and Arne sprayed the inside of the den as well as the entrance with diesel fuel. This basically made the snakes drunk on fumes and forced them out from their restful dens. When they exited their dens, they were confused and couldn't focus on their surroundings. This was the time when Arne and Bill struck out at the dangerous rattlers. They had some strange contraption ready to grab the snakes and then quickly placed them in inside their gunnysacks. Bill mused that it was an adrenaline rush and that Arne was crazy. This crazy, wild hunt was all for the adventure of it. They actually let the horned creatures go afterward. They returned home after a long day of hunting in the desert sun and heat to drink beer while telling of their snake stories, usually talking the other one up more than themselves. A great deal of laughter filled their home on those days. It was delightful.

The twins never had much money. They did what they had to do to get around, usually construction work. At times, they even sold their blood to blood banks just to eat. The twins were both lanky, and before going to the blood bank, they snuck small weights into the bottoms of their shoes to meet the weight requirements.

Arne worked for Skinny Jim at the junkyard in Natruna for a while. He also worked briefly painting houses, but the best—yet shortest—job that he'd ever had was the one at the Natruna plant when he'd worked alongside Bill.

Family and simple things seemed to consume most of the time for the Stone family

The children spent hours in the desert behind their house. Their mom pretty much let them roam anywhere they wanted. Everyone knew everyone, and for the most part, not a lot happened in Natruna.

Bill loved collecting things, anything ... but mostly junk. They had old toasters, wagons, chairs, cars, car parts, anything you would never need lying around their backyard, not to mention all the stuff packed into the garage.

It was great for kids. They used much of it to build their incredible forts and tree houses. They used hammers, old nails, and pieces of wood from the woodpile.

Bill supported their creativity and once told Carha a story about his own childhood and riding in the back of a trailer to pick up lumber with his dad when he was a young boy. He laughed as he described going through deep mud puddles with their large wooden wheels. He said that he loved every minute of the hard work since it was time that he spent one on one with his father. He bragged about how his dad talked to him about grown-up things like how the air force threw away perfectly good wood and it was lucky for them. They found all sorts of use with this free wood. They built barns, repaired fences, made front steps. He bragged that his dad was an artist when it came to lumber.

On one particular trip to pick up wood, little Billy was sitting next to his dad when they were pulled over by a policeman. Bill's father, Curly, had whiskey in a mason jar and quickly reached over to place it in between his son's little legs. They didn't get caught, but it spilled all over Billy's lap. Billy was shaking in fear, sure that he was going to jail for having to take the blame for being the one drinking the liquor, but he was prepared and willing. The cop let the two of them go, and Billy felt proud that he'd saved his father from getting into trouble. The times of impressing him were unfortunately infrequent. Billy never told his mother about the incident, which was difficult but important to gain his father's respect.

As a father, Bill's lax attitude about the yard's appearance allowed his own children the opportunity to build all of their brilliant forts. Luckily, Patria also supported their creativity. They placed chairs, tables, and dishes in the hideaways. They even hung curtains and pictures inside of their fortresses. Their forts were their homes away from home.

They also built amazing tree houses up in the salt cedars, the only cedar that could actually live in such highly alkaline conditions—a type of nuclear mutant cedar, if you would. It was a spindly, branchy tree with no actual leaves, but it had weak green needles that were coated in a salt residue. Those limbs were pretty yummy to kids after a long day of building forts on those hot summer days—not to actually eat, but to suck on.

As for animals, they had many dogs through the years, but their favorite was a yellow Lab named Yogi. He was the best. He was so much fun to play with and very protective but never aggressive enough to hurt anyone.

One of the kids would yell to Yogi, "Go get him!" and off Yogi would run and bark, chasing either one of the kids or their friends around the yard until finally he pounced on their backs, pushing them to the ground, and then he would jump on them and lick their faces.

Whenever one of the kids became sad or in trouble, they talked to Yogi. He always seemed to understand what they were saying or how they were feeling. They had him around for the longest time.

After many years, he acquired distemper like many other of the Natruna dogs.

Unfortunately, their father wasn't raised to spend money on animals. Bill waited for the kids to go to school and took Yogi out into the desert and shot him. The kids didn't get to say good-bye or have a grave to visit. This must have been hard for their father.

Patria loved having animals around the house. It reminded her of her favorite childhood memories. She adored her animals and took very good care of them.

Growing up, she had dogs and chickens and always had a horse or two to ride and for means of transportation.

The horse most special to Patria was named Dolly. Dolly was beautiful but also ornery and often bit Patria. Patria's shoulder received the hardest, deepest, and most unforgettable bite. Dolly also frequently stepped on Patria's feet, whether out of sheer meanness or clumsiness, it was hard to tell. Patria never really knew. She just knew that it hurt like hell. Patria never held a grudge, truly loved Dolly, and cherished the bond that they shared. Dolly made Patria happy and was Patria's favorite childhood memory. Patria always rode Dolly bareback, true to nature. She maintained skill, balance, and coordination and never fell or was thrown off.

When Patria was growing up in Denizen, everyone else drove cars or motorized vehicles of some type, but not the Traughters. They had horse and wagon.

On more than one occasion, while playing on the school playground, young Patria heard the clip-clop of horse and carriages coming from way down the road. She immediately hid out of embarrassment, knowing that it was her dad or mom. Her dad would tell her later that day that he went by her school to say hi to her, but she always made up some story about why she wasn't on recess and pretended that she was disappointed. She did feel very badly about it.

Bill never bought new cars, but at least they didn't have to commute on horse and wagon! *"But at least a horse and wagon would be more reliable"*, Patria often thought.

Their cars always seem to have ongoing problems. They were lucky to have a running automobile at all.

For years, they owned a yellow Volkswagen bus with a defunct starter. They had to park it on the top of every sloped parking lot in Natruna, sometimes having to walk quite a distance to get to where they were needed to go. All of the kids had to get behind the identifiable bright yellow bus and push it as hard as they could until they heard the motor start, and then they had to run alongside of it and jump in. They knew that their friends had to have seen this happen, but they never were made fun of, and thankfully, it was never mentioned.

Bill had difficulties spending money on professionals to fix things, like the cars. He tried to repair things but never finished his projects. He didn't believe in buying things brand new.

Patria never expected expensive or fancy things, but having things not work right made her frustrated. She never was one to bitch or complain. She just made the most out of what they had.

After the Stone's moved to Flower Street, they instantly made best friends with the neighbors. Carha's very best friend was Tammy Robbins. Billy became best friends with her younger sister, Amanda. They were the same ages as Carha and Billy but with a completely different upbringing.

Tammy and Carha were always together and adored

one another, but they also engaged in some pretty big battles, so big that their parents would have to separate them. This was painful for the two of them, having to go hours or days without playing with one another.

During these times that seemed like forever, they utilized a mailbox system. They kept this mailbox, which in actuality was a shoe box, on Tammy's brick fence.

They used a salt cedar limb for their flag. Having this form of communication saved them some of the agony of separation. They wrote letters all day until they could play with one another again. These letters were apologetic and remorseful. They reiterated their love for one another and their sisterhood. They wrote about the future ranch that they were going to share when they grew up and about all of the animals they would have. They wrote about what they were doing and what they wanted to do once reunited.

One of their favorite things to do was to sleep over at one another's houses. They made up plays or dances and performed them in front of their families. Even Billy and Amanda participated. Sometimes, they took place in Maggie's closet, with a small light hidden away in the back and a brush for a microphone, usually standing on a suitcase to make them feel like stars, and they either sang louder than the record player or lip-synced while dancing.

It must have been awfully boring to their parents and the rest of the Stone gang, but their audiences never let on. They watched attentively and clapped no matter what at the end. Sometimes, the two families joined together for the showings and even had to pay to get in.

Other times, they were just actresses performing some skit they watched and copied from *I Love Lucy*, *Laverne and Shirley*, or *The Carol Burnett Show*. Their families made them feel like stars.

When they took their baths, they spent hours lathering

one another's backs with soap and then drawing pictures while making the other guess what the drawings were (or letters of the alphabet).

Before falling asleep, they tickled each other's backs for hours, laughing and whispering, their hands so tired, feeling as though they could fall off.

Carha always felt sorry for Tammy because her parents were stricter than hers. Tammy was always sent to bed much earlier than Carha, and Carha dreaded this when she stayed the night with Tammy. It was almost torture to miss out on the world at such an early hour. However, it was a trade-off because Carha loved eating toast with butter and honey in the morning. Honey was just one of those items that Patria never bought.

Tammy's family was of incredibly strong Christian faith. They went to the Baptist church faithfully every Sunday, every Wednesday, and anytime something else was going on there. The Stone kids were always invited to attend and usually enjoyed going and participating. It was safe, fun, and interesting.

When the kids were younger, they attended the E-Free, well that's what the kids called it, it was the Evangelical church. They would all attend with their mother, but for some reason, Patria stopped going at some point and never chose to go to the Baptist church either.

Patria said that she felt disappointed and disillusioned with what people at church said and what they actually did. She felt they judged too much and many didn't follow God's word and they spent too much time pretending.

As she was growing up, her father, Fred never attended church but he said that he believed in God. Matter of fact, he bellowed and praised how God had once saved his life before he met Ethel.

Patria's father, Fred was born to the Tarahumara people located in Chihuahua, Mexico, in the late 1800s. He only knew the

Tarahumara Uto-Aztecan language.

Villa's forces ruled over parts of Mexico like a medieval warlord. Villa financed his army by stealing from the endless cattle herds in northern Mexico and selling beef north of the border. He found plenty of US merchants willing to sell him guns and ammunition out of their fear of him and his mob. Faced with a stagnant economy, he issued his own money; if merchants refused to take it, they risked being shot. Fred refused to be part of these executions, which Villa often ordered on a whim. They were usually left to his friend Rodolfo Fierro, best known by his nickname El Carnicero ("the Butcher"). Fred ended up riding with Pancho Villa for a while but for some reason hit a point when he refused to ride with his posse anymore. This caused a rift, and Fred was on the run and running in particular from a new rival by the name of El Carnicero. Once in an attempt to escape from Mexico for good, while swimming the Rio Grande River, Fred was shot once in the back by this well-known assassin. Fred arrived in Texas, barely alive and bleeding to death. Some good Samaritans found him and delivered him to a Catholic priest in hopes that there could be time for his last rites to be given.

The priest said that he heard the voice of God tell him to save this man who wore the cross over his chest. To the surprise of the priest, this man eventually healed, but before leaving the priest, he was sworn to a new name and identity forever. He could never return to Mexico again, never see the wife and five children that he'd left behind. He knew that if he did, he would be shot in a heartbeat or, worse, his family would be slaughtered.

He slowly learned English, but it wasn't easy, and many people could hardly understand what he was saying, but he didn't give up.

It wasn't long after that when Ethel and Fred were introduced to one another and it was an immediate match—maybe even fate or destiny. Fred was alone and lonely. Ethel and Ruby, just two years old, needed a man around.

Fred Traughter stood five feet six and was not a big man but was forceful and strong in his being. He was described as the depiction of some famous Indian man who played in old Westerns. He had thick, wavy, salt-and-pepper hair, little features, little lips, big dark-brown eyes, little ears, and little yellow "corn teeth." He took pride in his cleanliness and had a daily ritual of beginning each day with a nice clean shave. He mostly wore slacks. They weren't always in the best condition, but he tried. And of course, he bore the scar in his right shoulder from the bullet wound.

Patria was always intimidated by her father but loved him all the same and she thought of him often. Years had passed since his death and at times, it was still hard for her to believe that he was gone. She believed in God but had her doubts about heaven. Her father used to say that a person doesn't have to go to church to believe in God and many ungodly people go to church. Patria began thinking that maybe her father was right.

Even though Patria quit attending church in her late 20's, Carha and Billy continued going and even sang in the church choir and participated in the Christmas plays. Once, Carha sang a duet with Tammy in front of the entire congregation.

Good thing that wasn't recorded. Carha could never sing or carry a tune, but that didn't stop her from trying. She took after her mother in that sense. When Patria sang, her voice booed a combination of uneven whistles and scratched messed up vocal cords making it difficult to listen to. It was worse than nails on a blackboard.

Carha and Tammy enjoyed playing with little Billy and sweet Amanda. They were easygoing kids and did whatever Carha and Tammy asked them to do.

Once, Carha and Tammy dressed up Billy and Amanda for a marriage ceremony. They first arrived to the ceremony in a "covered wagon," which was really a wooden box sitting sideways on one of the play wagons. They had bread ties for rings, and after the wedding ceremony, the girls made them seal it with a kiss. They were pretty compliant, and it was a beautiful ceremony.

Carha definitely became the leader in the friendship from the beginning and most of the time led Tammy into trouble. She wasn't the best influence, but she loved her best friend and was loyal to her. She would have done anything for her friend.

It wasn't until the girls had turned nine years old that Mr. and Mrs. Robbins stopped drinking alcohol and frequenting the bars.

They both had a problem with monogamy while drinking. Once, Beverly Robbins tried French-kissing Patria over their wooden fence. Patria never told anyone about it but never became buddy-buddy with Mrs. Robbins after that. It was a good choice for the Robbinses to quit drinking.

Bill had many quirks; another one was that he took their trash to the dump but only after dark, and there was a very good reason why (that will be explained shortly). The kids were always so excited to go with him. It was a bonding and special time, yes … going to the dump with their father.

At times, he only took one of them at a time to spend alone time with them. He was an excellent listener—not just pretending but *really* listening and staying engaged for as long as it took. This was important for the girls, since talking was a huge part of their existence. They must have taken after their granny, Ethel.

On their way back, sometimes he pulled over at the Natruna Cemetery. He and Carha just sat outside the fence, talking about life, death, and God. She asked him personal questions, wanting to know more about him, but these were never openly answered. No matter what the question or how it was worded, he answered vaguely and briefly. It wasn't about him, it was about them … her. That was okay.

Bill usually had an Olympia beer can between his legs and a few more within reach behind the seat. The kids never cared. It seemed that when he drank, he was more relaxed, and the more relaxed he was, the more attention they received.

Carha remembered a conversation she had once with her father outside those cemetery gates, when her dad admitted that he didn't believe in a God. He said that he felt that after you died, you went nowhere. It was like before you were born, you didn't exist. Even as a young girl, Carha didn't believe this, not for a moment, but she wouldn't ever argue with her father. She looked up to him and respected and cherished all of his beliefs and feelings.

Since the kids lived about a thirty-minute walk from the cemetery, they visited it pretty regularly. Usually Billy and Carha went there together, but not always. At times, Carha went by herself.

They didn't know anyone there; really, they just wanted to go to visit those who passed. Carha never felt that they were gone; she just felt that they were not present physically here on earth.

She visited with a young girl whose name was Anna, who had died as a young girl. She was her friend but had never met her in this life. Carha became familiar with many of the graves and was drawn to certain ones. She just stood there and talked to them as if she knew them.

The cemetery was a special place for Carha. It felt like a peaceful and selfish time. Whether alone or with her brother or father, it made Carha feel calm and consider with veneration so many others who left this world too soon. It made her think of her own mortality and gave her an appreciation for still having time in the physical world. She thought of this, even at a very young age.

On their many trips to the dump, as they drove by that unattractive, dull, dry, cemetery to her left, she would always take a deep breath and feel an extraordinary amount of peace and love for all of the souls that left those bodies to go to heaven and this made her look around at her family all packed inside that van excited about their upcoming adventure with appreciation. She knew she was lucky. She was wise beyond her age in that sense.

Going to the dump held valued and unforgettable memories for the family. Yes, going to the dump! Their dad called out into the big house, "Who wants to go to the dump?" All the kids would scramble around, fighting for the brightest yellow flashlight. They all piled inside of the car or van—even their mom—and off they went to the Natruna dump … an exciting time to be treasure hunters.

They spread out over the hill and on top of the mounds of trash, but as soon as they saw headlights coming their way, someone would yell, "Car! Car!" Off went the flashlights, and everyone ran to the outskirts of the dump and huddled down until the people threw out their trash and left.

They were trash diggers, but had their dignity too. No one could ever find out. It was their family secret. They didn't even tell their best friends. Tammy didn't even know. Even the cars that pulled up to dump their trash increased their excitement and anticipation, especially if it was someone with money.

The kids found dolls, toys, decorations for their rooms, and even clothes. All they needed were a hard scrubbing, and they were usually as good as new. Sometimes they even found presents for one another if it was something that one of them wanted more than they did.

It was a fun time, a time of giving and a time of receiving. Even the smell of trash mixed with the dirt stirred up sensations of delight!

They didn't wear gloves and hardly got sick. Heck, they probably had tough immune systems from tolerating the knolls of germs, viruses, and bacteria they faced on a regular basis.

CHAPTER 9

*A*S SIBLINGS, THE *Traughter kids were as close as they came. They were continually playing together, coming up with new adventures and spending time doing their favorite things with each other. They loved rolling around and playing roughly on the grass. The smell of fresh grass created a mind full of fun times that made Patria smile inside and out. Collecting lightning bugs was another favorite memory. The kids could fill whole jars full of them. They challenged themselves to see if they could create even more of the mystical, dancing yellow lights than they had the time before. They respected the small creatures and feared that if they kept them too long, the insects would smother. It felt magical to watch them bounce away into the night skies.*

Going to the doctor's office or dentist on the other hand was not something that was done.

When Patria was very young, she had the most horrible and excruciating toothache. She waited as long as she could until the tooth was rotten. She told her parents about her troubling tooth day after day, but they just disregarded her moans and said that it would get better, but it didn't. She came home from school one morning and begged her daddy to take her to the dentist. She couldn't take the agony any longer. He finally gave in, gave her a little money, and said,

"Just go!" She painfully walked three long miles to the dentist's office, but they refused to see her without a parent present. She then had to walk all the way home to plead with her mom, "Please help me!" Her mom, still reluctant, gave in, and the two walked the three miles back to the dentist's office, and finally, the dentist pulled the damned nasty tooth out. It was a nightmare of a day.

They never had much money or food. Breakfast consisted of corn bread and beans or whatever the leftovers were from the night before— usually corn bread and beans. Potatoes were another common meal, usually fried in a pan full of oil.

Sometimes all they had to eat for days on end were either pig tails or crunchy pig ears. On a good day, they had both. Fred had store credit but rarely paid on it. The butcher let him get away with it and even threw the charge tickets away. He really cared about Fred and the family. He knew all of them by name, watched them grow, and wasn't blind to their poverty.

When they had flour to spare, Fred made the thickest, yummiest tortillas on the cookstove, and then he perfectly cut them into small pieces. The kids loved and devoured them. There wasn't ever enough to eat, not once. Patria fantasized that the next time he would make so many that she could eat and eat until she couldn't fit another single piece into her stomach. That would be a dream come true.

Ethel made the thickest, heaviest, flakiest, biggest, and most perfectly round biscuits ever. Patria said that if aimed just right, she was sure that they could knock someone straight to the ground. The kids were always on guard when eating them for fear of chewing into one of those common disgusting balls of baking soda.

Having meat on hand was a rarity, but when they did, they had their favorite dishes. Fred made amazing hamburger chili, and Ethel made her famous chicken and dumplings. Sometimes they came across the blessing of a pig to butcher. They didn't have many eggs, but when they did, they wolfed them down, feeling empowered by their richness.

During the school year, Wylie worked in the cafeteria, where she could sneak free lunches for all of her siblings. She was never afraid that she would be caught. She just felt it was her obligation given the circumstances.

Whenever one of the kids would become sick with a cold, their daddy would make another one of their favorite treats: kerosene candy. It was made out of kerosene mixed with sugar and fried in a cast-iron skillet. It was thin and hard like peanut brittle, and they loved it! He preached to them that it would get rid of their colds. They really never ate candy other than daddy's kerosene candy, and as adults always wondered what else the candy had gotten rid of…maybe a few brain cells?

Patria remembered, "Sometimes I would be so hungry that I would eat an onion sandwich, just onion and bread."

The family never ate out at restaurants, not once. They never went on a vacation, but then again, they only had a wagon, which would have made going anywhere virtually impossible.

Growing up, Patria said that they were the only family in Denizen that lived in history and never changed with the times. They even had their own gardens and grew the best fruits and vegetables ever.

Mrs. Gold was Patria's fourth-grade teacher. She was a heavyset, woman and very sweet. Patria began to dislike academics with a passion. She had no use for learning at all, especially math. She had a friend do all of her work and didn't pay any attention in class. One day, Mrs. Gold wrote some problems up on the board and asked that Patria go up there to solve them. Patria hesitantly attempted, with the steady persuasion of Mrs. Gold—"No, child, that's not right!" Then Mrs. Gold whipped Patria on her butt with her big fat hand in front of the entire class. That day didn't make Patria like going to school any better or want to try any harder.

Thankfully, some of the role models for the Traughter kids were what they considered positive. The Traughters were very close to the Matrons and felt them to be just like family. Ilene and Cal had kids ranging the same ages as the Traughters' children. Ilene Matron was the practicing midwife that delivered Patria and most of her siblings into this world. She also pierced Patria's earlobes. Patria felt they had a bond, and she really looked up to this kind, smart, beautiful woman.

Patria still looked up and admired Wylie. They were still extremely close. Wylie had a way of persuading all of the children to help around the house. All of the kids had chores, and for some reason, chopping wood, carrying it in, and stacking it next to the cookstove became Alfie and Patria's daily chores. Ethel and Wylie did most of the cooking. All of them attempted to keep the house clean, but it was nearly impossible due to the cramped spaces and the water situation. Even washing their clothes was difficult.

As Patria became older, she became more particular about her appearance. She washed her clothes, hung them on the line, neatly folded them, and then protectively placed them inside a cardboard box which she kept in the corner of her room.

All of the kids had to pitch in and do the dishes, even the boys. They didn't like doing them at all but knew that if they didn't, they would receive a walloping from their dad, so they did as they were told.

Patria proudly bragged that she was her dad's favorite child, his "pet." She was the toughest and worked the hardest. She was his number-one helper. Her daddy felt that Wylie was on the lazy side.

Three thirty in the morning came early with the sounds of her daddy's voice calling out to her, "Pat-ty, time to get up and go to work now." They were off to the Gullets'. Fran "Smiley" Gullet was the kindest, most generous woman. She handmade the girls' clothes every year. She made them the most beautiful sundresses. Every year, she and her husband took the girls to the shoe store to buy the brown oxford shoes. The kids never liked the "plain poor-people shoes," but they felt lucky to have something covering their feet, so they never protested and were always thankful.

Patria felt that she worked just as hard as her dad. She loved knowing how proud he was of her. She adored watching him laugh to show off all of his corn teeth. He didn't make much money, but having food for the family to eat was the most important thing to him and he tried his best to always provide.

The kids also assisted in gathering food when they could and when they were hungry. They all grouped together when it came to their crawdad-hunting outings. Usually one was nominated to sneak into the kitchen to snag any meat that they could get their hands on; bacon was the big score. Once the meat was in hand, the kids excitedly headed for the lake.

They were captivated by the small lobsterlike creatures. Time flew by while the kids diligently worked as a team, collecting as many as possible. Their break times consisted of playing with the crawdads, swimming, and talking innocently among themselves. After the hard day of work, the kids took the crawdads to town and sold them to the fishermen in Shaward.

Patria enjoyed riding her green bike around the neighborhood. It was a marvelous, used, twenty-four-inch girl's bicycle. It was rough at first, but after her dad put in a little tender loving care, along with some hard elbow grease, it wasn't too shabby. Patria said that she never understood why the heck he painted it such a funky green, but she treasured that bike.

Patria remembered her father as a modest man. When Fred bred one of his horses, he always made the children go into the house so that they would not witness the actual act. How could someone gentle in so many ways be so mean to others?

Years later, Fred's "Black Chalk" as they called it, had grown to become quite famous in Denizen not only to the hobos but also to prominent folks in town. The homebrew was called that due to its dark rich beautiful color. Even Mr. Oden, Patria's third-grade teacher's husband, indulged. He and Fred drank for hours under the big oak tree that was beside their house. During that time, Denizen was a dry county. Fred pulled in quite the income from this little side business.

The process began in the kitchen in a big galvanized tub, and then it relocated to storage shed out back. And when it was just right, it was strained into jars. This was one of Patria's preferred chores. As long as she worked, she could drink, even at age ten. She remembers that "happy, without-a-worry feeling."

As an adult, she began drinking more often than she should have, to drink away her frustrations and worries. She didn't drink everyday but as she hit her thirties, something happened and she began to lose coping skills that she once had. She worried about things more and more and drinking seemed to help her cope. She wasn't aware that it was only burying her worries deeper into her core creating bigger problems.

It didn't stop her from her active hardworking life style. She just kept that balance…at least for a while.

Being married to Bill, Patria learned how to work on cars, fix appliances, repair plumbing problems, and work on the heating and air conditioning unit, and she did the best that she could do.

For all of their weirdness, they were an extremely close family. There was an abundance of love in that green house on Flower Street. It is amazing how things that seem so strong and enduring can crumble in the blink of an eye and no matter how hard you wish for it to be the way it once was, it will never be…

CHAPTER 10

THE GOMEZES MOVED out to Pioneer when the children were small. They built a nice ranch-style home across from the horse corrals. It was roomy and peaceful out there. All of the children had their own rooms, but Willie, being the boy, had the smallest room of all. The resentment toward his sisters just never diminished.

The kids also had desert to roam in and plenty of rocky mountains to play on. They were much like the Stone children; they spent almost every waking hour either at school or playing outside.

Pete still worked at the plant, and Audrey was a stay-at-home mother after giving birth to Willie. She always kept busy caring for the kids, the house, and Pete. She took after her mother in many ways, waiting on her husband and having every meal ready and warm. She really spoiled him.

They had a good relationship, though it wasn't overly affectionate. Willie didn't see them hug or kiss, but he knew that they loved each other.

The family did what many families do together. They ate meals together and watched television together. They took trips as a family various times throughout the year, which they all looked forward to and appreciated the break from the desert heat.

They took their weeklong fishing trip to Nevada once a year and vacationed in Mexico every year, playing in the ocean and on the beach. They also took the yearly trip to Idaho to drop Willie off at his grandparents' ranch and pick him up at the end of the summer.

Both trips to Mexico and Idaho were long drives, which the kids never looked forward to. Once there, of course, they forgot about the trip and enjoyed themselves.

Growing up on the ranch, Willie learned to care for and respect animals at a very young age. Every summer, he stayed there for almost three months, working and learning cattle ranching. Changing sprinkler pipe, putting up hay and working cattle was hard work.

He was extremely close to his grandparents. They were kind and loving toward Willie.

His uncle Hugh wasn't as sweet and he nurtured in a different way. Hugh woke the boys up using an electric cattle prod, also called a hot shot or would throw cold water on them, always referred to them as 'hey girls', and once even dropped a bale of hay on one boy's head because he was moving too slowly. Hugh had a way of pushing their buttons and loved it when it would piss them off. They left not knowing if they hated or loved him, couldn't stop thinking of him, and then couldn't wait to get back to the ranch the next summer.

For all of the good that surrounded Willie, for some reason, he sort of snapped at around thirteen years of age. He became short tempered and angry at the world. He didn't understand it, and no one could explain it to him.

His grades began to drop, and punishments changed from the whippings to his dad sitting him in their utility shop and shaving his hair without a clipper comb attached to aid in a steady, even shave. It was pure, unadulterated blade to scalp. Some hair strands were kept long purposely and some shaved so closely that his scalp became excoriated.

It was his father's way of saying, "You think you're that cool? I'll show you how cool you are."

It was the hardest punishment for Willie, who was self-conscious anyway. You wouldn't believe so with him being so handsome, but he was. Plus he began having acne and couldn't get control of that, either.

His acne came on just as puberty did. His voice deepened, and he began getting hair in strange places around his body and on his face. The acne wasn't just on his face; it was on his back, chest, shoulders, and neck. He felt his acne was horrible and he couldn't hide it so it affected his self-esteem on a daily basis. Not knowing anything about dermatology or acne skin care, his treatments were beginning to leave permanent scars, which made matters worse.

He didn't just have whiteheads; he had blackheads, papules, pustules, nodules, and worst of all, cysts. The cysts were large, very painful, and filled with pus that was visible to all that looked at him. He couldn't hide them.

He was at the age that he began liking girls too, which didn't make his situation easier. In his mind, all he could see was them looking at him seeing a huge pimple and feeling grossed out.

He tried everything that he could. He tried gels, soaps, pads, creams, and lotions. Nothing seemed to help. It seemed that they just burned his skin, dried it out, and caused redness. So then, he not only had pimples and cysts everywhere, but he also had dried, flaky red skin. And then to top it off, he had his fathers induced baldness, if that's what you call it.

Like this was going to make him feel better and more at ease, right?

He finally went to the doctor about his acne and was told it was just hormonal—testosterone, to be more exact. The only thing that seemed to help at all was washing his face morning and night and applying benzoyl peroxide to it afterward. The doctor also prescribed an antibiotic called tetracycline, which he was on for way too long.

Needless to say, Willie was a mess.

After his father shaved his head, it took months for his hair to grow out completely. He walked around school looking like Quasimodo from "The Hunchback of Notre Dame."

His grades weren't picking up at all. As a matter of fact, it might have stirred more anger inside of him.

Plus there were a group of girls at school that gave him the nickname "the Atomic Fig." That didn't help matters much.

Luckily, the girls usually let up some in between the shaves.

Willie had a fondness for the outcasts of school, maybe because he felt like one. He never refrained from defending the underdog. If people were being picked on, it didn't matter who they were or if he knew them—he had to teach those bullies that their behavior was just not acceptable. That only landed him into more trouble.

Willie always seemed to show a solid resistance against authority and authority figures.

It was this attitude that brought Willie and a few friends to feel that the Natruna police had too much time on their hands. They started a small explosives-manufacturing business right there in the Natruna mountains.

They would look for old beer bottles in the desert or at the dump so they could whip up Molotov cocktails. They had plenty of testing ranges to make sure they would explode with just the right amount of boom—never planning to hurt anyone, just to get the local cops' attention.

They carried these explosives around in backpacks and sometimes even to school, but they didn't tell anyone. After school and just after the sun went down some and they found that perfect spot, they soaked cloth that protruded from the bottle with gasoline, and then toss one of the improvised incendiary weapons smack into the middle of a quiet street. When the bottle smashed in the middle of the road, on impact, an ensuing cloud of petrol droplets and vapor ignited, which caused a startling fireball immediately.

Families from almost every home came running out, surprised and confused. When the cops arrived, the boys were long gone.

This became quite the war. The bombers had to really plan out their next locations. They weren't old enough to drive, so strategy was of the utmost importance. They got away with it for months, never hurting anything or anyone, just driving the law enforcement mad, until one day, Willie lit his bottle's cloth on fire and prepared to throw it by reaching as far back behind his shoulder as he could, then as the fuel leaked down his shoulder and arm, the flames followed burning his hair and partially singed his right arm and part of his eyebrow.

Luckily, his bombing mate John acted quickly and threw Willie to the ground and rolled him over on the sand, pouring more sand over him and patting the fire out.

Willie suffered painful second-degree burns, but they got away with no one ever finding out that they were the Natruna bombers. Willie doctored his own burns, never revealing his secret to even his parents. But that was the end of that syndicate.

Willie was an average athlete. He played football all four years of high school. This was about the only sport he felt comfortable playing, since he could cover his face in the helmet and face guard. He enjoyed traveling on the school bus to faraway schools and checking out all of the girls there.

His downfall in football, just as in life, was that he didn't like being told what to do. He was kicked off of the football team several times because his hair was too long and he refused to cut it or would disobey school rules.

When he was around sixteen, he did not have a car or a driver's license (he had been kicked out of drivers education after only two weeks of beginning the class) and he refused to ride the school bus. He began hitchhiking to school. Some mornings, he was successful, and some, he just couldn't get a ride, which caused him to be late to Mr. Myer's homeroom class.

At first, Mr. Myer wrote tardy slip after tardy slip, and then after too many of those, he just sent him to the principal's office, which became way too familiar with Willie Gomez.

Eventually, Mr. Myer didn't do anything at all. He just rolled his eyes and continued teaching, while Willie took his seat. They had a very understanding relationship.

By this time, Willie's parents, frustrated and disappointed, basically gave up. They too shook their heads in defeat time after time.

Willie wasn't a bad teen. As a matter of fact, everyone who knew him liked him. He had a way of making even grown-ups feel special.

For all of Willie's rebellion, he never did drugs up to this point, rarely drank, and detested cigarettes. He genuinely cared about people and didn't mean to stress them. He himself was confused about why he did the things that he did. He knew there wasn't any excuse. And for all of the bad things that he did, he rarely got away with anything. Sometimes he was accused of doing things that he didn't even do, and he couldn't talk his way out of those times, either.

You would think that he would learn his lessons, especially since he kept getting caught and punished. Some people just seem to sabotage themselves; guess that was Willie's way.

Even the best people make mistakes, but unfortunately, some of them don't live through them.

Thanksgivings were memorable at the Gomez home and usually the home filled with a few out of town family members. Audrey was a good cook and always made a handsome spread. Cousins played and enjoyed their visits and being in the openness of the desert while experiencing the uniqueness of Natruna.

The Stone family also made cherished memories during holidays and on Thanksgiving, Patria always went all out and made the exact same traditional meal every year which was delicious.

The house became active with family and friends. Music was always playing on an old record player. A little bit of country, a bit of rock 'n' roll, and even some current hits from the time, everyone enjoyed talking, dancing, laughing, and of course eating lots of wonderful food. Smiles were on everyone's faces. Kids ran in and out of the house as they always did but even more so during the holidays. They didn't want to miss a single minute with their uncles, especially Maggie with her Uncle Arne. She didn't leave his side. Everywhere Arne was, Maggie was holding on to his leg or arm.

Although Thanksgivings were a special time and a time of celebration, Patria and her siblings would be sure to take time to join one another in remembrance of their father.

Just after the table was set, Arne would usually lead the family in prayer. He reminded everyone is his deep, gentle, soothing voice, "Please hold hands, bow your heads" and then he would recite something like this: "Dear God, Thank you for our food today and for every meal you have generously given to us. Thank you for this blessed Thanksgiving and for allowing us to be here once again together and with our dear sweet momma. We pray that our daddy who left us on this day so many years ago has been embraced, forgiven and healed by your loving grace. God have mercy on his soul and please keep us all safe and filled with the spirit of your all mighty and on the path of righteousness, in Jesus name, Amen."

Arne never ceased to amaze Patria. He did pay attention all of those fidgety mornings sitting on those church pews.

Patria had memories of the last time that she saw her father at the age of fifteen. He was out in the back under the tree that he loved so much all by himself drinking some of his homemade brew. He was sitting reclined in an old woodened chair with his legs propped up on an old wooden bucket. He was wearing his favorite faded overalls and straw hat which he always wore when out in the yard. He appeared relaxed and unaffected that his daughter was leaving Texas for California to join her big sister Wylie and her husband, Sidney.

He knew that Patria was strong willed and stubborn like a thick nail refusing to go all the way through one of his 2x4's. There wasn't anything that he could say or do to stop her from leaving.

He loved her and his heart was breaking, inside he felt the pain badly but on the outside, he would not show it. He wanted what was best for her but knew Wylie would watch over her.

She was puzzled to his aloofness and figured he was just a miserable, unhappy mean drunk that didn't care but she also knew deep down inside of him, there was love for her.

While knowing her ride was anxiously waiting, she quickly dropped her suitcase and hurried down the hill to say good-bye to her father which she had been dreading all week.

She said, "I'm leaving daddy." He just looked up at her and shook his head. She asked, "Aren't you going to say good-bye to me?" He looked at the ground and grunted. He rocked the old foot stool forward and back while continuing to grunt. Patria almost cried. She bent down and wrapped her arms around his growing belly and rested her head on his big shoulder and just felt him, felt his energy, briefly smelt his unique smell which always smelt like his favorite musky, spicy soap. His long wavy hair touched against her cheek. He patted her arm, not saying a word. She knew that was his way of saying that he loved her. She quickly stood up, twisted around and ran up the hill to meet her friend waiting for her.

She never did cry. She never looked back. The bus took forever but she wasn't afraid at all.

She wasn't nervous like many girls at her age, leaving home and everything that she knew for the first time. She was quite the opposite.

Wylie, woven from the same cloth, wasn't shy or timid. She took pleasure in the attention that she received while displaying her unspoiled body, sunbathing smack-dab in the middle of their apartment complex, displayed for all the men to gawk at and woman to hate. She definitely wasn't introverted when it came to her body. Sidney knew what men said about his wife but never became bitter or irritated at her or them; he knew his wife was stunning, and he felt honored.

Neal Hogan was the most electrifying man Patria had ever encountered. He also wore the thickest glasses she had ever seen, resembling Buddy Holly a bit. Neal was the sweetest and most generous man. He took Patria on motorcycle rides to the Pacific Ocean, which was most invigorating. She began to feel that the skies were the limit. They went to the hippie espresso cafés around the area just to kick back and hang out. She was having the time of her life. She felt secure living there and was treated respectably by everyone.

She quickly landed a job at a plastic factory, and she was delighted to receive her own money and never had a problem with working hard.

Judy lived down the street and became Patria's best girlfriend. One day, they were all hanging out at Wylie's when Patria decided to take a ride in some gorgeous guy's car. He was Judy's cousin and was visiting for a few days from out of town. Anyway, when Patria arrived back at Wylie's, she found her best friend and very sweet boyfriend together, practically naked on the couch. Neal and Patria were history and very soon after, and Neal and her best friend Judy were joined in holy matrimony. She never saw Judy's cute cousin again.

Life in California seemed like a dream come true. Finally there was a little money, food, a clean place to live. The girls often talked of visiting their parents, but it seemed the days would just roll by, one faster than the last.

On Thanksgiving 1960, a telegram arrived for the girls informing them that their dad was in the hospital and was asking for them. They were trying to make the arrangements to go to him, but while in the middle of the chaos, they received a second telegram telling him of his passing.

It was too late.

According to Ethel, he had been out of his heart pills for some time because they couldn't afford them. He had done this before without any repercussions, and they thought it would be okay. They had a wonderful Thanksgiving Day, and everything seemed fine until he began complaining of chest pain and a bad stomachache. At first they thought it was just indigestion but it wasn't going away. Ethel called for an ambulance. They said he had a heart attack.

He was only sixty-seven, and it was so unexpected for everyone.

The girls made it back for the funeral, thanks to Sidney's help.

It was hard on the family, especially Ethel. She mourned his death, and it was obvious that her world as she knew it had changed. She had good and bad days, good and bad hours, even minutes. She went from crying, to sleeping, to sobbing, to telling stories of her beloved husband.

The funeral took place inside a Catholic church. The words were foreign and impossible to understand, but the girls were relieved to be there. It wasn't an easy trip. There laid Fred, aged and frail, in an open casket for the whole congregation—people that he didn't even know—to see. Why? Patria thought. What was the purpose in displaying this empty shell of a man, her father, for these strangers to gawk at? Ethel was as skinny as ever and obviously weakened emotionally and physically by the loss of her husband and the father of her eight children. She was apparently grief stricken but appeared numb and without any tears left. They seemed to have stopped and no longer existed. She shed not one tear during the funeral. This created confusion among the children. How could she be this way? This caused a wall of misunderstanding, as it always did with death and their tender yet strong mother.

At the time of his death, his real name was unknown, and his birthplace a mystery and the truth died with him. It is said that his real last name was Garcia when he crossed that border. His name and the names of his long-lost wife and children were also gone. Through many years of Fred's life, he and his best friend, Mr. Cisco Morales, sent numerous letters attempting to make contact with his family in Mexico, only for them to be return home unopened. The whereabouts of the letters were hidden, lost or thrown away, as were the clues to who he really was.

The children stayed by their mother's side and were supportive for as long as they could be. She had to get on some governmental assistance once again, which wasn't much at all. It was difficult. She still went around the house and talked to Fred as if he were there, and when confronted out of concern by one of her kids saying, "Momma, you know Daddy's gone," she would softly reply, "I know he is still here with me in spirit."

Many nights after Fred's passing, Ethel not only saw Fred's rocking chair rock back and forth, she could hear it creaking and cracking at all hours of the night. She heard his footsteps and felt his presence and didn't doubt at all that he was with her.

For all of his violence and abuse, she loved him.

Ethel's faith in the afterworld and in spirits visiting their loved ones kept her going. One night, when she was rocking in her rocking chair on Sheep Street, she heard a little knock at the back door. She got up to answer it, only to see backside of a little girl running off in the distance under the clothesline, caressing the white, freshly washed sheets. She effortlessly turned her head back toward Ethel while grinning and saying, "Momma, come with me." Ethel never hesitated and knew that it was Annie, her beloved baby girl.

Annie was wearing a beautiful, sheer, lacy white dress with matching socks and shoes. She had long, wavy black hair that bounced freely as she walked. Ethel followed after her. Annie grabbed her hand and said, "It's all right. I'm fine." The cool breeze softly blew, bringing a peaceful and calm sensation that surrounded Ethel like a warm blanket; it was pure perfection in every way. Ethel knew it to be the truth. She was relaxed and felt enjoyment and liberation in watching Annie.

After some time passed, Annie told her mom that it was time for her to go but not to ever worry about her and they would be together again someday.

Ethel and Annie Marie walked hand in hand toward the run-down wooden steps leading to the back door. Ethel let go and turned to Annie, but she was gone.

Ethel smiled confidently while telling of her meeting with her long-lost baby girl. There wasn't an ounce of sadness.

Patria taught her own children to believe in life after death and miracles. She was a strong believer in dreams coming true. She showed them that life is not limited to just what you see but believe in what comes from your heart and your imagination. Be open to the unbelievable, if you believe, it could happen.

CHAPTER 11

PATRIA HAD A way in making Christmas magical. The kids absolutely knew that there was a Santa and he came to their house on Flower Street once a year.

On Christmas Eves, the Stone children hardly slept at all. They usually huddled together on Maggie's bed and had long discussions about Santa Claus, the North Pole and all the presents that they were going to receive. They were so excited! At times, they swore that they could hear reindeer landing on their roof, but they weren't allowed to come out of their bedrooms until in the morning.

The kids all woke one another up as early as possible, shaking and yelling, "Get up! Santa came!" They practically ran from their rooms wearing their pajamas, hair all messed up, but they didn't care; they just wanted to see the beautiful lit-up Christmas tree with all of the colorful presents underneath it. Sometimes they had so many gifts that they were spread out everywhere in the living room— bows on the tops of dollhouses, bikes, skates, Barbies, Barbie vans, clothes, and all kinds of toys. It was amazing. Their stockings were filled with candy canes and assorted nuts.

The house was warm and smelled of fresh pine. Their mom and dad smiled from ear to ear, feeling as thrilled about it as the children were. With wrapping paper all over the place and toys to occupy the kids for the entire day at the very least, they were in heaven, and they loved each other and their lives.

The kids were unaware that the majority of their gifts were repaired, painted, and refurbished dump items. It wouldn't have mattered anyway. Their parents must have been busy for months in preparation for Christmas.

Birthdays were always special too. The birthday girl or boy had tons of attention and love for the day! It was their day. They had their favorite cake, candles, and their "Happy Birthday song" sung to them while sitting at the head for the table. The candles danced in the dark. Smiles swarmed the room, along with laughter and joy of life. It felt glorious.

Gifts were special too, but not as special as the attention from their family and friends.

Their father once told Carha of a very special birthday- It was Billy's eighth birthday, everyone pitched in to buy him a football. His dad stayed outside while everyone else went inside as the day was winding down. They played football until it was dark, regardless of his dad's ailing health. Billy knew that his dad was in excruciating pain but constantly tried to hide it, especially on that day. Billy said, 'On my birthday, it was special. My dad found strength inside of himself to kick that football to orbit—and just for me!"

When Patria was growing up, celebrations in the Traughter household were few and far between—no birthday cakes, no presents, and no Easter eggs. To Fred and Ethel, they remained like any other day. There weren't ever explanations, and the children never asked for any.

On occasion, people from the church arrived to the house on Christmas Day, dressed up like Santas to deliver presents to the kids.

This was excitingly welcomed and appreciated by the kids. It was also a gift in itself that would always be remembered and cherished. Were times so different then that people turned a blind eye to what obviously went on behind closed doors, only to assist in minimizing their guilt by delivering gifts? Back then, minding your own business was true to its word.

Halloween was something that the Traughter children looked forward to all year long. All they had to do was put on old clothes or whatever they had around to make costumes, and off they went collecting all of the candy that they could on this one night a year. Patria recalled that the boys claimed to be dressed as hobos, yet they really didn't look much different from the way they usually looked, with worn shirts, jackets, jeans, or overalls and worn leather boots.

They worked hard on this night, putting on sweet, innocent smiles while opening their gunnysacks wide, all the while secretly praying for the most amount of candy or for the best candy that home had to offer. This was the only candy they had all year besides the kerosene candy, and they really only received that if they were sick. They worked it. They usually went home exhausted and proud, only to have their hard work eaten away in just a few short days, but they never had any regrets.

Fred never got anyone anything on their birthdays, but one year he bought Patria a used, lime-green General Electric AM tabletop radio from a local pawn shop. The case was made out of hard plastic, and the dials were accented with gold-colored inlay. There was a gold background behind the radio station tuner dial. The label on the back wasn't even readable, but it still blared some pretty damned-good tunes like "Rock Around the Clock" by Bill Haley and His Comets and "Oh! My Pa-Pa" by Eddie Fisher (on whom Patria had a huge crush), "Secret Love" by Doris Day, and "Mr. Sandman" by the Chordettes. This fantastic radio also lit up from seven tubes from the inside when turned on.

Once, he also gave her a beautiful gold-tone Stratton compact with an enameled burgundy wave design on it. It had a hinged-back mirror *with the original sticker on its powder puff and sifter. It came with a little black wool pouch to protect it. Shortly after receiving it, she sadly and accidently dropped it underneath a bridge that lined a highway and followed the train tracks. There wasn't any way she could retrieve it. She never had the heart to tell her dad that she had lost it.*

These gifts meant the world to her. She knew that they really represented his respect for who she was.

Growing up, Patria never really set foot outside of her home town. They never went on vacations, nor did Billy while he was a child.

Bill, Patria and the kids never went on vacations either unless it was one of their many fishing trips, which was fine by them. They loved it. They never ate out at restaurants or went to Disneyland or the zoo-it was just too costly. Their vacations were all centered around fishing. Any chance that their father had the time off, they went fishing and camping. Sometimes the trips lasted anywhere from two days to six days.

They usually went to Bishop or Lake Isabella. Both of these places were not very far away, but for the children, they felt like hours to get to.

Bishop was the most fun and had the best of memories. Bill drove for hours on bumpy dirt roads looking for the perfect spot. Being kids, they enjoyed this part of their trip the least.

They usually camped somewhere along the Owens River. There were many turnouts leading to the swift, never-ending river. The dirt roads and each camping spot had their own unique and special features. Bill wasn't ever in a hurry and usually had his beer between his legs to enhance his relaxation and slow his drive.

To help alleviate their impatience while driving, the kids played games. There was this one that they made up where they hung their bodies out of their car windows while they grabbed dried-up cow patties as they drove along, the bigger and the more intact the cow patty, the greater the winner.

Sometimes, the kids could find one as wide as a ruler. The trick was to pick it up in one piece.

They seemed to spend more time driving than fishing or camping, but when they finally parked, it was all worth it.

Bishop had great fishing. There were deep undercut banks, perfect for pulling in large trout that were just hanging out and waiting. The night fishing was heart pounding and surreal. The catfish were huge, and they were fighters. There were dams, ponds, streams, springs, lakes, and large deep, pools. Many of the ponds in which they caught the majority of bluegill and perch were dominated by vegetation collectively known as "tulles"—huge and massive, growing eight feet high and in swaths ten feet wide. They were like water jungles to get lost or hung up in and to explore.

The family had their favorite places to camp, fish, swim, and bathe. They usually didn't stay in one camping spot for longer than a night. They had to pack up every day and look for the next-best spot.

There were river beavers, songbirds, waterfowl, shorebirds, frogs, rabbits, snakes, elk, and deer. There were possibly even wild, hungry animals watching them from the surrounding willows and cottonwoods, but the kids didn't have time to worry about that.

There was an old bridge that was in a horribly decrepit state. It should have had a sign in front of it, stating, "Unsafe to Pass." Bill drove across it anyway. This proved too much for Patria, who had never learned how to swim, so she insisted on getting out and walking across, leaving the children in the car to drive across. Perhaps she believed that God would protect her children but not her. The bridge was so high up that if it had broken, they all would have most likely died from hitting the water, and it wouldn't have mattered if they knew how to swim or not.

While camping, Bill took his old .22-caliber rifle and taught all of the kids how to destroy cow patties with one single bullet. They could blow them apart. Powder everywhere! They also learned to shoot at other targets and be comfortable with guns. They learned gun safety at early ages.

In the evenings, under the stars, they told stories and sang songs. It reminded Patria of nights back in Texas when her family members spent most of their nights outside sitting around the bonfire. They told stories and sang songs. Ethel told the scariest and most intense stories; even the tough boys became frightened and didn't try to hide it.

She always kept the stories new and interesting. Fred tried to tell them too, but he never came close to being the storyteller that Ethel was—and his English was so poor that even the kids couldn't understand him at times. The cool night air, dark sky, crackling fire, and coyotes echoing from beyond the shadows added intense ambiance and thrilled the kids every time.

Ethel yodeled like no other. It was intriguing to hear and watch her carefree show. It seemed that the tunes were always different, and the family wondered in awe where they came from. There was never confusion, delay, or tension in her musical expression ... it was pure and heartfelt. She also sang beautiful hymns. These were usually the same songs repeated in the same imperfect yet comforting way. Her favorite was "The Old Rugged Cross." She never really said why this was her favorite, but it was the one song that she sang most often and from her soul.

> *The Old Rugged Cross*
> *On a hill far away stood an old rugged cross*
> *The emblem of suffering and shame*
> *And I love that old cross where the dearest and best*
> *For a world of lost sinners was slain*

So I'll cherish the old rugged cross
Till my trophies at last I lay down
I will cling to the old rugged cross
And exchange it someday for a crown
O that old rugged cross so despised by the world
Has a wondrous attraction for me
For the dear lamb of God left His glory above
To bear it on dark Calvary

The Stone children sang while driving in the car but not as much around a camp fire. If they stayed awake late, it was usually because they were fishing or frog gigging and they usually got up at the crack of dawn to fish some more!

They all slept in sleeping bags under the stars, never inside of tents. They didn't even like their bags too close to one another. They preferred their own personal space, which was rare at home, but they stayed close enough to one another to chat some before falling asleep.

During the summers, in the morning, they'd wake to the hot, bright sun shining on their faces. They would try to cover their faces inside of their sleeping bags, but then they had a difficult time breathing. There were usually flies buzzing around too on those mornings, which were their annoying wake-up call. Enough was enough.

The kids were excellent anglers, all except Maggie; she didn't like anything about the outdoors.

Bill and Patria patiently fixed broken fishing lines and untangled the kids' lines, never appearing to be irritated. The kids didn't like to waste time, so they became self-sufficient fishers at a very young age.

One of their favorite camping spots had an old horse that roamed around and seemed to not have an owner. He looked pretty neglected. He was brown and tan and barely had an ounce of fat covering his bones. He was thin and old, but he was one tough horse! Dana and Anna felt that he belonged to them. They fed him, walked him, and even rode him, going on some crazy, wild, and scary rides. Sometimes both of the girls rode him at the same time. He didn't seem to like that at all. He dropped Dana right to the ground one time and kicked high in the air after the fact, letting them know that they'd better not do that again, but the next trip there, they did. Dana almost broke her tailbone once while Anna watched nervously.

The children ran around wherever, and they had great adventures on the various trails and in between the many types of tulle. There were snakes to be mindful of, but they just kept their eyes open just like at home. It wasn't a big deal.

Their granny frequently joined them on their camping trips. She fished while wearing her dresses and aprons and covered up her fragile head and face with a bonnet. She still carried her Folgers can with her to spit her tobacco into; she never spit on the ground. She still talked a lot. She talked when no one was around and just continued when you approached her. She acted as if you were always there. She talked when you were there, and if you left, she continued without pause.

Maggie stayed in the car most of the time and slept. One camping trip, the mosquitoes bit her up so badly around her eyes that they swelled shut. No one else was bit up at all. She cried because it happened right before a big school dance. She wasn't a happy camper.

Bill told her what he told all of the kids: "It's a state of mind. If you don't think about getting bit, you won't, but if you do, you will." He claimed to never get bit and never used bug spray. The children played along with him but figured that he just didn't feel the bites because he was too intoxicated.

They always took sunflower seeds, lemons, cream sodas, and Fig Newtons on their trips, and Patria made the best fried chicken and potato salad to take along.

On another one of their many fishing trips, Maggie ate sunflower seeds whole (without removing the shells), lots of them. After eating pounds of unshelled sunflower seeds, it came time to pass them. This was not an easy task for Maggie in the outdoors without outhouses. Her bowels became irritable movements with blood, pain, tears, and regret. The family had to leave for home early on that trip, and everyone was mad at Maggie, who lay in the back looking like a sheep with the bloat.

One night while camping, everyone was fast asleep, except for Carha.

She heard their mother crawl into their dad's sleeping bag. They were whispering and breathing heavily. She kind of knew what they were doing, though she didn't really have the full concept, but it made her happy to know her parents wanted to be together and that they loved each other in that way.

All of the kids were very curious and not easily grossed out. They not only caught fish but would dissect them and explore the inside of their slimy bodies. The removed body parts and eyeballs and even played with the eyeballs. Sometimes, they removed the fish's "air bubbles," as they called them, and took them home with them to see how long they would stay inflated. They usually kept the sacks on their laps all the way home so that the sacks could be protected.

One might think that this would deter them from eating fish, but it never did. Even stinky water creatures tasted delicious when coated with Patria's special seasoned flour mix and then deep fried in a pan of hot oil.

For as much as most of the kids loved the fishing

adventures, they dreaded going home and unloading the vehicle. They were usually very tired and dirty and just wanted to shower and rest. Besides unloading a vehicle packed for a family of seven, they also had to clean all of the fish that they caught, no matter what time they arrived home.

One late night, after returning home from fishing, they all went to bed, except for Maggie. She was washing her hair in the kitchen sink. It was fairly dark throughout the house. She heard a noise from behind the freezer.

The twenty-four-cubic-foot chest freezer sat along the wall in the kitchen, with its end situated only inches from the back door.

Maggie asked, "Who's there?" She repeated, "Who is there?"

She became frozen with fear. There was no reply so she questioned again, louder this time, "Who's there?"

At that moment, up popped a very big man from behind the large freezer. He was wearing an army suit and had long, black, wildly curly hair.

Maggie ran, trying to open her parents' door, but it took her a long time due to her hands not working the way they normally would. It must have been the combination of suds and shaking.

She finally got it open and yelled to her dad. He jumped out, grabbed his rifle, and ran out.

The man had already run out the back door, dropping and breaking one of Bill's old watches, which the man had attempted to steal. It turned out that the robber had been hiding in the small laundry area off from the kitchen the entire time that they entered into their home and unloaded, cleaned fish, and went to bed.

They never found out who he was. This seemed to just be the beginning of men prowling around the Stones' home—most often when Bill was working, but that's another chapter.

The kids were all doing well in school. They were well liked and had many friends.

Carha was extraordinarily shy around strangers, with the exception of when she was chasing boys, but then again, she didn't have to speak while chasing them. She still had a speech delay and couldn't pronounce her *r*'s any better. She was a very insecure girl but wouldn't give up in her endeavors to be like everyone else.

Carha looked forward to recesses. She began chasing John Sanchez, and he was a challenge. He had the prettiest smile and white teeth. He too was quiet but fast.

Around that time, Maggie began cutting and styling hair. She didn't take classes but felt she was good at it. Their mother insisted that the girls help in Maggie's training and let her cut their hair.

It was supposed to be shag; those were in style at the time. Well, she cut Carha's hair way too short. To fix the problem with Carha's now not just thin and straggly but extremely short hair, her mother picked up a home perm kit so that Maggie could add curl and body to Carha's hair.

Carha sat in this tall chair in the kitchen with tiny, pink rollers on her head. Dana and Anna were hiding in the hallway and would jump out, peek their heads around the corner, and giggle. That was bad enough, but after the rods came out, what was left of her hair was now tightly stuck to her head.

The devil demon sisters had a field day. They now called her "Stick Poodle."

To top it off, after Carha returned to school, John Sanchez didn't run from her anymore. He just hid behind the merry-go-round. She tried and tried, but it was over, and she knew it was because of her hair.

CHAPTER 12

HAVING HAPPY, HEALTHY *teenage girls occasionally brought back mixed feelings and memories about Patria's own teenage years.*

After the loss of Patria's father and at the age of fifteen, life seemed to be stagnating and she felt uncertainty for her future. She didn't really know where she was going, should she stay or should she go? She worried of her mother, she felt like a third wheel at times with her sister Wylie and Sydney, although they never complained.

While still in Texas after her father's funeral, she, Wylie and Sydney went to the skating rink in town, and there was an older man working there who was overly attentive to Patria. He stared and made it apparent that he found her attractive. She was laughing and purposely ignoring his attention until finally he approached her.

He looked weatherworn and not very attractive, but he knew his words and how to place them together to be charming. He had thick, curly, sandy-brown hair that sat high on top of his head. He had an elongated face, flattering blue eyes, and a tall, thin, yet big-boned stature.

He asked for her number, and of course, feeling lucky, she gave it to him.

Chuck Vaught called the very next day and then the day after, and eventually, they were dating on regular basis. He wooed her and promised to provide her with a home, food, and security. Hey, she was in for that. What else did she have? She began feeling as a third wheel with Wylie and Sidney. He seemed to have it together. Why not?

A few months later, Wylie signed consent, and they were married. Did she love him? No. He was older by twenty years and wiser, and he wanted to take care of her. She was sixteen years old, and by the time she found out that she was pregnant, it was too late. She had discovered who Chuck Vaught really was. She learned of his habitual lies and frequent rages.

They lived with his mother but in the garage, which had been converted to a small apartment, if you could call it that. She knew that they would never have a real home. He bounced from one job to another, and no one really liked him. She was ashamed and angry of her situation. At that point, like her mother before her, she had nowhere to go. The further along in her pregnancy she became, the more psychotic he became, accusing her of thinking of other men, of thinking that he wasn't man enough to please her. She desperately wanted out and didn't know what to do.

One night, while big and pregnant, she told him, "Chuck, I shouldn't have married you. I don't love you. I'm sorry, but I can't stay with you." He became so enraged that he took out his gun and threatened to kill her and their unborn child and then himself. He said that this way, they would all stay together forever. He was crazy.

The gun he pulled out was the one that he placed under his pillow every night.

He grew into these fits of rage frequently, but one particular night, Patria had to call for his mother. She begged for her help; she feared she would be dead if she did not. His mother immediately came over, calming him with her words as she regularly did, pulling him out of his delusion and into the real world.

After that night, Patria knew she had to leave him.

Margaret (Maggie) was born on November 1, 1961. The delivery went without complications, but now Patria had to make a plan. How was she to leave him and protect her new baby from this man?

Ethel, proud of her new granddaughter, asked that Patria take the baby to church to be blessed and accepted by the elders. Her mother insisted that it was important that they both become closer to God. All of the church members were kind and accepting, even giving young Patria a rose in celebration of her new life. Patria was the youngest mother to ever attend that particular church.

After giving Maggie a bath that very same evening, Patria found that rose cut to pieces, laid out on their bed. The cut-up rose was lying on top of a newspaper that had black paint splattered on top of it. It was too bizarre and made no sense.

On the opposite side of the room sat Chuck with his gun in his hand. He was playing with it, moving it in between in fingers, rotating it round and round.

Patria held Maggie tightly, her heart in her throat, and began to pray aloud while tears rolled down her beautiful high cheekbones.

Chuck's eyes had that madness in them. He said, "Patria, you think those churchgoers care about you? They don't know what a lying slut you really are." He took a drink of his whiskey bottle, spilling part of it down his chin. Not concerning himself with the mess, he continued, "You think that I don't know your plans and how you think of leaving me for another man and how the church is helping you leave with him?"

All Patria could do is tell him repeatedly, "No, that's not true. I'm not leaving." She tried to stay strong, calm, and believable. He began to cry, slobber, and beg. He again told her that if she ever left him, he would shoot her and Maggie. He explained that he couldn't ever live without them.

That night, Patria didn't have to call his mother over. He luckily passed out drunk. Patria tried to ask him to get help many times before. She pleaded with his mother to take him to a doctor. His mother just said, "Patria, you're wasting your time. He doesn't need help; he just needs you and Maggie."

Chuck didn't pay much attention to Maggie. He didn't even pick *her up or look at her much and had never changed one diaper.*

He hadn't had a job since before Maggie was born, and Patria continually begged him to find work. Chuck had a brother working in California. Once he had mentioned that he was thinking about moving them there to be closer to his brother.

Patria talked him into moving there.

She told him, "We will be so happy there, it will be different for us … a new opportunity." She knew how to get to him. All she had to do was bat her big brown eyes, pout, and move her sultry, shiny, long black hair side to side, and he was putty in her hands.

After the birth of Maggie, she quickly returned to her prepregnancy weight and was actually more curvy and sensual than before. She was absolutely, unadulteratedly beautiful.

Maggie was still a newborn when they packed up and headed to sunny California. Patria asked if they could stop to visit Wylie on their way. Chuck faithfully doted on her, but only if she played the subservient, devoted wife part. He reservedly agreed.

They stopped to visit, but unbeknownst to Chuck, it was a visit planned for months. Patria even hid his gun in the trunk during one of their many stops.

Once they arrived at Wylie's and made small talk, the plan was for Sidney to stand up to Chuck and tell him that Patria and the baby were going to stay there and that he would have to leave without them.

This had been the plan for months, and of course, it didn't happen like that at all.

Sidney told him, exactly as rehearsed, while Patria hid behind Sidney and her sister.

Chuck smiled freakishly like it was a joke, like Sidney was a joke. Sidney nervously advised Chuck to leave. He told Chuck, "Just go now and leave them. They are not going with you."

Chuck chuckled and countered, "Oh yeah? You really think so, you little man?"

Chuck smoothly and quickly weaved around Sidney and Wylie

and snatched Maggie out of Patria's arms with one strong pull.

Patria ran after him as he walked straight out the door, not looking back once. He walked straight down the sidewalk toward the car. She pleaded, "Please don't take her, please. I'm sorry!"

He coldly looked at her and said, "Then get inside of the car and come with me."

While Patria was begging Chuck, Wylie was back inside of the house on the telephone with the police, explaining the situation. The police advised her to tell Patria to go with him and play along and the police would catch up with them.

Wylie quickly ran outside, shaking to death and pulled Patria aside after pleading with Chuck to just give her a minute to say good-bye to her sister. Wylie hugged her sister and whispered in her ear exactly what the police had advised.

It all seemed like a bad dream; Patria was actually getting back into the car. Patria and Wylie just glared at each other as she and Chuck sped off out of the driveway and down the street.

Chuck had decided to take them all to his brother's. Chuck was furious, and his mouth was going nonstop about how she would never leave him. "How stupid do you think I am? You will never see your sister again."

They pulled up at the last gas station located at the edge of town.

Wylie and Sidney slowly yet frantically trailed behind. Patria jumped out of the car, bent over, and reached for Maggie, but before she could even get to her, Chuck intercepted after he spotted Wylie and Sidney pulling in. He tried to grab Patria, but she pulled away and began running toward her sister.

He jumped inside of the car and locked himself inside. Thankfully, Maggie was sleeping peacefully in her sitter.

Patria began sweating in the California heat. Chuck sat inside the burning car with all windows rolled up, motioning for Patria to get into the car. Sidney was thinking, pondering what to do. Should they leave her?

Finally, the police showed up and blocked him from driving away.

The time passed slowly. They paced. Sidney proudly came up with a plan and assuredly walked right over to the hood of the car, lifted it, and began pulling wire after wire while Chuck just angrily watched. That car wasn't going anywhere.

After what seemed like forever, Chuck surrendered.

A police officer handed baby Maggie to Patria while another was putting Chuck in handcuffs. As they drove off they could see Chuck sitting in the back of a police car, head down and leaning against the back cage.

Patria and Maggie moved in with Wylie and Sidney, who were always loving and supportive. They acted like parents to her and Maggie, and she never felt like a burden to either of them. The thought actually never crossed her mind.

Chuck was taken to jail briefly after the incident; Patria filed restraining orders and watched her back daily. It took a long while for them all to relax, but they eventually did.

Little did the family know that the evilness that possessed this man would someday cause him to do the unimaginable.

Chapter 13

IN 1972, ALMOST seventeen years after the death of Fred, Ethel was reintroduced to an old acquaintance, Mr. Jay Kuykendall. He had been recently widowed. He was a feeble elderly man but very kind and generous. He hummed all of the time and recited Bible verses. Ethel always said, "Don't mind him. God is talking through him." He treated Ethel with great care and respect. He was quiet and accepting of Ethel and her family. They were married in no time, and Ethel was happier than she had ever been.

After almost a year of blissful marriage, Ethel and Jay both became very ill with pneumonia. The two were hospitalized at the same time. She was released, but he never left the hospital. She had to return home without him. Due to continued weakness from her illness, she was unable to attend his funeral. It was a solemn time, and her strength seemed to weaken after his death. She missed him deeply. It was apparent to the family that his death was the hardest and most difficult for her to bear.

What made her life even more difficult was that she had to move in with Tully and her family. Not that they weren't kind and caring, but it was just different for her to lose her independence in addition to her husband and best friend.

Later that year, another tragedy struck. Patria's sister Wylie was living in Texas and taking care of her three children, who were all growing up too fast. Her oldest son, Randy, was in junior high, and Teah was in grade school. Wylie's youngest, Grady was five years old.

The family had just returned from a hunting trip. They didn't have any luck hunting, but they'd had a great time. They unloaded the truck and were relaxing that evening when Wylie remembered that the rifle was still in the truck.

She went outside to get it, reaching in over the back seat and pulled it up towards her, unaware that it was loaded. It went off, shooting her up through her chin, through her face, and out the top of her head.

This was the story that was told about how it happened. Many years later, another story was told.

Patria, Ethel, and the other siblings flew to Texas as soon as they received word.

She was critical, but alive.

The doctors told the family that if she were to survive, she wouldn't have any personality. She wouldn't be the same person, would have permanent brain damage and be grossly disfigured.

The family stayed at her bedside. They took turns, shuffling in and out.

They held hands and prayed over her still comatose body. They couldn't see her face or head for it was wrapped layer after layer in gauze.

Days passed, and then weeks, and then months.

After two months, three days, seven hours and twenty-three minutes, Wylie woke up.

She couldn't talk, she only moaned. She couldn't eat, walk or even sit up for months. The hospital staff did a phenomenal job taking care of her. They rolled her side to side, moved her extremities to keep the circulation moving and kept her stimulated with frequent conversation. The family visited her daily.

For all of the poor choices that Wylie made when it came to men, she was a good person. She was a kind, caring and loving human being that wouldn't hurt a soul. She was beautiful.

Patria made several trips back and forth that year to be with her sister. It took a long time healing. Many skin grafts had to be taken from her thighs and buttocks. Most of the right side of her face was gone, including her eye. She had many years of surgeries ahead of her, not to mention all the psychological scarring that she was left with. She was in constant pain, not just from the gunshot but from the grafts. She was on many medications for pain and for reoccurring infections in her eye socket. She was unable to wear prosthetic eyes due to the nonstop draining that couldn't be controlled. She wore a white piece of gauze, with a single piece of tape diagonally across it, over the area where her eye used to be. Occasionally, she took it off to let it dry, but it just drained green stuff and was startling to look at. The right side of her face was sunken in and badly scarred, and her mouth drooped on that side. She had a difficult time with her speech and controlling drool that would slyly leak from her drooped mouth. She didn't have her right ear anymore. Basically she lost the entire right side of her face and head.

Wylie was never the same after the accident. She remembered her past, her family, and her life, but she did not remember the accident.

The man that was supposedly a good man left her and the children while she was in the coma.

The children went to stay with Ruby and her family.

Patria said that Wylie wasn't the same. She didn't have

the reasoning skills that she once had. It was very hard for the entire family.

She eventually, over years learned to talk (with slurred speech) and walk again. She had her children, lived on her own but wasn't the same.

With their mom back home and things as good as could be expected in Texas, the Stones were bracing for another year of School.

Carha was in third grade now, getting good grades while staying out of trouble, until her teacher, Mrs. Lake, accused her of spitting on a boy. He only said that because he wanted Carha's attention. Carha knew that he liked her, but she didn't want anything to do with him.

The teacher made her stand in the corner of the room in front of everyone for something that she didn't even do. She didn't argue because she knew that that would be discourteous. It was embarrassing and even worse because she was accused of spitting on someone, something she would never do.

She stood in the corner, angry, thinking the entire time about how she could get vengeance on the teacher who punished her for something that she obviously would not have ever done. She cared even less about the boy who wrongly accused her.

The next day, Carha snuck into Mrs. Stupid Teacher's lunch bag while she was in the back setting up the four round tables for art time. All the kids were grouped and focused on painting.

Carha pulled out her teacher's wax-paper-wrapped bologna sandwich from her brown lunch sack, which the teacher always kept on the left side of her desk next to her can of pens and pencils.

Carha hurriedly opened the sandwich. She turned, facing the blackboard, and dripped copious amounts of her saliva over the greasy, cold meat.

Danny Lee witnessed the entire event and never said a word; as a matter of fact, he didn't make any expression at all. Carha was certain that he wouldn't. He must have thought that she was crazy.

In the cafeteria that day, Carha chose to sit closer to the teacher's table. She had a clear view of Mrs. Lake as she took bite after bite of her now much-juicier sandwich. Carha watched in great satisfaction as her teacher chewed, and she delighted in every bite. Carha felt that all was better in her world now.

Carha's mother, Patria had spent much of her own childhood in trouble. Mrs. Oden was Patria's cranky ol' third-grade teacher and didn't appreciate Patria's social popularity at all. She was constantly in trouble for talking too much. That year, for her punishment, Mrs. Oden made Patria change seats and sit super close to Louie, a little Hispanic boy, who did not know a lick of English. Patria did not like this one bit, as the boy was never able to converse with her, which just made her more anxious to visit with her friends just as soon as the opportunity arose. It was a vicious cycle, really. The more she would talk, the more she was isolated, so the more she would talk and act out.

Carha on the other hand, wasn't too much of a talker but more of a listener with her own friends, especially in a crowd. She was still very close to Tammy Robins and spent almost every waking minute when not in school wanting to be with her best friend, "sisters" they really called each other.

In August- later of that year, Carha and Tammy were playing in her room when her mother came in to tell them of very sad news. Elvis Presley, their music icon, had died of heart failure. It happened in his Memphis mansion, Graceland, sometime during that morning. He was only forty-two years old. It was implausible, and the world around them was crushed. Everyone seemed to be suffering from the loss. Sadness was in the air.

Carha and Tammy played "Love Me Tender" on their record player over and over for days to follow and cried. It was the first time that Carha had experienced the feelings associated with grief. It was a new, uncomfortable feeling that she didn't like at all. Although, having Tammy going through the same grief gave great comfort to Carha. She was thankful for her friend.

Thankfully, Carha got along with everyone except one, you could say that they were rivals of sort. It started all the way back in kindergarten, when Charlene tripped Carha on the playground, and said "Oops look at the stick fall". Carha didn't do anything back on that day, we was more stunned than anything. She could only think that maybe she had done something unwarily to Charlene to make her angry at her. It had to be her own fault because somebody couldn't be so mean for no reason at all.

Then in second grade, Charlene took it upon herself to replace Tammy in pushing Carha on the swing during recess. While Charlene's friends watched, Charlene pushed Carha but not softly. Carha yelled for her to stop. She tried to anchor her feet to the ground, but couldn't. Charlene just told her that she was being nice and to "shut her big flap if she knew what was good for her". Tammy asked Charlene to stop but she wouldn't and barked at Tammy to back off. How could this little girl be so mean? By this time, Carha knew that she hadn't done anything to this mean girl and had she done something, it must have been a long time prior and an accident.

Charlene pushed her hard over and over again while Carha continued to yell to her to stop. Charlene continued making fun of her, mocking her and saying, "Make me".

Carha was sure she would fall or flip out of the swing

but luckily the bell rang and the yard duty came over to remind everyone that recess was over. Charlene and her clan ran off while Carha finally slowed down. Her heart was pounding and her stomach hurt. She felt as though she was going to vomit and of course, she had tears rolling down her redden cheeks which she tried to wipe as soon as she could. Tammy hugged her friend and asked, "Are you okay?" Carha just shook her head while looking at the ground humiliated and stunned.

She never told anyone what happened, never got revenge and just tried to stay clear of this mean, evil little girl.

Over the next few years, both Charlene and Carha continued to be very competitive in sports. They both ran track and played soccer, softball, and basketball. Both were quite athletic and enjoyed playing vigorously and competitively. This was when Carha felt confident and great about herself. She didn't like to talk but knew she was good at sports and other kids wanted her on their team.

Charlene and Carha seemed to always be chosen as the captains or team leaders for whatever game or competition they were participating in.

In fourth grade, while playing basketball, Carha and Charlene butted heads as they commonly did.

The fight that day was over the ball and how it accidently hit Charlene in the chin. Charlene had a mean temper and in retaliation kicked the ball back at Carha, calling her a dummy. Carha didn't like the name at all and was tired of being picked on. She didn't plan for it but punched Charlene right in her big nose. More punches followed until they both were separated by the yard guard.

They both ended up in the restroom, instructed by the supervising yard guard to place cool paper towels over their wounds. Carha was frustrated that she couldn't get the best of Charlene. Charlene was strong and had muscles that even a fourth-grade boy didn't have and more importantly shouldn't have. She lifted weights with her dad and brother.

It took a day or two to get past the episode, but they did, and both of them never got into trouble for the fight. The two were never friends and remained fierce competitors.

The Stone children continued being close and like many kids their ages, enjoyed playing outdoor games, like cowboys and Indians, unga bunga, ditch 'em, stuck in the mud, and frozen statues.

One summer day while playing unga bunga (which was a game the kids made up), Carha was running to safety, when her left hand slipped, breaking completely through Curt and Beverly Robbins's bedroom window. Blood was everywhere, and Tammy was freaking out. Their parents were gone, and one of their friends' mothers who lived across the street took them to the hospital.

Carha's index finger was barely attached, and her thumb was pretty cut up, as well. After many stitches, finger splints, and rolls of gauze, she was fixed up.

Carha's father had no pity for injuries. For some reason, it angered him and discouraged him that the kids let something like that happen to disrupt his life or cause him worries and concern. It did make Carha feel stupid that it had happened, but it had happened, and she would have liked some attention from her dad.

Things were simple in Natruna and the kids went everywhere either on their bikes or on foot.

One summer day, while Carha and Tammy were riding their bikes to the liquor store—not for liquor but for the candy—they found a kitten that had been run over.

The middle of the kitten's tail was barely hanging on, and there was quite a bit of blood.

Carha took the kitten home to her mother, who loved animals too. Patria instructed the kids to stay in the house while she took the kitten to the garage.

For some reason, Carha didn't know what she was going to do and felt protective. She entered into the garage just in time to see the sledge hammer coming down to sever the hanging tail. With that, the kitten let out a terrible scream, and that was that. Patria doctored the cat's tail, and it never became infected. Carha named her "Kitty" after the redheaded woman from *Gunsmoke*. She loved that cat. Kitty climbed through her bedroom window and visited with Carha; she knew whom she belonged to.

Older sisters and brothers are probably the main contributor to any sibling's psychosis.

For example, one day, the desert demons, Dana and Anna, must have become bored and decided to tie Carha to a tree in the desert behind their home. She hadn't done anything to them to promote the behavior. It was probably for cheap entertainment.

The rope wrapped around Carha's hands, which were tied behind her back, over a large salt cedar limb, and then connected to an extremely large cactus that dangled over her head.

If Carha were to untie the rope herself, there was a very good possibility that the cactus would fall on top of her head, especially if she had to do a lot of manipulating of the rope. She was brave at first, but after hours of being alone, the heat, hunger pangs, and fear that she would die out there began to produce panic and tears.

It was almost dark before her mom discovered and untied her.

Patria was hardly the disciplinarian, however, on that day; the demon girls had earfuls from their sweet mother and were placed on restriction for an entire week. This brought some pleasure to Carha.

Even though Carha was probably the skinniest girl in the 4th grade, she always had a number of boys vying for her attention.   She was definitely a very cute girl, but it could also have been her Boston accent.

Chris Baker was in Carha's fourth-grade class, and he stared at her an awful lot. He was the skinniest boy in class and also had bucked teeth. Once, he wrote a note to Carha asking her to meet him on the steps behind their class after school; he said he had to tell her a secret. So she met him.

He whispered in her ear, "I have a secret, but you have to promise not to tell."

She said, "I promise."

Then he made her double promise and then triple promise. Finally, he gave her a quick peck on the lips and ran.

That was Carha's first kiss, and it sort of hurt. It was so hard and fast, almost like a blow to the mouth. It shocked her, and she didn't really like it at all.

Later that year, Chris glued his eyes shut with superglue and had to go to the hospital via ambulance. Before that school year was over, he moved away, and that was the last time Carha saw Chris.

Sometimes during quiet and precious moments between Patria and her girls as they were growing into young women, Patria shared personal stories about when she was growing up and her own experiences. The girls listened and laughed to a point of almost peeing their pants! Patria had a way of telling stories that were humorous, all adventurous, but mostly they were surprising. She was one of a kind that was for sure!

Her first crush was on Keith Clair. When she told the story, her eyes glazed over and there was a sweet smile that softly swept over her face. She literally appeared to have left her body for a spell.

When she was a young woman, she was naturally beautiful. Her hormones began moving about inside of her and stirring feelings up in funny ways just as they were for her own children when they became teenagers.

Next to her junior high school was the popular hangout, the local cheeseburger stand.

Sometimes Patria earned some change while working with her father, and she looked forward to heading to the stand to hang out with her friends.

It was there that she met dreamy Keith Clair. He had coal-black hair, mesmerizing eyes, and a car that he drove all the way from Carson, Oklahoma, just to see her.

He fell hard and fast, and Patria liked him very much at first, but she was beginning to feel her beauty and enjoy attention from other boys, as well. In the end, she broke his heart.

As a teenager, Patria was beautiful but also could be uninhibited and spiteful at times. She didn't filter much of what she felt to what came out of her mouth. She pretty much said whatever came to mind. She didn't care if people like or didn't like her. After being so poor and picked on for such a long time and being around her rowdy brothers, she could feel tough and defensive at times. She was tougher than most girls her own age. She was also naturally beautiful with gave her an edge.

Some stories were told to Patria's children years...many years later or maybe as tales are told from one to another, these were eventually put down on paper.

When Patria became fifteen years old so, she decided that cigarette butts weren't going to get it anymore. She walked right into the grocery store and bought her own package of cigarettes—Pall Mall long, unfiltered in the red box.

When she didn't have money, she charged them to her daddy's charge ticket. This didn't last very long before the store clerk ratted on her and told Fred. He didn't say much, other than "Pat-ty, don't do that anymore."

Patria came to like a boy named Harvey. Everyone called him "Babe." She and he became an item for a while. Patria got wind that Colleen Pratt was spreading rumors that she (Colleen) had sex with Babe. This didn't set well with Patria at all. One day, she saw Colleen at the train depot and quickly came up with a plan for retribution. She urinated inside of an empty Pepsi bottle, cornered Colleen, and told her that she needed something other than nonsense words inside her big mouth, and she made Colleen drink her pee. Colleen drank every last bit in fear, crying.

Patria knew that Colleen and Babe were probably having sex because that was the kind of girl Colleen was, still she felt badly afterward. A few days later, Patria dumped Babe after he admitted that he was, in fact, sleeping with Colleen.

Patria kept busy with her friends. One of Patria's best friends at that time was Carly Nunn. Barns Run at Lake Texoma was another well-known hangout. She loved it there. There was a concession stand, music blasted over loudspeakers placed in all different directions, and hot boys were everywhere.

One day, the two girls double-dated. While looking good in her little bikini and strutting around, Patria's confidence grew by the minute.

Carly gracefully strutted to the edge of the lake and perfectly swan dove in. Patria felt pressure to follow suit, aware that the two boys— and most likely more—were watching. She was oblivious to the actual fact that she couldn't swim, and she dove in behind her friend. She did okay for a few moments, and then the flaring, kicking, choking, yelling, and water out the nose took hold. She never did learn how to swim.

Carly quickly came to her rescue, only to be held underwater herself by the hands of Patria. They were both going to die until a young boy observing from shore swam out and rescued the both of them.

Carly never invited Patria to go to the lake with her again.

Patria's youngest sister, Tully, was sent to live in a girls' home during that time. She was too much to handle at an early age. It was sad, but Patria was so busy doing her own thing and so much into boys that she didn't let it distract her much. For a very long time, they didn't even hear from Tully and rarely saw her.

Back at home, things seemed to be getting worse for the family. Ethel favored Alfie, and everyone knew it. She tried to help him by babying him, but naively, it was just causing more hostility between him, Fred, and the twins. The teasing just became more intense as years went by. The twins became harder on him, and the beatings from Fred worsened.

Times were hard, and food resources were low, but they had to eat. Arne learned to hunt and help feed the family. They used to call him "the Big White Hunter." He was the best at killing pigeons and rabbits but didn't hesitate to kill anything that they could eat.

Winter was especially good for rabbit hunting because the snow slowed down the rabbits. They were delicious fried up; in fact, that's how they cooked all of their meat.

Once, Arne came back with a dead armadillo, and they fried that up and ate it too. When you're hungry, you're hungry. It's a powerful force.

On one particular day, their stomachs were burning. Patria was feeling empty, lightheaded, and even experiencing that dreaded "hunger headache."

Fred told Arne to go into the pen and kill two chickens for supper. It was a celebration, and the whole family was excited, their mouths watering.

Arne felt like a stud as he butchered, cleaned, and helped cook the feast. They all sat around the table anxiously waiting, well-mannered as they always were, when the picture-perfect cooked chickens were placed in front of them. Patria hurriedly reached for a piece and took a big bite when she felt and tasted odd, grainy bits inside of her mouth. She spit it out, turned to her proud brother, and asked, "What the hell, Arne? Did you forget to clean the grain from the chicken's neck?" He laughed and laughed, showing his big pearly whites. She began laughing too. She wasn't going to let grain or guts get in the way of eating that chicken.

As adults Patria remained close to the twins but there was a special bond between her and Arne. Even though she lived in California and he was back in Texas, he still made frequent trips to visit her, Bill and the children who adored him.

It was the late 70's and Arne had been dating a gal named Sherri off and on. It had been several months since they had been on, and Arne was living back in his hometown of Denizen which was hours from where Sherri was living. Out of the blue, Arne received a call from Sherri, asking him to go visit her. She told him that she missed him and wanted to see him.

Arne's friend Charles Nears warned him to not go there. She was trouble. Arne reassured him that everything was going to be cool and that she sounded like she could be in some kind of trouble.

Concerned, Arne left for Shaward.

Arne arrived to Sherri's home late afternoon. While sitting in the living room and catching up, Sherri confided in him that she needed help to get out of the messed-up relationship that she was in and didn't know who else to call.

He hadn't been there but fifteen minutes when someone kicked opened the front door and fired a gun directly at Arne.

It was as if he had been watching him somehow. He knew exactly where he was.

Arne always carried a small handgun in his boot for protection. Being on the road, it was always safe practice.

He immediately ducked and rolled, pulling his small gun out from his boot. He fired a shot back at the man, but not before receiving a bullet to his right thigh.

Sherri ran for cover, making it to the back bedroom.

Arne shot the man in the shoulder, but he was weakened and bleeding profusely. He fell to the ground, and the man then fired two more bullets into Arne.

Arne Traughter died on October 17. The man who killed him was Chuck Vaught, his ex-brother-in-law and Maggie's biological father.

Patria, her mother, and all of the other siblings sadly attended Arne's funeral in their hometown of Denizon, Texas. There was a pronounced emptiness inside of their hearts, especially Patria's. Arne was always present in her life from the time that she could remember, knowing this had always created peacefulness within her.

Not only did she lose her closest brother and a friend who always loved her totally, but she was also gradually losing even more than that but couldn't acknowledge it. It terrified her too much.

Ethel, just as during previous losses in her life, turned to her faith in God. She cried, she mourned, she was fragile, but there wasn't ever one indication that she wouldn't get through such a horrible time. It was God's path, and that was the way it was.

For Patria, watching her mother at the funeral only puzzled her more. She couldn't understand her mother. How could she be standing so strongly? Did she not love Arne as much as Patria loved him? She again felt a little resentment toward her mother, feeling that she was too naive to really feel the death of her son. He was gone and never coming back! Didn't she get that? It was so frustrating and confusing to Patria, but she would never say anything to cause more grief to her dear, sweet mother.

She was also afraid of what Ardon would do. He was struggling, and there was dark hatred in his eyes. He wanted to get revenge for what Chuck and Sherri had done and for them to pay. He wasn't the only one feeling this way.

Ardon, Alfie, and their longtime best friends Charlie Nears, Joel Grant, and Randy Hoskins were the pallbearers. These men weren't a group of loyal brothers you wanted to reckon with. They were solemn yet moved with intention through the ceremony.

The boys were silent while the girls' moans and cries echoed throughout that foggy old decrepit cemetery.

Patria was bent over at times with her arms folded across her abdomen, for her core felt excruciating hurt. She could hardly bear it.

During this time, Bill reflected on his feelings in regards to death. He felt a protective wall shoot up in front of him, maybe from inside of him like a shield. This is the only way that he knew how to deal with this loss. He loved Arne. He was closer to Arne than he had been to any man in his entire life.

He didn't realize he put up a wall, a protective wall of sorts. He didn't mean for it to go up but it did and when it did, it somehow blocked off his wife and children.

He never could realize how the death of his own father affected him and created the same sort of all wall to go up and to never completely go down.

When he was only sixteen, Billy went to live with Toby to ease his mother's financial burden after the death of his father.

He refused to grieve or cry about his life or what had happened. He just built this emotional wall around him and continued to do what he was supposed to do.

Soon after receiving his high school diploma, he did what many other eighteen-year-old boys did at that time: he enlisted in the service, the United States Air Force.

He trained to be a military policeman and was stationed in England. He had many friends and became the joker and life of the parties. Everyone adored him. He drank a lot, played cards, smoked cigars, and became fond of boxing. He dated little, but there was one steady English girl. Her name was Lisa Elizabeth. She had long blonde hair, a perfect figure, and also a wild streak. She would have married him in a heartbeat had he asked her.

He began living his own life, having some control of it, which was a blessing. He still looked forward to that next drink that would take him away from his reality, the past, his family, his father. It was a relief to forget about it, and alcohol did that for him.

Then one day, he was called before a military review board and they drilled him about why he came from "communistic blood." He remembered sitting in an interrogation room with the bright light blinding him while being asked question after question about his dad. Who were his father's associates while alive? Where did his dad frequently travel to? Who made regular visits to the house? How did he feel about communism? How about Toby?

This didn't just happen one time but many times during his enlistment. People began to talk. Bill, no longer Billy, never received an explanation about why this had happened. Honestly, he didn't know, but it did happen, and when it happened, it brought not only humiliating shame but also mounds of anger toward his father and the confusing unknown.

He didn't talk about his father, and when the subject came up, he instantly felt exposed, as if people were going to judge him. They may have thought that he himself was weak and unstable too. He was forever branded with the mental and emotional work of processing his father's death internally.

Over time, he came to place his father on some heroic pedestal to make him feel better for what his father had done. "He did this for his family, a selfless act," he told himself. This subconsciously made him feel that he could be more accepting of his father's abandonment. It was the only way that he could make sense of it all. If he were a perfect being, then he was beyond any blame in his mind.

"He was in too much pain and didn't want to burden his family with medical bills." He couldn't say, "He left us because he was too

weak, mentally ill, or didn't love us enough to stay."

With Bill, he never could admit that his father wasn't perfect and that it was his imperfection that pulled the trigger that day. The shame, defectiveness, and inappropriate guilt began to grow in him like some dysfunctional seed, and he didn't even know it.

This wound of rejection, the contamination of shame, and the coating of contempt formed a layer of emptiness and overwhelming loss just below the surface of his consciousness. He saw himself as a young boy who he really wasn't at all. But he was too hurt to see and understand. He didn't discuss it; therefore, he didn't have anyone to explain it to him and help him to sort it all out.

He learned to not ask directly for what he needed or wanted and not to ever expect to get it, for he wasn't allowed. At this point, he was in survival mode. He learned to keep his feelings, questions, and confusion to himself. This way, he wouldn't be let down. He learned and settled with expecting only this. This sadly became his comfort zone and the only zone he learned to become familiar with.

Nonetheless, while in the Military, he was having the time of his life outwardly and was popular. He was the joker and never serious. People enjoyed being around his happy-go-lucky personality, and he didn't dare discuss growing up. He didn't even want to think of it and surely would never speak of it. No one had a clue to the hurt buried deep inside of him, and that's just the way he liked it.

After the death of Arne, they all returned to their lives after the funeral, still unsure of what consequences lay in store, still preoccupied and concerned. For the time being, Chuck was incarcerated and awaiting his hearing. Sherri was nowhere to be seen.

Soon after returning from the funeral, Bill and Patria called a family meeting. They sat all five of their children down on the floor one next to another. They seriously and calmly pulled up chairs to sit side by side and centered in front of their children.

Family meetings like this rarely occurred, and the kids

knew that it must be serious. Patria spoke. She explained how she had been married before marrying their father and that when she was married before, she had a baby. That baby was Maggie.

She continued to explain how she met Bill only a few years after Maggie was born, how Bill adopted and raised Maggie as his very own, and that it didn't change anything.

Bill and Patria were aware that there were things being said about how Maggie's biological father killed their uncle Arne. They needed to explain.

The kids knew something was different and causing a tenseness among them. They didn't have a clue that Maggie wasn't their full biological sister. It didn't matter to them who killed their uncle at that point because they were distraught that Maggie wasn't their true-blooded sister, and on top of it all, they felt deceived by their parents. They felt that their entire lives were based on this huge lie. They didn't understand why they weren't aware.

Unbeknownst to the other children, Maggie had had a private meeting with Bill and Patria the night before to discuss all that had taken place. Maggie had vaguely remembered that date years ago, going to court where her biological father eyed her. He was only a stranger to her and had always been.

Maggie had repressed or ignored the awareness of having a different father. This was basically new information to swallow. She was the bigger, stronger sister—and a teenager to boot. This created confusion in an already confused head. Her biological father, her blood, shot and murdered her favorite and closest uncle, whom everyone loved and adored? What did this mean? She pondered this along with the feeling of being now an outcast and somehow responsible for the murder of her uncle.

On the day that Carha discovered Maggie wasn't her real sister, she cried all of that day and all of the next day until her small little eyes became swollen and red. She dwelled on it for a few days, but then it became a part of the past and forgotten. She knew that it didn't matter to her or to her sisters and brother; Maggie was their real sister, as real as they all were related.

They were bonded by memories and absolute love. They were all the same but slightly different. They were as close as their hands and feet. They knew each other's hearts more than anyone else at that point in time.

It again was one more stump to hurdle over as a family. The hurdles seemed tolerable in the beginning and, like many of Carha's friends, seemed to be spread out just enough to gather some momentum before having to jump over that next hurdle. There really weren't any hurdles to know of before that year, and it was a little scary and unsettling

After Patria and Bill had gotten together and married, it was important that Maggie take Bill's name before beginning kindergarten. They hadn't ever heard one word from Chuck at that time and never received a dime, but they needed to contact him if Bill wanted to adopt Maggie.

They got a lawyer, and when Maggie was four years old, they went to court.

Chuck shockingly showed up. By that time, Patria was frightened that he was going to have a gun and really kill her. She warned the bailiffs, and they watched out for her. Chuck had not a chance. Sadly, he didn't even approach Maggie. They couldn't understand why he even showed up. It seemed that he had aged ten years from the time she saw him last, riding away from that gas station with defeat and anger written all over his face.

Patria thought about Chuck over the years, and sometimes, she could see him in Maggie's face. She didn't want to, but she did. She

thought of the stories his mother told her of what he went through while he served in the Korean War.

Patria had flashes of the scar on the inside of his left ankle from an implanted plate. He almost lost his foot. He never talked about it and never even told her that he was in the war, but she knew. She not only heard the stories from his mother but found the box with all of the memorabilia hidden away in the closet. She found the Bronze Star with a golden eagle wrapped tightly around it. She found an old book of matches, some gun shells, and a torn black-and-white picture of eleven soldiers—some smiling, some serious, but all young and handsome in their uniforms. Chuck stood in the very back row on the far left. You could hardly see his face.

Then there was a nicely folded certificate kept in a plastic bag. It was in fairly good condition. It read, "Awarded to Army Sergeant Chuck Vaught, Kishingdong, Korea, November 28, 1950. Company D, Eighteenth Infantry Division. Risked his life to destroy an enemy gun emplacement and allow his squad to finish their objective. Protected his squad by running into the line of fire to discard an active grenade."

Chuck Vaught was on the front lines defending a country he never knew and people he had never met. He was damaged from the war; the plate implanted inside his foot along with all of the other scars over his body weren't anything compared to the pain and injury his personality suffered. Maybe it wasn't just the war; maybe it was just him. Nonetheless, what was done was done and he was damaged. He was damaged when he threatened Patria and their new baby.

He was damaged when he murdered Patria's beloved brother, Arne. And she wanted him to pay regardless.

CHAPTER 14

AS THE DAYS went on, the anger and pain slipped beneath the surface but the kids went back to being kids. They spent almost every waking moment playing in the desert, playing with their friends, and going to Vale Springs Pool every chance they possibly got.

After the last gas station came and went in Pioneer and approximately eighteen and a half minutes north of Pioneer- was where this popular recreational area was nestled among a mound of the tallest of all salt cedars. It was the most magical place in the world. The pool was in reality a huge storage tank used by the chemical corporation as a place to obtain water for their potash and other mineral extractions.

Beyond Vale Springs Pool, the next gas station wasn't for another ninety miles on an isolated road. This lonely highway lay in a long, narrow basin 288 feet below sea level, yet it was walled by high, steep, rugged mountain ranges. The clear, dry air and sparse plant cover allowed sunlight to heat the desert surface, creating temperatures as high as 130 degrees. No one wanted to run out of gas or break down on that stretch of black asphalt.

Trying to catch rides wasn't always easy and sometimes took some wheeling and dealing. At times, people arrived, piling out of cars one after another. It was amazing that they fit. It was really too far to walk due to the scalding heat, but there were the crazy few that attempted it. Riding bikes wasn't safe, either.

Some days the Stone children worked hours of hard labor for their next-door neighbor Beverly Robbins in return for one round-trip ride to the pool. Most of the time, Patria took the kids without hesitation, but there seemed to be those rare times when bargaining was their only option, and Mrs. Robbins benefited from those times. The Stones' hours of work usually only resulted in an hour or two of pool time, if they were lucky.

When their mother took them, they stayed all day long, usually from morning to just before sundown. As they became older, she just dropped them off in the morning and picked them up in the evening. They didn't care if they ate or didn't eat. The pool had a drinking fountain full of ice-cold water, and that was their only necessity.

Hitchhiking was an option, just not for the Stone girls if they wanted to live. They wouldn't dare to even consider it, due to the value they placed on their own young lives and knowing that their protective father would have ended their precious beings from this world, if they had they even attempted to hitch a ride.

The large, unmarked, unrestricted dirt parking lot was usually packed with many of the six thousand residents of Natruna as well as the out-of-towners who drove all the way from Ridgefield. They weren't sticking their noses up to Natruna then!

The whole recreational area was surrounded by a tall chain-link fence that was virtually impossible to climb over.

There were various picnic and entertaining areas, all

directly on top of a good old Natruna bed of sand, grit, and rocks of various sizes.

There was a huge concrete slab wrapping around the swimming pool.

The pool of water itself was separated by metal bars, dividing it by depth. There was the baby pool, the three-foot, four-foot, and the largest of them all, the six-foot pool.

The pool was at least 180 feet in length and 120 feet wide—that's about 1,079,568 gallons of brackish, chlorinated water.

The bottom and sides of this gigantic tub were painted the most glorious deep sky blue.

The blue skies above and the blue waters below with the only separation being the crisp, clean, cool, and refreshing saline water made for a heavenly, vitalizing experience.

Natrunans knew how blessed they were.

Almost every few feet, there was a head bobbing up and down during those hot summer days, while parents attentively sat under the covered benches, observing their little ones. They socialized, relaxed, and appeared to enjoy the break away, as well.

There was the regular blowing of the whistle, followed by "Stop running!" or "Off the bars!" or "No swimming in between the bars!"

Wet footprints of all different sizes temporarily imprinted the common walkways. You couldn't stand for very long, or the bottoms of your feet became burned. And forget flip-flops; most of the time, there just wasn't time put them on.

Skinny boys in their cutoff shorts played rough, hardly preoccupied with the girls in their small bikinis lying all over the place on large beach towels, glowing from the mounds of cocoa butter, baby oil, or even cooking oil slathered over their young bodies.

No matter what, there wasn't one Natruna kid who was too cool to swim. Everyone swam, played, and enjoyed cooling off.

The wooden dock surprisingly tolerated the weight year after year of all of the many people who ran and jumped from its sides. Its hollow echo could be heard with each and every stomp. Occasionally, they replaced the worn, fake blue outdoor grass which covered the dock, the pool's stage. This was where most eyes peered to see who and how someone was jumping off. Was it a perfect dive, straight-legged jump, or a great big bomb that blasted anyone in its path?

The rope, as is was called, floated across the six-foot pool, approximately sixty feet from the dock and partway to the end of the six-foot pool. The goal was to see how far you could swim underwater after jumping off the dock. The closer you came to the rope, the tougher you were. Like anyone noticed.

Sitting on the thick, rough white rope gave you some rest and time to catch your breath before either going all the way to the end of the pool, hanging out under the large white clock, or heading directly back in the direction you came from. Sitting on it, however, required some balance, a playful swing dance of sorts while just passing time.

Everyone knew the few parts of pool where your feet would slide if you were trying to ascend the sides. The thick, slimy algae were impossible. There were also the parts of the pool to avoid where the concrete was sharp and jagged. The triangular corners of the pool were eased with partial underwater steps that made nice conversation retreats.

Inevitably, someone was dunking someone until one of

the lifeguards blew their whistle and yelled, "No rough playing!"

Nothing really bad ever happened there, and it was a magical, watery land.

Blind man's bluff or Marco Polo was actively in motion on the left side of the dock. Anyone could join in, and no one was ever discouraged or turned away.

The three-foot pool was the best for games of chicken. The whistle never blew during that game. The lifeguards watched responsively and on alert, but they always seemed to enjoy the entertaining competitions.

The pool's recreation hall was a nice retreat from the sun and water. The smell of the cheeseburgers carried all the way to the pool area, calling out your name! All that swimming sure stirred the appetite. The bun had just enough crunch and just the right amount of mayonnaise, mustard, and ketchup, crispy lettuce, firm tomatoes, sweet onions, crispy pickles, and fat slices of cheddar cheese, slightly melted. The fries were impeccable, and they had the best fountain drinks—perfectly crushed ice in the white foam cups. The foam created the best flavors of soda and ice.

Mr. and Mrs. Long and their kids ran the rec hall and were also caretakers for the pool. Everyone was jealous of them. All that good food and ability to swim day or night made Natruna children wish they were Kelly and Mike. Although they weren't popular at all, they were still admired.

Walking down the hot plain gray concrete path toward the snack bar was a bit exciting. This recreation room had an open floor plan with all concrete flooring to tolerate all of the wet feet and constant drips from bathing suits. There were scattered puddles of water and different shades of wet footprints everywhere. It smelled as though the ocean were somewhere, hiding. Echoes were heard throughout, pool sticks hitting balls, girls giggling while they whispered and watched, light ping-pong balls and paddles in synchrony, and of course the famous jukebox playing all of the greatest hits by singers like Bob Seger and the Silver Bullet Band, the Commodores, the Bee Gees, Andy Gibb, John Travolta and Olivia Newton-John, Eric Clapton, Billy Joel, and of course the Rolling Stones.

Their music and familiar voices repeatedly heard over the very tall loudspeakers dominated the entire recreational area and were songs that accompanied unforgettable memories that could be recalled in just a flash and took you right back to where you were—that moment in time at Vale Springs.

Bats were commonly seen and avoided at the pool. They slept among the treetops or rock enclosures during the days but at night swooped down to drink and eat insects or scorpions or maybe to just scare the crap out of people. Their long, muscular, brown, silky bodies came down and up and were joined in bat gangs. Their webbed wings with their white curved claws threatened all those below them. Their narrow, ratlike faces intentionally pointed in your direction. Their beady brown glowing eyes purposely messed with you. Their teeny sharp teeth had "poison" written all over them. Their ears appeared bigger than a dog's. Sometimes they slowed flight just enough to allow a glimpse of a conspicuous penis or nipples in the middle of their discolored breasts.

Yeah, being at the pool at night was not that appealing.

For the long days when stranded there at Vale Springs, although no one ever looked at it that way, there was the outdoor shower to get the salt off your skin and suit. There were picnic areas, basketball, tennis and volleyball courts, horseshoe pits, shuffleboard, a playground, and even a golf club located next door. Yes, and it too was a dirt golf course.

The Natruna golf course was a unique experience. There was a sign by the unlocked front gate that read, "Caution: Rattlesnakes," and you had better believe it! There were also bobcats, foxes, and even jackrabbits that passed the time by watching the avid golfers come and go. Occasionally, even the animals would entertain the strangers who visited the golf course.

The desert course was maintained strictly by volunteers. They were dedicated and glad to collect the fee that gamers slipped in the slot before heading out to the dirt course. Originally, the golf course was developed as a recreational outlet for company workers who lived and worked in the town. There weren't any fairways, just desert with elevated greens and tees—an environmentalist's dream. There weren't too many hazards: a stray junkyard dog, nearby chemical plants, and many red fire ants busy at work.

It was where Natruna's very own Pete Gomez sunk a 230-yard shot for an eagle from under a salt cedar tree. That day he scored an overall score of thirteen under par, the course record. They created a plaque for him and hung it in the course pro shop; I guess you could say he's famous.

The golf course had other notable incidents- like it was where Leanne Mears became pregnant with baby number two and where Greg Malone punched Dr. Hanes in the nose over an affair that he was supposedly having with Mrs. Malone. Dr. Hanes and Mrs. Malone denied it to the entire town, but the two ended up saying "I do" a year and half later. It was scandalous.

Also, in later years, it was the scene of a crime. Willie Gomez and his best friend, Geno, stole all of the liquor from the golf club bar, only to get caught days later when one of the boys, who drank much of it, ratted on them all.

Willie ended up having to pay the price, since it was stored in his apartment. He had to work the incident off by hard manual labor under the hot summer sun.

What was amazing was the one day a year that the pool closed to the general public and only opened to the corporation's employees and their family members.

They supplied all the food and fun activities. Balloons and ribbons dangled from the sky. There were mounds of free cheeseburgers, hotdogs, sodas, and ice cream bars. They even had carnivals come in, and everyone rode the rides for free.

They buried change in the sandbox, and each child got to make one scoop with a little bucket, running it through the sand in hopes of picking some of the money. They could see pieces shining in different places of the sandpit. Then the kids filtered the sand through a screen to discover the treasure. It was thrilling!

They also placed coins in balloons, blew them up, tossed the balloons into the pool and yelled out, "Ready, set, go!" All of the kids jumped in after the balloons. Or the staff simply threw money into the water and let the kids dive in after it. It was like being at Disneyland for the day.

Vale Springs was such an incredible part of all of Natruna's children's lives and most cherished memories. For every child who grew up going to the pool year after year, there will always be times in their adult lives that trigger a memory of the pool and special times while there. They, like many other parts of growing up in their exceptional desert town, are undoubtedly memories that are both happy and sad.

CHAPTER 15

ETHEL MOVED OUT of the Stones' home and into a tiny rock house in Argos, and life slowly began to return to normal, but something had changed. There seemed to be a gray hue gradually clouding the inside of their loving green home. It wasn't anything that could be pinpointed but more like a sense or progression of more negativity like dark clouds coming their way.

Although the kids were sad that their granny moved out of their home, it gave each one of them time to spend alone with her and they loved staying nights with her in her little rock home. They loved listening to her stories and eating TV dinners, which they never had at home. They cooked anything they wanted to and even drank instant coffee with lots of creamer and sugar with her in the morning and at night. That would never happen at home.

It was evident that she enjoyed their company, as well. Usually, only one of the kids stayed with her at a time; her little rock house was just too small. It was nice to spend quality one-on-one time with her and to have a break from sibling rivalry.

She usually had two or three cats living with her at a time. She loved her cats and treated them like her children. She talked to them too. She kept a rolled-up newspaper close at hand to take a sweep at one or another if they got out of line. She usually just scared them while explaining to them why they were in trouble. She believed that they understood her explanations. Most of the time, they hid under the bed the whole entire time the kids were there.

Her front yard was made of hard dirt embedded with a variety of different-sized rocks. When the kids played ball with her dogs, all of the balls rolled down the grade and landed up against her slanted chain-link fence. She usually had one or two dogs guarding her front yard too, and she liked them enough, but she was more of a cat lady.

Her neighbors were kind to her, and many stopped by on a regular basis just to visit—mostly children. Ethel told stories of them stopping by and what they did and talked about. The grandchildren never really liked it. Maybe it was jealously; maybe they didn't trust the childrens' intentions.

At night, Ethel rocked in her rocking chair and chewed her tobacco. She watched Westerns and told story after story, which were difficult for the children to keep up with. Usually, after the first minutes, their minds wandered elsewhere.

They usually went to bed before their granny. She climbed in bed late at night or even in the early morning hours. She only had one bedroom and one bed. The kids never minded sleeping with her. Upon entering the room in search of her nightgown from her closet, her stories resumed where they left off even though her grandchild was fast asleep. They probably fell into and out of dreams containing some character from one of her stories. Her stories usually were repeats of a Western show that she had watched and how they somehow correlated to her real-life past.

She still spoke her father, Ves Dawes and told stories of how and when her parents met and fell in love. It was obvious that it made her happy to remember them and to share who they were with her grandchildren.

The grandchildren never became tired of hearing about them and imagining their granny as a little girl.

It was always fascinating to them how she told these stories and laughed as a distant look clouded her eyes, changing even their appearances as she told these stories and went back to when they took place. It was as if she were there.

Her father, Ves was twenty-four years older than Azlee when they met and fell in love.

Ves already had two young children, Mae and Peggy, whom he was raising on his own after the passing of his wife. He was a strikingly handsome man. He had russet-brown wavy hair that didn't have even a hint of gray, blue eyes, and a friendly, happy-go-lucky attitude. He always wore a Stetson hat and puffed on a hand-rolled cigarette. All of the women of the town—even married ones—flirted with him, but there was only one woman that he had eyes for. Having worked for the railroad and doing manual labor most of his life, he was a fit man.

Ves and Azlee were in love, and even the financial struggles of raising a family didn't put a damper on their affection for one another.

Ves's male friends quickly nicknamed Azlee "old maid." It didn't bother her. It actually made her prideful that she was different from other women.

It wasn't until she was thirty-five years old that she gave birth to Ethel Dawes. Ethel recalled, "My daddy loved my mammy. They always got along real good."

Five years after the birth of Ethel, Azlee began having frequent falling spells. Ethel remembered having to do all of the cooking, cleaning, and caring for the family. She said, "I must have been little, because I had to stand on a wooden box just to be able to reach the wash pans and table."

Ves felt that Azlee's health would improve if they moved away from Kansas, and he heard that he could get some work at a cotton gin in Texas. So they ventured out across prairies in a covered wagon for days and days. Young Ethel slept most of the time, but while awake, she entertained herself by watching the many prairie dogs pop their heads up from their small, volcano-like dirt cones that sat on top of the dried, hardened sand. She could hear their echoing barks and yapping calls to one another. She also remembered going through prairies, being amazed by all of the small brown birds that she called prairie chickens making strange, loud booming sounds. They hid in the grass and had nests.

The family finally arrived in Texas, exhausted but hopeful. Ves's age, along with the health of Azlee, began taking a toll. The two never complained in the presence of their children—or to anyone, for that matter. They were loving and sweet to one another...always.

Their struggles continued for a few more years until they couldn't any longer. They never had enough to eat, and Azlee couldn't care for them anymore. They had no choice but to consider farming the children out.

This was a sad time for Ethel. She recalls the day when the only sisters she ever knew, Peggy and Mae, left with some strange woman from the county. She recalls her parents' tears and guilt. Later that year, they received word that Mae died, Ethel never knew why or how. They lost the whereabouts of Peggy.

Ethel remembered this one conversation with her mammy. She told her mammy that she was going to have two kids someday, a boy and a girl. Her mammy replied, 'No, daughter, you will be pregnant at least seven times, but create even more beautiful souls to love forever and remember my little bird, Life and death are one of the same but may appear to be different." Ethel said that mammy knew the future but didn't make much sense at times.

Their granny too believed that people could see the

future and that dreams had meanings and some people could see their deceased loved ones and even have visits with them.

Ethel asked that the grandchildren help her to put her storytelling down onto paper. The children didn't mind at all. At different times, each and every one of them would read, edit and teach their granny how to improve her writing during visits.

Ethel never really went to school and never learned to read or write. She eventually learned how to do both with the assistance of her grandkids and even Patria helped her too.

Her stories were difficult to comprehend; only parts were somewhat comprehendible, but she put her heart and soul into them, and her family appreciated that.

The children didn't mind her never-ending stories and were never impatient with her. She was unequivocally caring and loving to them, never scolding or lecturing. They didn't really talk too much while with her; there wasn't much room for that, but that was okay with them. They adored her.

Not everyone around Natruna was so nonjudgmental of Ethel. Once, while shopping at the Argos grocery store, Patria overheard two women from church talking and laughing at her mother. She couldn't handle it, and again, Patria felt that Ethel was naive to how cruel people could be.

Patria hurried her mother to check out and got out of there as quickly as possible, but once they sat in the car getting ready to drive off, it was too late. Her blood was at a boil.

She returned to the inside of the store to find the two prudish, middle-aged women checking out. One was wearing her hair in a high-up do with what looked like the entire can of hairspray on it, pulling her face so tightly that there were tons of broken pieces of hair outlining her made-up face.

The other one wore large, fancy, plastic-rimmed eyeglasses that covered her long, thick fake eyelashes, and she wore a heavily starched, two-piece wool skirt suit with shoulder pads. *Really, this is Natruna?* Patria thought to herself.

Patria walked in between the two, looked them both into their surprised faces, and said, "You'd better not ever talk about or laugh at my mom again. If I find out you have, you will go to sleep one night and never wake your sorry asses up. You both should pray to God and ask for his forgiveness for being such sinful, hypocritical bitches."

She turned and walked sternly and confidently toward the glass sliding doors, noticing that the store became utterly quiet, eyes following her as she exited the store. That's when the tears began. Her breathing became heavy as she tried to catch her breath, stop the tears, and get hold of herself as she opened the car door and sat down next to her mother. Ethel looked over at her, her face concerned, and asked, "Patria, What's the matter?"

Patria replied, "Nothing, Momma. I'm fine. Let's go home."

It didn't take but a few minutes before Ethel returned to her normal self and begin telling stories. Was she really unaware of the cruelness of the world, or did she not bother herself to care? By the time they were pulling into the gravel driveway at the little granny home located only blocks away from the store, Patria was feeling better. She quietly listened to her mother and asked herself, *How could anyone ever be mean to my mom?*

Patria thinks back at stories her mother had told to her when she was younger that made her sad. She thought, *if only people knew what her sweet mother went through, nobody could be that cruel to still tease and belittle her, right?*

Ethel was only eight years old when they buried her mother, Azlee, in an unmarked grave in a small cemetery located in Texas. The death certificate said that it was "a death due to cancer of the stomach," but Ethel swears that she died of tuberculosis.

It was then only Ves and young Ethel. Ethel had to run the house, take care of her dad, and do all of the things that a woman would have to do. At times, she even had to do things that a man would normally do because her father was away for days at a time, working whatever jobs that he could.

She tried to go to school, but it wasn't consistent, and she finally stopped going altogether when she was around ten years old. She didn't have time to take care of herself like many other girls her age. She didn't think of it. It was surviving the best that she could.

Ves continued to work hard. Things seemed to be looking up, and they had food to put on the table. One day, Ves was working for a railroad company when a large wagon of rocks fell on him, crushing many of his ribs and causing internal injuries. The doctor told him that the ribs on one side were out of place. Ethel witnessed as the doctor inspected her father's hands. He appeared concerned and serious. He said, "Mr. Dawes, I see that you are a hardworking man, but you won't be able to work hard anymore."

John Smith was a good friend to Ves and he trusted him with his life. When Ethel was just fourteen years old, her father told her that they were moving away and asked that she pack all of her belongings.

They pulled up to the Smith family home and unloaded their belongings with plans to stay for a while. It wasn't long before John's oldest son, Roy, took a liking to young Ethel. He decided that she would belong to him. Ves didn't care for him but didn't discourage him away, either.

Ves was a stubborn and independent man. He told Ethel that he was uncomfortable there and didn't want to impose on anyone anymore.

Not long after that, Ves asked Ethel to come outside with him. He kneeled down, looked Ethel straight into her eyes, and began crying. He told her that he was headed to the poor farm in Dallas or Greenville. He explained that the government had places for people like him, where he could live since he couldn't work anymore. He told her that the Smiths would look after her. He said that he couldn't tend to her anymore.

Ethel refused and begged, "Please, don't leave me here! I'll be better, please!"

He again just repeated, "You're too young to be on your own."

She remembered watching as he rode off in their covered wagon. He looked back at her and replied, "I wish you good luck, Ethel!" She never saw or heard from him again. At that time, he was seventy-three years old.

Ethel's heart was broken yet again, and it caused a deep emptiness inside of her soul. She told herself that her father did the best that he could do and that he couldn't give much more than he had been given himself.

Ethel couldn't say, "He left me because he wasn't man enough to take care of me." She had to say, "If I were more worthy, worked harder, or ate less, he wouldn't have left me."

She began feeling that something was wrong with her. It was too painful to say out loud.

With Ethel, she never understood that her daddy wasn't perfect and that it was his imperfection that drove him away that day, not hers. The shame, defectiveness, and inappropriate guilt began to implant in her like a seed.

She soon came to understand that her father gave her to Roy, who quickly took ownership of Ethel, body and soul, as if he had won her as a prize somehow. He was a jealous and unruly man. He hung around with rowdy friends and swung her about like she was his trophy.

What could she do? She had nowhere to go and no one to turn to.

Roy and Ethel wed in front of the justice of peace and then moved *to an old, run-down shack in town. Times were trying, and Ethel despised Roy Smith with all of her being. He eventually began to abuse her emotionally, physically, and sexually.*

Time passed as slowly as buds on a tree after freezing weather. Ethel finally got some relief when Roy shot a man during a bar brawl and had to spend some time in the Huntsville prison. He threatened that when he was released, he would kill her if she didn't take him money while he was in prison.

Ethel, being illiterate and with nowhere to go and no skills, did what she had to do, the only thing that she was able to do was with her God-given body.

It was during Roy's imprisonment that Ethel would hang out in bars cleaning and working the back rooms when she met some guy who was a well-known gang member. She remembered all of the guns that he kept in the trunk of his car. Ethel swore that the group were really good people and that they just liked to help the poor. Their names were Bonnie and Clyde, and she continued to have a relationship with the bunch for some time after.

When Roy Smith was released from prison, she became pregnant and she was always worried about whom the father might be-worried mostly that it would be Roy's.

She was in constant fear of him. He continually watched her every move, the way she spoke, the way she cleaned, the way she fixed herself, the way she interacted with others, what she ate, what she didn't eat. The relationship was unhealthy, and now that she was pregnant, he seemed even more controlling and belittling since she was carrying his child. She felt self-loathing, helplessness, desperation, and isolation. He used fear, guilt, shame, and intimidation to wear her down and keep her under his thumb. Of course, he made sure that she didn't have any friends or anyone to confide in.

The beatings continued even while she was pregnant. He just avoided her enlarging abdomen and didn't push her as hard when he beat her.

Ethel wasn't ever emotionally connected to this abusive pig of a man, but she just didn't have anywhere to go. She took a desperate leap of faith. She confided in her sister-in-law, not knowing which side June would be on. The baby growing inside of her needed her; it was a powerful influence in motivating her to get out of this horrid relationship.

While he was away for a few hours, she did it. She packed her things and left for June's.

It wasn't easy getting away and keeping Roy away, but with the help of his sister and brother-in-law and Roy's criminal history, he quickly learned to comply.

Ethel soon learned that Roy's intimidation and her deathly fear of him was a delusion in a way. He had her believing that he was so powerful that he had control over not just her but the world that she lived in. She gradually believed this to be the truth. After only a few confrontations between June's husband (who was even much smaller than Roy), she was awakened to the fact that he was in reality a coward and that she had been a fool.

Ethel gave birth at the age of eighteen to a healthy baby girl whom she named Ruby Smith.

She had to get some government assistance to take care of herself and her baby. She remembered picking up a card once a month that allowed her to get groceries. She felt this was truly amazing and that she'd never had it so good. Once a month, she took the card and picked up powdered milk, a sack of flour, cornmeal, cans of beef, cans of chicken, cans of powdered eggs, real butter, and cooking oil.

She remained living with Roy's sister and became very close to her and her husband. June had three children of her own and was an experienced housewife. She taught Ethel how to clean and care for baby Ruby. Ethel was happier than she had ever been and loved her precious baby girl.

Later in her life, some of these stories Ethel would not put on paper and some she chose to.

CHAPTER 16

BACK ON THE home front and later that year, things seemed going upside down. Maggie went away for a while to stay with Toby and Joan, Bill's brother and his wife. It was strange to the other kids that she left in the middle of the school year and out of the blue. They were never separated as siblings for very long. Strange things seemed to be going on—maybe because the girls were becoming teenagers, maybe because Arne died, Ethel moved out, or Bill and Patria's drinking seemed to start earlier in the day and continue further into the night. They didn't seem as happy anymore. They hardly talked. She still got up in the morning with him to see him off to work but didn't walk him to the back door anymore and kiss him. She sat his lunch pail on the small black table and kept preoccupied with dishes or cleaning the kitchen. Their house felt sad now.

While Patria was growing up, she didn't really experience the feeling of having a grand, happy childhood and then it being taken away. It was always dysfunctional in a normal, functional way. It wasn't surprisingly sad; it was just always messed up.

Of course they had some ups as well as downs. They were too close as siblings and even though their father was a hard ass, they loved him and their mother.

The Traughters were without a doubt ashamed of their lives, their parents and the way they lived.

And they lived differently from most which didn't make it any easier.

Dallas Pew was one of those kids who didn't want Patria to forget how different she was. When Patria was a child, she swore that he had the devil in him. He yelled profanities at her, told her to go back across the river where she came from, and never failed to add that she was a dirty little wetback. He ran around her, pulled at her hair, and was the ugliest kid that Patria ever had wished bad things upon. She never had the guts to be assertive with him. She tried to walk away from him, but he just followed her. Through the years of cruelty, the fire within her began to stir and build. She somehow became less sensitive to violence all the way around.

As the Traughter girls hit early adolescence, the welfare building became their shopping mall. There were boxes scattered all over this barren room, with a variety of beautiful donated clothes inside. They loved shopping there but were always afraid that someone from school would recognize one of their outfits. Patria found her favorite white "cancan" dress there. Her good friend Phyllis loved it so much that she even borrowed it.

By the time she was eleven years old, Patria was smoking cigarette butts on fairly regular basis. She began to feel any softness within her slowly fading away and being replaced by meanness. She didn't understand why.

She regrettably remembered fighting over the one lone heater in their living room that they all huddled over on one very cold morning. She didn't feel like sharing, and Wylie was in her way, so instead of pushing her out of the way, she pushed her sister directly into the heater, scarring her arm. And all of the times before, Wylie forgive her little sister again.

Wylie acted more like a mother than a sister but at other times, it *was the opposite. She took her to the movies sometimes and on many of those outings, Wylie just left her there, swore her to secrecy, and then took off with one boy or another. Patria never dared to tell on her, for that was her only way to get out.*

Wylie babied Patria and stuck up for her, even lying in her honor, like one time when Patria was jumping on the bed and broke a window. Wylie didn't want her to get into trouble, so she took the blame. She had a good yelling from her dad but never strayed from her story.

They were best friends and confidantes. Wylie was her protector and provided constant security. Yes, they shared their ups and downs, but they were devoted to one another. Wylie was the first person Patria turned to when she needed an ear. Wylie was always ready to provide a shoulder for comfort and gave sensible advice and a sense of perspective. No one knew Patria better than her older sister.

Ella Randal and her family moved to the "white" end of Sheep Street. Wylie began walking to school with Ella, and that is how she was introduced to Ella's much-older and more-mature brother, Sidney. Once she hit age thirteen, Wylie began distancing herself more and more from her family.

At first, she hid the relationship from her father. They weren't allowed to date. She began lying and sneaking around. She was spending more time with Sidney and less time at home. This alone created tension at home. It wasn't long until she was caught. The fighting between Wylie and her dad intensified, and it was her excuse to get out.

Fourteen-year-old Wylie and twenty-five-year-old Sidney were married. It was a quick justice of the peace ceremony, and they were off to California to stay with family friends who offered to help them find work. This devastated Patria.

Ethel's oldest daughter Ruby had been married to Lee Massey for quite a few years by this time, and had just given birth to their fourth child, they named Sheryl. Lee wasn't different from Ethel's first husband; he was extremely violent and began being abusive to Ruby.

She came to stay with the Traughters, along with her children, trying to figure out her next step. It had only been a day or so when evening came and the bullets began piercing the walls of the family home while the family was eating dinner. Fred quickly instructed everyone to hit the floor and take cover. The children were crying and screaming, but that wasn't stopping the gunfire from hitting all parts of the inside of their home. Glass broke, the gunshots were loud, and the kids were covering their ears and heads, praying to live through it. Finally, the police came. They arrested Lee and placed him behind bars for some time, giving Ruby time to start a new life, now with four children, no father around, and no job. She moved in with June Smith once again since there wasn't an inch of room to spare on Sheep Street.

Alfie mainly just kept to himself. Sadly, the boys never played with him. The twins often chased after him with horse's apples—big, fluorescent green, and heavy—and threw them at him. The twins were cruel at times to their youngest brother.

Fred was mean to Alfie, as well. Alfie could never do anything right. If he didn't work hard enough, Fred grabbed hold of a shovel or the handle of a hoe, whatever they were working with at the time, and beat Alfie with it. He did the same with the twins, but definitely not nearly as often. Alfie was sometimes irritating in his demeanor, somehow slightly repulsive to others. He wasn't a bad or mean young man in any way; he had a big heart and even protected the girls without any hesitation if a situation arose.

One day, Alfie came home from grade school with a fine-looking bicycle. Fred asked him where it came from. Alfie said a boy gave it to him, but Fred replied, "No, boy, tell me the truth, damn it!" Alfie admitted that he'd stolen it, and Fred made him take it back to the boy he'd taken it from and apologize. The entire school got wind of what he had done, and the kids called him a thief and began picking on him too.

Fred wasn't this way with the girls. The only time he ever hit one of them was years earlier when Wylie was flirting with one of Fred's male friends. After the man left, Fred whipped Wylie with a gun holster while explaining that her behavior was unacceptable and would never happen again.

As the years wore on, the more that Fred drank, the more violent he became.

As the children got older, Fred would send the kids to a lady named Laura Quinn. Her house was hidden deep in the hoary woods east of town. One of the kids hesitantly knocked on her creepy, decaying, splintered door. She slowly opened the door with her dirty hands and long yellow nails and just studied them up and down with her big protruding eyes. They quivered while telling her that they were there from Mr. Fred Traughter. She quietly instructed them to stay put, and then she walked past them, not saying a word, and disappeared into the forest for what seemed like eternity.

She returned holding the jar of white lightning out in front of her ripped, dirty dress. After handing over the jar, she turned over her big, filthy hand and just blinked her eyes, never saying a word. One of the kids then placed the money in her hand, and they practically ran home with their hearts pounding. None of them liked going, but they knew they had to do what they were told.

Eventually, no words needed to be exchanged. It was a given what they were there for. It seemed this mysterious woman in the woods never changed. She seemed to wear the exact same thing, have the same dirt dispersed over the same exact body parts, have her hair the exact same unbrushed and ratty way, and she never aged a single moment.

Fred seemed to partake in this illegal moonshine more often than not. It was known for its high alcohol content and low price. At around 150 proof—75 percent alcohol—it was quick intoxication at a minimum price and he began preferring this over his lighter homebrew.

If not manufactured correctly and contaminated with poisons, people could become blind or even die. The mash was cooked with birch bark to give it a minty flavor, disguising any taste of toxins. It seemed that the more Fred partook in this homemade whiskey, the more out of his mind he became.

CHAPTER 17

IN 1979, BILL'S older brother, Toby, was doing well and had just opened his own security business; it grew so quickly and became so successful that he quit his chiropractic practice altogether and sold it. Bill was so proud of his big brother—not so much for what he accomplished but for how he worked so hard for his accomplishments as well as for his strength and his willpower.

Patria's sister, Wylie became single once again and moved to Natruna to be closer to family.

Yes, although she was scarred and messed up, she still had men and was still desirable. Incredibly, Wylie never lost her sex appeal.

She and her three children, Randy, Teah and Grady, stayed with the Stones for a while until they could afford to move into a place.

Carha was only nine years old when she began admiring her older cousin Teah. She was fascinating and had been out there in the world traveling from town to town. She was pretty and carefree. Teah had long brown hair, dark skin, full lips, and big brown eyes. She was thin yet curvy and seemed to be constantly happy and smiling. She laughed a lot—not a loud, boisterous laugh but more of a sweet and dainty laugh. She wore real sterling silver with innumerable colored stones, from necklaces to dangling earrings to rings on almost every finger.

Carha and her mother went to Ethel's house to visit with Wylie and the kids who were visiting for a few days. While going to the bathroom, Carha saw some of Teah's jewelry sitting in a small decorative shell bowl on the shelf beneath the mirror. It was just beautiful. One thing led to another, and before she knew it, she was wearing some rings on her fingers. Wearing them made her feel like she was free and beautiful just like her cousin. She couldn't pass up the opportunity to keep feeling that way, so she made the decision to keep the rings. Teah had more, and she wouldn't miss the four rings.

Carha slid them into her jeans' pocket. She didn't even have time to wear the stunning rings before being cornered by her mother and her aunt Wylie about the stolen jewelry.

Carha didn't waste any time before admitting that she had taken the rings and was very sorry. She admitted to admiring them and her cousin. That didn't prevent the two raging women from slowing down with their lecturing. The lecture seemed to go on and on. The conversation between the two repeatedly mentioned jail time and even a stint in prison, but it didn't stop there; they went on to describe the inside of prisons and what the experience would be like for a pretty young girl like her.

Carha never stole again after that, ever. She respected Teah even more after that for not ever mentioning what had happened or acting differently toward her.

Her devil sisters weren't as loving or forgiving. They not only called her "The Toothpick Robber" for weeks, but also called her "The Cousin Crook" in front of their friends and they all laughed. Carha thought that everything in families shouldn't be shared knowledge.

One time, Dana and Anna had had a few boyfriends over, and Carha was bitter and feeling ignored, so she wrote in her diary that she didn't want to live anymore. She opened it nonchalantly on her bed and left the room, hoping they would find it, read it, and feel bad for her. For sure, they then would want to include her.

Well, they all read it all right, even the boys. Then they laughed at her, teased her, and unsympathetically asked her for days that followed how she planned on doing it.

Every morning, the girls left out of the front door together, smiling while saying good-bye to their mom. Once past the upper block of Flower Street, Carha knew that her legs wouldn't ever catch her older sisters and that she had to follow the little sister etiquette and stay a certain distance behind.

As they became older, smoking cigarettes seemed the cool thing to do, so of course Anna and Dana smoked. Carha knew not to say a thing, or life would become even more humiliating.

The demon sisters never detoured from entertaining themselves at Carha's expense. One afternoon, Carha was sitting on the toilet minding her own business while thinking of her many nine-year-old thoughts when out jumped Anna and Dana, screaming and yelling from behind the shower curtain. They scared her so badly that her face turned red and she cried. That only fueled the mean spirit in them and they made fun of the way that she cried.

Carha hatched a plan to repay them both, so she waited for the perfect opportunity.

One day, she lay down inside of the bathtub and waited and waited. She knew eventually the brats would have come in and they would be together, because they did everything together, and they did.

Dana was busy primping in the mirror and Anna sitting on the toilet. Carha could barely hold back her laughter; this was going to be good. She waited for the right moment. She was getting close to making her move while listening to their stupid talk about boys and school when their conversation changed focus to a conversation about Carha.

They whispered, "When are Mom and Dad going to tell Carha? She is going to be so upset. Our room is going to be bigger now! She is so dumb and needs to go away. Maybe we will be nice and go visit her at the Sunshine House." Carha knew full well that they were referring to homes for mentally retarded children. She didn't think that she was retarded but it made her wonder. Maybe she could be to some degree?

Carha couldn't stand it any longer. She ran out, yelling at them, "You both are lying!" They acted surprised and startled.

Carha found her mother and told her what happened. Her mother assured her that she wasn't going anywhere and that the girls were just teasing. Deep down Carha knew that, but still, her sisters were pretty believable.

That little adventure also entertained the girls for years to follow.

Maggie finally came home a few months after she had left. It was good to finally see her. They all missed her. She seemed different. She was growing up and growing even more serious.

After lots of question with few answers, Maggie let the older girls know she had an abortion while away. No one except the girls and their mother knew about this until many years later.

Patria couldn't help but be haunted by her own demons when she thought of her own daughter and what she was going through. She couldn't help and recall an event in her own life that she tried with all of her might to forget. She did well at not speaking of what happened, but as far as the flashbacks, they would forever haunt her whether she tried to forget or not.

At age thirteen, Patria preferred to stay away from her house as much as possible. She was interested in boys but still trying to figure out what they were all about. She and Babe didn't last long, and she definitely wasn't ready to have sex, but she still liked the attention that she received from boys.

One night, she asked her father if she could stay the night with her new best friend, Ella. Her dad said that it was fine but reminded his daughter, "Pat-ty, you better be good, you hear!" He may have been abusive, but he was also protective of his girls and family. Patria was always terrified of getting in trouble and was very careful when she did wrong.

Ella was older, more experienced, and a little more on the wild side. Keith Clair invited Ella and Patria to a party in the woods. He and his best friend, Pete, drove all the way there because Pete was crushing on Ella big time.

That night, the girls snuck out of Ella's house and caught a ride from the boys. Driving there was exhilarating. Patria felt the wind in her hair and freedom in her veins while riding in the back of Keith's truck. This was living, and she was having a blast.

They made sure that they were way out of town and deep in the woods so that they wouldn't be harassed by the local cops. They were having an awesome time, and the group was growing by the hour. It was a popular meeting spot for partiers.

One of the older guys, Donald, was spending way too much time looking at Patria. She didn't like it one bit and felt that he was strange. He had to have been in his mid-thirties. He had huge bug eyes and oily dark-brown hair that was cut straight across his forehead, just above his eyes. He was dirty and creepy.

He finally approached Patria and tried to talk to her, but she politely dismissed him and turned around to find Ella. Ella and Pete seemed to keep disappearing in the crowd, and Keith was nowhere to be found.

Patria was getting tired and wanted to leave. She searched and asked if anyone had seen Ella. Creepy Donald told her that he knew where she was and to follow him. She hesitated but really wanted to get out of there. It was getting cold too. She followed Donald as he led her away from the party. She began feeling nervous and told him, "No, I don't believe that she is out here. I'm going back." He kept reassuring her that it was just a little farther. Finally, Patria said, "I'm going back." She had a bad feeling. He replied, "No, little darling, you're not going anywhere." She could smell his foul breath as he grew closer to her face. His teeth looked rotten. She turned to run, but he grabbed her by the arm and slung her to the cold, rigid ground. He sat on top of her, his legs and knees strongly pinning her to the ground. She began crying and yelling. He placed his hand across her mouth, his other arm pressed firmly across her chest. He was so strong. He moved his hand to her throat and placed pressure. She thought that he was going to strangle her. She began to struggle for air.

He let up on the pressure and whispered, "If you don't shut up, bitch, I'm going to kill you. You'd better be quiet, or I will snap your pretty neck in half."

She was powerless. He unbuttoned his filthy pants, pulled out his penis, tore her panties off, and entered into her time and time again. She wanted to die, the pain was horrible, and it felt like her insides were being ripped apart.

He finished and told her, "If you tell anyone, I will slit your throat and your slutty friend's throat too." He stood up, zipped his pants up, smiled, an evil smile, and walked away.

Patria could barely stand, her legs were shaking, and she was traumatized and ashamed. She started to run, and kept running. She was lost and in shock. She ran for hours and at dawn, the skies began to light up and she could figure out where she was to make it home.

She snuck into her home before anyone was up. She cleaned the *blood from between her legs and tried to scrub off the dirty sick feeling from inside, climbed into her bed with her siblings, covered herself up with the blankets, and never wanted anyone to know her shame ... and no one did, not a soul. She felt that her dad would disown her or her brothers would kill the man for sure, and she couldn't stomach the thought of either one of those options.*

She knew that she shouldn't have gone there that night and that she had been wrong for going there. Then she started feeling that it was her fault, and the shame was difficult to bear.

She withdrew from her friends and family even more. She didn't even know Donald's full name or where he was from. She couldn't get revenge. She couldn't do anything except to put it out of her head, so far out that she forgot about it consciously, but she became angry inside.

Because she didn't know any better or talk to anyone about what had happened, she didn't know what she was experiencing had anything to do with the rape. Was she normal? Hormones were changing, this was just life stuff. Stop dwelling and move on, she told herself.

She had difficulty thinking and sleeping. She was jumpy and on edge. Her emotions were all over the place, but dealing with the ordeal or even thinking of it made her sick to her stomach. She had to push the memories away. She began feeling numb and detached from what had happened until, in her mind, it hadn't happened.

She was relieved that she didn't become pregnant. If she had become pregnant, how could she keep it? The thought of carrying that man's baby in her haunted her and made her feel like a terrible horrible being at the same time.

Abortions were illegal and she couldn't have afforded one anyway. She had heard horror stories about how terrifying and expensive illegal abortions were. She heard that they could cost up to $1000 and many women died from hemorrhaging or infection. Many women who did recover ended up sterile or chronically and painfully ill. What would have she done? Her father would have killed her and the ugly man *who raped her if he ever found out.*

She spent much energy worrying about this as she did trying to get up and go through her normal daily activities. When she finally started her period, she felt she could pass out from overwhelming relief but couldn't even tell anyone. Starting her period however, gave her a little more desire to move forward and have hope that maybe her life could be normal again.

CHAPTER 18

CARHA HAD JUST turned ten and school was going pretty well. She had many close friends, her speech problems were improving, and she kept busy with all kinds of sports.

She still seemed to compete to no end with Charlene. For some reason, Charlene just did not like her. One day, they were playing soccer up on the blacktop, working hard toward being big champions, when, by accident, Charlene ran into Carha and tripped. Charlene immediately became angry and went into a rage. She called Carha a "beaner," which Carha never understood. Carha was still as white as could be with lots of freckles, and she couldn't get a tan if she tried. It was a blank in time before Charlene was beating Carha up. Carha tried to defend herself, but that's about all she could do. It was again broken up by a yard guard, and they were both washing their faces once again in the girls' restroom. Carha never really understood what she did to piss that girl off.

While their core family unit was changing, the extended family was rapidly growing. Patria's younger sister, Tully, arrived with her new husband and their two children. Joseph was Carha's age, and Rose was Billy's age. They all got along well.

Their uncle Ardon seemed to visit more often seeing that all the family was there. He was loving and patient. He played with the girls and gave them an abundance of attention. He was handsome too and had dark, friendly eyes and a big smile with slightly crooked teeth.

As always, it was a big celebration day when the family got together. Ardon was affectionate with the girls, even braiding their hair and complimenting them. He made them feel good and self-assured about who they were as they were awkwardly developing.

Patria always cried when he left. She worried too, even more so now that Arne was gone.

Chuck Vaught never went to prison for very long. They called it self-defense. This was also painful to the family and just downright unbelievable. There was always a fear that Ardon would avenge his brother's death but for some odd reason, he didn't.

On one of Ardon's visits in particular, Patria was sadder than usual; he told her not to be sad and that he would be back before she knew it.

He gave her his favorite ring; he took it right off his finger and placed it on hers. It was a mystifying stone of a deep brownish orange, a tiger's eye-gold electroplated ring that he had worn constantly for years. She never knew where he got the ring but was aware that it meant something very special to him.

Patria thought to herself, *He is going to be lost without his ring.* He never took that thing off, but it made her feel good too. She knew he loved her.

Soon Patria's youngest brother, Alfie, joined the clan. He was with many women, women of all ages, sizes, colors, backgrounds, and foregrounds. He was also a fine-looking and distinguished man. He worked construction and kept fit. His downfall was that he drank too much, and when he drank, what little confidence that he had went out of him entirely. He wasn't a pleasant drunk, but boastful, sloppy, and embarrassing to his family.

He was working on some apartments there in town when he introduced his young niece Maggie to a handsome guy working on the job from out of town. She was smitten from the first time she laid her eyes on this mysterious out-of-towner whose name was Brad. He was tall, dark, and had a head full of wild, curly jet-black hair.

Bill was not happy in any way. A rift began, and it wasn't just between Maggie and her father. Because her mother was accepting of the relationship with this older man—and a mixed-raced man—arguments followed between Bill and Patria. These arguments were seldom witnessed and kept private from the children.

It never made a bit of sense that their father was so prejudice towards any other race, other than white. How could he be with their mother and have children with her when she was of mixed blood? They never had the guts to question him and when they asked their mother about it, she replied stating that she didn't know why. That was it.

After Bill arrived home from work, he usually went straight out to the garage or to his workbench. He was always doing something outside. The kids hardly saw him and their mother spending time with each other anymore. It was so gradual that they didn't even realize it.

Even though things were strange, Bill still made all of the kids laugh. He called them "googleaumas" and other crazy names. They never knew where the name came from, but it didn't matter; it made them laugh anyway. He told them that he loved them so much that he wouldn't trade them for buckets of rusted old nails. He had a thing with his face that he would do and he would say, "I tawt I taw a puddy tat—I did, I did, I did." It made every kid in the neighborhood laugh and want to see it.

He also played the harmonica incredibly well. It was wonderful to watch and listen to. He said that he played while stationed in England. The kids loved to listen to him.

Bill spent so much time outside that he began sleeping outside, even in colder weather. He bundled up in his sleeping bag and just slept under the stars. Sometimes, the kids visited him out there after dark, and he would explain to them about all of the different planets, the names of stars, and so on, just like he did when they went fishing.

Little Billy slept with Patria and never in his own bed.

The children loved their dad so much and loved to be with him, but they could sense that their mom and dad were growing apart. They didn't talk to each other like they used to. Their mother seemed withdrawn and sad since Arne died.

Maggie began hanging around with a whole different group of friends and still trying to act more mature than she was. She began to experiment with marijuana and drinking too. She didn't seem happy much. Maggie was also spending more and more time at the Hortas'. They were a Hispanic family full of secrets and evilness.

There was Old Man Horta, who used to work for the railroad until he had a back injury and sued the company for a few million. His wife, once sweet and well liked, was now in early stages of Alzheimer's disease. There was the oldest brother, Rusty; he had two young girls and a wife that was committed into a psych ward across the state. Then there was the big guy with tattoos all over his body. His name was Ted, and it was said that he worshipped the devil. He had a bad reputation for violence and for beating his last wife. He had a son, Eddy, with his former wife.

None of the family really kept jobs for very long except

for the youngest one, Mike. He worked locally for the post office and never married, and rumor had it that he preferred men.

All of the men (except Mike) had a reputation for beating their women. No one liked them in Natruna, and everyone would have been pleased to see them all leave.

Bill and Patria were unaware that Maggie was hanging around with the Hortas but knew that she was not the same girl that she used to be. It seemed that she transformed from this cute and talkative preteen into a creature who was filled with complicated emotions, wanting to distance herself and to constantly challenge her parents' authority.

Bill and Patria were trying hard to show her love and understanding while still disciplining her, but nothing seemed to make it better. They felt unfit and incompetent as parents.

Patria felt that Bill was withdrawing his love from Maggie and causing her to rebel, and Bill felt that Patria was too supportive and protective of Maggie, allowing her to do bad things.

They were doing the best that they knew how to do but constantly feared that Maggie's path was going to lead her down a very wrong road, or worse, get her hurt.

It was scary and stressful. They felt as if the family was completely out of control.

Maggie became best friends with Sylvia Gomez in high school, and she always seemed to be wherever Maggie was. Willie had somehow found it in his heart to forgive Sylvia for all the time she and Tabitha got him into trouble, and they were actually very close in high school.

He and Tabitha, on the other hand, weren't close and didn't get along at all, ever.

Will also hung around with Sylvia and Maggie pretty often. They occasionally visited the Stones'. Usually, they were brief visits, maybe hanging out while Maggie grabbed something or was checking in.

Will secretly had a little crush on Patria. He felt that she was a very pretty woman. He admired her for the way she took care of her family and home. As years passed and he visited more, he vaguely got to know the rest of the family. He felt Dana and Anna to be connected at the hip and that Carha to be connected to her mother's hip. He didn't pay much attention to baby Billy, only because he was a baby, and Will at the time was a normal teenage boy, not into babies.

As a favor, he did babysit once for a neighbor that had four boys. It didn't go very well. They were wild and didn't listen to him. They must have been able to sense that he didn't have an ounce of experience or any patience whatsoever for children.

He was sitting on the couch reading *The Lord of the Rings* for the third time. His reading must have irritated the boys. They grabbed hold of his book and tossed it outside. When Will went outside to get the book—he was pissed by that time—the boys locked all of the doors and even the windows. He didn't stand a chance. He was about to leave the little brats but decided against it and stayed on the front porch until their parents finally arrived home. That never happened again! He swore to never have children, ever, after that.

Will, Sylvia, and Tabitha were all exceptionally attractive and popular. Will already had somewhat of the reputation with girls and Sylvia with the boys.

They all had smooth dark skin due to their father's Hispanic pedigree. Their mother's family was mostly Irish, but she valued her husband's Mexican's roots and traditions more.

She learned how to cook from Pete's mother, who was

said to cook the best Mexican food ever and felt it her God-given right to have anyone and everyone eat it. Her house always smelled of corn tortillas and delicious spices. She loved to gather the kids up tightly against her large breasts to express her happiness and sincere love for them.

Pete's father was not that way whatsoever. He felt that kids shouldn't be seen or heard.

The Gomez children had scattered freckles over their shoulders, backs, and arms. They had inviting, deep, dark-brown eyes which lightened some in certain light to a friendlier and innocent lighter shade of golden brown.

They had thick, shiny, undulating wavy black hair, perfectly straight white teeth, and beautiful lips which uniquely puckered and protruded right in the middle of their upper lips—a Gomez family trait.

Will smiled and laughed a lot. Maybe it was part nervousness. It was cute nonetheless. Their noses were somewhat thick near the ends yet fit dreamily to the sculpture of their faces. They had the unadulterated bodies and tone. They apparently took pride in their physical appearances.

Will appeared as though he lifted weights—not too much, but just enough to define his muscles. They were evident in all the right places.

Will was hairy but not overly so, just enough to show that he was a man. He wore a five o'clock shadow, which made him look handsomely rugged like Clint Eastwood and he felt it helped cover the scars remaining from ongoing bouts of acne. He had perfectly proportioned ears, a nice strong neck with a masculine Adam's apple, broad shoulders, and a deep voice. He spoke well and in an educated way.

Will worked hard labor from a young age and always pushed himself to outdo anyone else. He had large, strong, sturdy hands that could get dirty during the day but wash clean at night. He enjoyed reading books of all kinds and learning about people, philosophy, and life. He respected people for who they were and was an active listener. He loved David Bowie and had posters of him all over his room, which his mom despised and made her have doubts that Will was straight. She had no idea how many girlfriends he really had, since he didn't bring them home.

Will was extra nice to everyone, polite, and had a way with women. Young or old, they all were attached to and interested in him. He knew what to say, how to look at them, and how to make them feel beautiful. He was one of those few men that could relate and even understand women. He loved them so much that he took time to learn about what they were all about by listening, reading books, and closely examining them.

It was apparent that he respected them for who they were. That was sexy! He wasn't macho and wasn't feminine. He was modest, didn't brag, and was totally cool. All Natruna women wanted Will Gomez, but he wasn't a one-woman man. He enjoyed women—just not one at a time for any length of time, that is, so forget commitment.

Will had many friends, but even some of his best guy friends were jealous of his popularity. He also still had problem with rules and that created problems in his relationship with his parents. They were highly respectable people in Natruna.

Will's father, Pete, was the president of the golf club, and his mother was actively involved in the volunteer program at the club. They loved their small town and raised their children to have the same respect, and the girls really did.

While Will and Sylvia were sweet, unassertive, and quiet—maybe a little introverted but well liked—Tabitha had more of a hard disposition and only had a few close friends. She just didn't really care what people thought. Will and Sylvia maybe worried too much about how people were feeling, especially if they cared about them. They would take the shirts off of their backs to help people.

Will occasionally went to the Hortas', where he began running into Maggie more and more. He only went there to hang around with Mike, who, despite his crazy family, was likable considering ...

Will really didn't like seeing Maggie or his sister there. He even lectured them a few times, which was out of character for him, but hey, he knew that the Hortas were bad news. Will grew very uncomfortable there over time because it was too dirty, and he felt that the Hortas were scum.

They had foster-care children whom they treated as slaves. The boys had to work all of the time, were yelled at, and were publicly mistreated. Well, then Rusty married one of the girls who came to live with them. She was the one who ended up living out the rest of her life in the hospital for the mentally ill.

Once, Will went over there and observed that their pet Saint Bernard, named "Dino," was lying very still in his doghouse, which he was chained to. There was a huge swarm of flies not only on top of the doghouse but also on the dog, which wasn't moving.

Will hit Mike in the arm and said, "Hey, dude, something looks wrong with your dog." They walked over to it, and sure as shit, it was dead and had been for quite some time based on the smell. It was that hot time of the year, and Will noticed that the water bowl was bone dry.

Will despised the family even more after this.

Will continued to struggle through high school. He finally was transferred to the continuation program that was still providentially located on the high school campus. Most of the teachers really liked him and wanted to see him graduate. They were trying to assist him in receiving his credits so that he could at least receive his diploma. By this time, Will was pretty disappointed in himself and knew that he wasn't going to walk with his classmates anyway. He really wanted to walk with his classmates and his friends with whom he'd bonded since kindergarten, but at this point, it just wasn't going to happen.

Mr. and Mrs. Gomez felt embarrassed of their son's behavior. Going home only made him feel worse. Will wasn't blaming anyone for his behavior but himself. He knew he had choices. His emotions just took control over his actions, and he didn't know how to gain control over his life. He wanted to do right; he didn't want to hurt his family anymore but just couldn't seem to grasp it all.

It was during the second semester of twelfth grade when his luck ran out and tolerance ended in a flash. Mr. Long yelled at him in front of the PE class, instructing him to go into the locker room and change, followed by, "I have had enough of your attitude!"

That was it for Will; he lost it. Without thinking at all and using all of his might, he threw the soccer ball that was in his hand directly into Mr. Long's thin, fragile face.

The lenses of teacher's eyeglasses cracked, the frame broke, and he had a bad bloody nose, he was utterly shocked. Mr. Long did not expect this behavior from this young man whom he'd known since he was a kindergartener. It was disheartening for Mr. Long.

Mr. Long, like many of Will's other teachers, was keenly aware of Will's intellect and potential, but the school had no other options but to expel Will.

After his expulsion and his parents putting an end to the comforts of home life, he no longer had a home, a car, work, or financial support. Will was in a pickle, to put it lightly. He stayed with a few of his friends on several occasions, but it wasn't long before his friends' parents politely said, "He's got to go."

He couldn't bear to face his sweet, respected, and loving grandparents in Idaho. He obviously despised rules, but he didn't have a choice if he wanted to eat and have a roof over his head.

Will could only think of one thing to do—and that was to join the United States Army. This would definitely be interesting!

CHAPTER 19

THANK GOODNESS FOR school sports! All of the Stone girls were actively involved in them and on cheerleading teams, and had lots of friends. Their interest in boys was steadily growing and their father was struggling. Their mother was struggling too but more with their father than the kids. They were both drinking more and more. Patria began hiding her liquor in strange places around the house and was already tipsy by the time the kids came home from school.

Carha could remember when she was in first and second grade and was typically the first to arrive home from school, and she looked forward to coming through the front door, knowing that her mother was taking an afternoon break and hadn't started drinking yet. It was her time to relax for an hour or two. Their mom watched her afternoon Western like *Gunsmoke* or *The Big Valley*. The curtains were closed, the house smelled of Pine Sol, and it was cozy.

It was a special time for Patria and Carha. Carha would take her shoes off, climb across her mother's legs on the couch, and cuddle underneath the soft, warm blankets.

They softly rubbed each other's feet until Carha fell asleep for her afternoon nap. It was relaxing.

When Carha awakened, her mother was already going again, getting ready for the arrival of the rest of the kids.

As they day progressed, it seemed that Patria would find her familiar place at the dining room table to have her afternoon drink and it didn't take any time for her to become emotional and teary eyed about her life. She wasn't the same anymore. The life seemed to be leaving who she was.

Patria saw Arne one night in her dream. It was a beautiful dream. She was awakened from this dream from a dead sleep by the presence or feeling of Arne being near her. She opened her eyes, and there he was, plain as day, standing in front of the hot water heater. He looked great, relaxed, grinning from ear to ear, and showing off his pearly whites. He said, "Patria, I'm here for you. I want you to know that I am okay. Please don't worry about me." He said it several times, "I'm okay, Patria ... I'm okay, Patria. Stop worrying about me." He gave her a big smile and said, "I love you!" Then he vanished. She woke up crying. It felt so real. She missed him so much.

She used to call him when she was sad, sometimes even in the middle of the night and they would talk for hours.

She always felt comforted after talking to him and he had a way of making her feel lighter and encouraged her to not take things so seriously.

Patria wished that she could talk to him so badly and explain how she was feeling and how she and Bill were drifting apart.

He would be surprised. He also admired their marriage and loved Bill like his own brother.

Even though she could talk to him when she was down, she didn't ever dig deep enough to the root of her pain, not even to herself. She didn't know how. Neither did Bill. Had they reached down and pulled it all out, maybe it wouldn't have diseased their souls and effected their lives, marriage and children.

Alcohol was a Band-Aid that made it all worse. The more they tried to cover and dismiss their pain without facing it head on, they more it festered and grew so big that there wasn't any Band-Aid large enough to cover it up. It was destined to explode. It had to.

As months passed and sadness filled their home, the kids began to find relief by staying away from the home that they once knew as their sanctuary.

Carha became very good friends with the Edmonds' who lived on the corner of Flower Street, one block down from the Stones. They began spending a lot of time together after school which helped to pass the time. Devin and Darcie were twins and the same age as Carha and were a blast to be around. They were always up for anything, but one thing Carha wouldn't ever consider doing was inviting either of them to her home. They were half-white and half African American.

Bill was inherently prejudiced and wasn't reserved about his feelings, especially as the children were getting older. He referred to Devin and Darcie as "monkeys." This didn't sit well with the rest of his family. They found it crude and appalling. They still couldn't understand why he wasn't bias against their mother and her family, or having children with Patria. Again, this was never discussed with their father. They were too afraid, maybe because he always seemed so angry when he made his comments… that at that time, he began frightening them.

Where did this come from? The kids had heard a few comments through the years about "Nazis" and "Negros," but his voice was never so angry and offensive. It was odd and out of character.

As kids, they continued having fun, no matter. They were always thinking of crazy ideas. They dressed up and placed wild wigs on their heads and then ran all over the neighborhood to get the neighbors' attention. They laughed at themselves more than the neighbors ever did.

The kids dressed up mannequins that they had found at the dump, and sat them by the street in a chair and had them reading books, raising their arms and hands, and doing other strange things. They anxiously waited for drivers to pass by so that they could see their reactions. Thank goodness there were not any accidents.

There were many good times too. The kids were very close and even as teenagers still wanted to hang out together, but over time, they began to find their own independence, their own friends, and somewhat separated their lives.

Patria often had flashes of her own childhood, what happened after the secret rape and how things became even more difficult for her that year. Fred was drinking too much, Wylie had moved to California and worst of all, later that year, somebody discovered the body of Lizza Croner, their beloved hobo housemaid. She had been lying dead in the hobo jungles for months, facedown, her skirt and bottoms pulled down and around her feet and her shirt off. She had been sexually assaulted and stabbed numerous times. There wasn't a service, and no one claimed her as family, but the Traughters felt great tragedy and loss. They never found the person who committed this horrific crime, either.

Ethel continued to go through her daily life routines during those days, not arguing, not fighting, and not being angry with God or life. She was always sweet, honest, and kind. She never yelled, spanked, or disciplined the children. Chores kept her busy most days. Just washing clothes with the old scrub board was time consuming itself. She enjoyed rocking in her rocking chair and telling stories or combing and braiding her long hair.

She once told Patria, "Patty, I guess your grandpa Ves is dead now, but I believe that he is in heaven, for he was a good man and got along well with everybody." This was the first time that Patria ever heard her mother admit to the possibility that her grandpa was dead. Through the years, Ethel talked about him as if she were waiting for him to visit her and that he was still somewhere in Texas living on a poor farm.

She taught the kids to never lie and always hold true to their beliefs and values. She reminded the kids as they were growing up, "If you lie, you will go to the ol' devil." She often said.

Ethel had many superstitions and old wives' tales that she firmly held on to. Through the years, she repeatedly taught the kids to believe in them too. They didn't really believe in all of them, but some of them they couldn't help but believe.

Ethel would say, "If a hoot owl hollows at night, it is bad luck, so you must tie a knot in something to choke it." Ethel used her apron. She also placed a broomstick across the doorway to break its neck.

Ethel also said, "When a dog howls, there is going to be a death."

When Ethel was pregnant with Patria, she went to watch a picture show. There was a woman in it with pure-white hair. Ethel, not thinking, touched her tummy. She told Patria that because she did that, Patria would have gray hair at an early age.

If the kids had a dream at night, she told them not to talk about it before breakfast or it would come true.

If the kids got sties in their eyes, she would tell them to go to the end of the road and wait until somebody passed by and recite, "Sty, sty, leave my eye, take the next one coming by."

She believed that if you got a fever blister on your lip, you should leave a teaspoon outside all night and then use it the next morning on your lip to make the blister disappear.

If you were pregnant and went the movies, if something bad happened in the movie and you touched your tummy, you would mark your unborn child in some way.

Fred was just as superstitious, and also had many beliefs when it came to healing. He would always boil milkweed and placed the boiled down extract on any sores to help heal them.

The Traughters had it a bit tougher than most, but kids are kids. They were no different than most, when it came to giving their folks a hard time.

When the children were hard on their mom, as they often were as teenagers, she would say to them, "One day when you grow up to have kids, I hope that they don't treat you the way you treat me."

They didn't mean to be mean to their mom, but they witnessed time and time again their father's disrespect toward her. She never said or did anything; she just took it. They couldn't help but feel some disrespect and resentment toward her.

It would have been a saving grace if Patria and the other kids had somewhere else to live, to go to during times of violence, to have a safe, welcoming place to stay, to have support and the opportunity to openly talk about what was happening. There wasn't anywhere or anyone that made that invitation. They minded their own lives, ignored the dysfunction, and continued living their lives.

Eventually, the kids figured that their lives were normal and accepted it. There wasn't any other way. They became used to feeling alone, afraid, numb, and lonely.

Patria swore to never be like her mother. She would never be too nice or gullible. She would never let people take advantage of her or run over her. She would never let a man lift a finger to her or her children. As a matter of fact, she made an oath to herself at a very young age to be the exact opposite of her mom.

But here she was with a nice house, beautiful healthy children who adored her and a husband that supported her and the children and she wasn't happy anymore. She was drinking like her own father and in the middle of the day like her own father. She was an alcoholic and didn't even know it, or did she? Did she just not want to admit it? Why now? Why do this when the kids needed her to be a strong role model more than ever? Why was she falling to pieces now? Why?

CHAPTER 20

THE COCKROACH WAS a Natruna nightmare! These insects were approximately one and a half inches long and had oval-shaped, reddish-brown, hard, shiny shells. During the day, you didn't know that they existed, but after the lights went out at night and everyone was tucked away, they came out by the hundreds. It was astonishing that they could fit in the tiny cracks between the cupboards in the kitchen. You saw them nowhere else but the kitchen—yuck!

At night when it was completely dark, they covered the kitchen floor almost entirely, but the minute the light switched turned on, they scrambled using their six tiny pin-like legs. You wouldn't even be able to step in between them. There were just too many.

The exterminator would come, and the ugly, gross critters would disappear for months, only to reappear again. Their large infestations and movement to and from neighbors' prevented them from ever leaving for good.

Wow, growing up with them made you feel as though you were the only one that had them. Having friends stay the night was too humiliating. They could come over during the day but were convinced to leave by night. There were only a few exceptions to the rule.

Only a few very best friends of the girls were trusted to stay the night. That was it.

Laurie Hicks was one of them. With her long legs, she stepped between the crunchy critters by using a combination of ballerina and athletic moves. She would laugh while calling out, "Cocka-roaches! Cocka-roaches!" She never acted grossed out but was more flabbergasted that there were so many.

Roxie Van Laren admitted to having them too but not as many. She only lived a few streets over and through the years became like a sister to Anna and Dana. The girls got a kick out of how pure and innocent she was even after the crude exposure to other kids that weren't. It never seemed to change her true disposition which seemed be so natural and inherit to her. It couldn't be swayed. The girls tried and tried, but Roxie was Roxie, always surprised and amused by the girls and found them funny and NEVER at Carha's expense, which Carha genuinely appreciated.

Robin Mathews came over one time after school. Robin and Carha got it in their heads to fry up cheese, just plain cheese, in a frying pan. They did until it was thin and crispy. They had a good time, giggled a lot, and wondered why they didn't hang out more often. And the fried cheese was delicious!

Robin had been attending school with Carha since kindergarten. They played dolls together, lay next to each other during reading time, played on the swings together at recess, and were in many of the same classes after they advanced on to middle school.

Robin lived way out in Village Gully, and after elementary school, the two didn't really spend any one-on-one time together. Carha felt that she became stuck up and acted better than others. Robin's dad owned a few different companies around town, and they had more money than most. Robin was quiet and got along with everyone but didn't really have a best friend.

One year, something happened to cause some drama at school, and some of girls began teasing her by calling her names and running around her singing that song by Hall and Oates, "Rich Girl."

It's unclear what started the whole immature girl war, but it ended as soon as it began, it probably hurt Robin for a long time afterward.

Later that same year, Robin's parents separated, she became depressed and always looked sad. It seemed during that time, she didn't have many friends, either. She walked around with her head down. Kids can be so cruel.

Carha was one of the unkind ones who never really said that she was sorry for her behavior, but she was sorry.

The Stone girls were growing and developing. Boys began sniffing around the Stone home on a regular basis. Random boys visited Flower Street, walking to the top of the fence, but then where? There wasn't anywhere else to go. Like the Stones weren't aware of what they were really looking for.

The girls were certainly coming into their own. They were pretty, athletic, clean, had incredible senses of humor, and were polite. They were all on the homecoming courts and popular with not just boys but girls too.

With having four teenaged girls in the home, strange events began taking place, like the one night when Maggie was showering with the little French bathroom window cracked opened, as it often was. The window was situated slightly above eye level but too small for anyone to crawl through. It led to a small space which held up a swamp cooler that was in the fenced backyard.

Maggie was washing up, when a man's hand came through the window in an attempt to grab, most likely, one of her young, perky breasts.

Maggie came running out of the bathroom, dripping wet and screaming at the top of her lungs. Of course, their father was working, and all of the girls went into lockdown.

Patria sat on the couch with Bill's 22-caliber rifle on her lap, with all of the children surrounding her. She didn't call the cops, but waited and waited.

When questioning Maggie about what happened and what she saw, all Maggie could say was "It was a man's arm and hand and it was enormous and hairy!"

They never found out whose big hairy arm that was and why he was trying to grab Maggie, but they were all careful from then on out.

There was a new Foursquare Church preacher who came to town bringing along his wife and three children. Trent was the eldest, then Liam, and then Julia. The Carters were exceptionally kind and giving. They moved into a home at the bottom of Flower Street.

Carha and Billy befriended Julia, and they really liked and enjoyed being around the entire family. They even attended a few of the services at their church, which was within walking distance of their home. It made it convenient.

The church wasn't quite the fit as the Baptist church was for the Stones, so eventually they went back to the church they knew and felt more comfortable with.

Carha spent hours every day with Julia, listening to the *Grease* soundtrack over and over again, dancing, singing, and even watching the movie repeatedly. They pretended to be the sweet and innocent Olivia Newton-John and then switched gears and pretended to be the sexy Olivia Newton-John dressed all in black. They didn't have leather but acted as if they did.

The more time that Carha spent at their house, the more time she and Liam developed crushes on one another.

He knocked on the Stones' door once during dinnertime and asked for Carha. Carha was surprised to see him. He was sweet looking with his curly sandy-blond hair and brown eyes with long eyelashes, nervously looking at her. He was adorable, wearing a long-sleeved plaid shirt that was tucked in nicely to his light brown, flared corduroy pants.

He asked that she come out to talk with him. Dana and Anna were peeking out of the living room window laughing. Carha was puzzled by his strange behavior. He was talking about nothing but approaching her closer and closer until his face was right in front of her face. This made her feel so uncomfortable that she backed right into one of the sagebrushes.

She quickly jumped up and yelled to him, "What is wrong with you?"

He apologized and said, "I just want to give you a kiss."

Carha looked again at the girls with their nosey faces chuckling in the window. She looked back at him and said, "Well then, do it."

He came close; she closed her eyes and puckered her lips tightly. Then they touched lips. They moved their heads side to side as they pressed their mouths against one another's. It lasted a few seconds and was weird for both of them.

Then he took a deep breath and said, "Thank you." He turned around, stumbling, and walked quickly down the street without looking back. That was Carha's second kiss but her first real kiss.

The girls were proud of their little sister and pleased that they witnessed it. Their relationship began changing at that point. They didn't pick on her as much and maybe even began respecting her some.

Liam and his family moved away soon after. It was sad, but life was moving and evolving at a fast pace, and Carha was just trying to keep up with it all. She and Liam wrote a few letters, but that was about it. More than anything, she really missed her dear friend Julia.

To keep her mind off of her losses, she began going to the movies almost every weekend. This wasn't just any movie theater, it was magnificent and where all the teens hung out. Carha wasn't allowed to go by herself until around the end of the sixth grade and it was all the rave!

The Natruna Theater opened sometime in the mid-'50s and was then a part of the Fox Theater circuit. The generous chemical corporation purchased it, equipped and all. It contained more advanced features than any other theater of comparable size in the world.

Being built in the 1950s, the entrance to Fox Theater was bright and dazzling.

The dramatic effect of both the incandescent lights blinking on and off in a rhythmic pattern and the warm glow of the neon lights defining the letters in the Fox name made the lights really stand out.

The marquee was split, with each side mirroring the other. It was big and bold, and you could read what was playing from blocks away. The ticket booth was set dead center under the two opposing marquees; the booth was made of solid glass and stood out from the main doors like a crystal fortress for a gatekeeper set outside a castle.

Once you purchased your tickets, you would walk around the ticket booth and head straight to the concession stand. You name it, they had it—popcorn, candy, hot dogs, sodas ... it looked like an all-you-can-eat sugar buffet.

Once you purchased all your snacks and left the

concession stand, you would head to find your seat. You could enter the main theater from either the left or right.

The walls were tall and built of brick, and the ceiling seemed to be one hundred feet high. All the walls in the main theater had paintings of giant ferns with large green stems and leaves curling and twisting this way and that, just as if they were real and alive. It always felt so cool and dark. The ferns looked so real that they made it seem like you could walk right through them and into the jungle.

The chairs were all covered with light purple corduroy that always felt like big, soft sofa pillows. There were so many seats that no matter how crowded the theater, you could always find a spot all your own.

The screen seemed larger than any other screen they had ever seen (well, of course, except for the screen at the drive-in), and it had a large stage in front of it that looked as if you could put on a full play.

They always played "The Star-Spangled Banner" before starting the movies. Everyone would stand up and place their hands over their hearts and watch the short movie of the flag waving in the breeze, and then once it was over, everyone would cheer and take their seats, knowing that the movie would start any second.

Going to the Natruna movie theater was like going on an exciting adventure.

It was there one night where Sandy, Sheri, and Carha were waiting to purchase a ticket and Carha had to stand up for a new friend.

The sun was just going down, and there was still an hour or so before the theater opened its doors. Sheri gave the impression that she was slightly slow mentally. Her accent, short blonde hair, and thick glasses didn't help her image much. She had just moved to Natruna from Arkansas and quickly became friends with Carha and the group she hung around with.

Sheri participated in all popular activities and had nice clothes, a small frame, and very big boobs, which made all of the boys like her; therefore, all the girls her age liked her too. But some of the older girls found her to be a threat and began picking on her.

That night at the movies, the three friends hung out in the parking lot across from the show, minding their own businesses, until they became target practice for a group of girls a few years older than them.

The rocks were really aimed at Sheri. The name-calling followed. Carha and Sandy just moved out of the way, but after a few minutes of witnessing their friend's abuse, they yelled to the girls to stop. The girls came closer, packed together, and weren't going to stop. They were intimidating and aggressive. Sheri started crying, hiding her face and protecting her glasses from the continued rock throwing. Carha felt steam rise up but couldn't slow the bunch with words. There was only one thing that would work, and that was physical action.

Carha covered her face while walking as quickly as possible toward whichever one she could get to the fastest. Before she knew it, her fist hit one of the girls directly in the nose. The girl fell to the ground and had blood flowing from her nose.

Carha got another girl's attention, put her fist up in front of her face, got into a boxer's stance that her father had taught her and said, "Who's next? I told you to stop."

The girls ran to their friend's side, and one of them removed a piece of clothing and pressed it up against the upset girl's nose. They didn't say one word. They gave Carha many dirty looks but didn't say one word. They assisted their friend back across the street while whispering to her that she was going to be okay.

Sheri never said anything to Carha about what had happened. She was still hurt about the way the girls treated her, but that wasn't all she was upset about. It was more, and Carha knew it. There were things that her new friend didn't talk about—why she moved, why her dad followed months later but slept on the couch. Carha never asked her about her personal life. She just liked her and knew no one should be treated like that. It was wrong.

For all of the good and bad, Carha still felt an abundance of love from inside of her home, but there was that persistent overcast of sadness that couldn't be pinpointed or clearly understood. It was there like an unwavering heaviness that made it difficult to take a full breath at times.

Thankfully, the extended family continued to visit through the years which delivered a bit of a reprieve and inviting breath of fresh air for all of the family to take in.

Ardon was in and out as usual, doing what he did, traveling back and forth from Texas to Natruna. He was even settling down some and had a pretty serious relationship with a lady named Margie. She was nice, but the Stones knew that women in Ardon's life came and went.

Margie was really good to Ardon. She cooked, cleaned, and even shined his boots. They moved to Sacramento, California, to be closer to her family, which thrilled Patria to have her brother so much closer.

Patria worried about her brother, but she had to remind herself that he had been freight hopping almost his entire life. He had a survival guide imprinted inside of his beautiful head.

He, Arne, Alfie, and all of their closest friends train hopped without the slightest hesitation. It was usually their only means of transportation in times of economic hardship. Maybe that wasn't the only reason they did it. Hopping a freight train was crazy, dangerous, and an adrenaline rush for many.

Every year, the trains were excelling at even faster speeds, causing increased threat to all who attempted to jump them.

This was hard on Patria, knowing how dangerous it was, but it was such a part of the boys' lives that she had to accept it, especially if she wanted to see them. It wasn't just life-threatening but illegal. But, dang, it was adventurous, and the boys thrived on it. The ride also provided a freedom they craved. They were drifters and observers of spectacular, often unseen views of the country. You could say that they were addicted. Some called them "hobos." But these hobos were exceptionally nice looking, young, prideful, polite, particular, and clean as they could possibly be.

Ardon knew where, how, and when to jump the trains from almost anywhere in Texas. It was too risky to get into a car while it was just sitting. He had been caught too many times when he was younger and a newbie, and he wouldn't chance it. Those big sticks that the "bulls" carried around weren't just for looks. Those railroad police would certainly beat the crap out of you because they viewed you as a filthy hobo.

Ardon knew if he needed to get to the tracks on the other side of a train, to never, never crawl under a car— that was another reason to know where, when, and how to jump that train. He knew to never step on the coupling between cars if you wanted to keep your feet. He knew to avoid open cars, like flatcars, gondolas, or car carriers, and to stay away from trains that were carrying new automobiles. If there was one thing the bulls were on the lookout for, it was people boosting radios on the car carriers. And he knew to never jump into a car without inspecting it carefully. Some cars were very dirty, and once the train got up to speed, all of that dirt flew around like a sandblaster.

Regardless of how clean Ardon was boarding the train, by the time he arrived at his destination, he was pretty grubby. Guess there is a reason for the caricature of the dirty-faced bum.

Another challenge, among the many, was boarding with a gallon-sized plastic jug of water. It was a necessity not just to drink but also to wash with. Unexpected events could arise, and preparation was everything.

Empty boxcars bounced around very violently, causing the loose sand to hit you from every direction. It is almost impossible to keep your bottom on the floor of the car. Some travelers preferred to squat for many hours just to save their rear ends the torture.

Another item of necessity was a common rock of perfect size or one brake shoe. The hoppers would use one or the other to wedge into the rail where the doors slid on a boxcar. The boxcars would bang about brutally, sliding them shut and locking them in. Being locked in a boxcar during summer months could be like being locked in an oven at three hundred degrees, whereas being in a boxcar during cold months could be lethal.

He also knew to sleep with his feet pointed toward the front of the train when he was going to sleep in a boxcar. If it stopped quickly and he slid, he could break a leg or both, or even break his neck.

In addition, Ardon was experienced with the various types of people who traveled freight—the cons, the hobos, the hitchhikers, and the thrill seekers. He rode with hard-core criminals, soft-core criminals, rapists, and the mentally ill. He planned his sleeping position wisely. He also carried himself in a friendly, nonthreatening way, especially during the night. He even felt that the loud, screeching rails were comforting to his ears.

He had the skills perfected when it came to catching a freight train.

Timing was everything when jumping onto a train. He waited and waited until that last car slowly whistled by. He would sprint alongside with his long, bony legs—thick, black, wavy hair flowing behind him—while carrying an intense grin showing every single pretty white tooth he carried in his mouth. His heart pumped so hard that it felt as if it would burst through his solid chest wall. He would grab hold of the end ladder, feeling the full power of the train, while just at that right moment swing his body forward through the doors and feel, smell, and experience being home again. It was a huge adrenaline rush yet soothing at the same time.

Jumping off a train was a different story. Those smith wheel blades were sharp and heavy. It wouldn't take much, just one turn, for you to lose a body part. Shoot, those wheels rumbling by were only a few inches from a hand or foot. And jumping out onto the gravel and losing balance equaled bloody palms, torn clothes, bloody knees, basically your body being chewed up by gravel ... a very different type of road rash.

These guys knew the risk when they jumped these freight trains, and Ardon wasn't stupid by any means, but he wasn't invincible, either.

One day, Patria received a call from Ardon asking if his income tax papers had arrived. He always received his important papers at Patria's house; it was the only firm, concrete place that he knew, Patria explained that they hadn't come yet, and they visited for a while. He did as he always did, asking about everybody one by one, starting at the oldest, Maggie, and working his way down to little Billy. He told her as soon as they arrived that he would be on his way to pick them up and would plan on staying for a while.

Patria was looking forward to it and was already preoccupied preparing her shopping list. She loved to spoil him while he was there, making all of his favorite home-cooked meals. He loved cold fried chicken and Patria's potato salad.

It wasn't but a few days later when the phone rang. It was Marge calling to tell them that there had been an accident. Ardon didn't know the Sacramento railway, and he didn't properly prepare ahead of time. It was a combination of surprises that caused the accident to happen.

The ladder was on the side of the car, not behind it as he was more familiar with. He expected it would be there and he could land on the end of the ladder, but there wasn't one, and he lost his footing just enough for his foot, leg, and then body to be caught in the undercarriage. He was run over by the wheels, supporting one hundred thousand pounds of dead weight.

They were only able to identify him by his tattoos.

Ardon was only thirty-one years old at the time of his death.

CHAPTER 21

AT THE AGE of seventeen, Will's mother gladly took him to meet with the recruiter, and in no time, it was arranged for him to take the ASVAB test. Will expected to receive orders almost immediately, but due to scoring a 91 out of 100 on the AFQT (Armed Forces Qualification Test) and demonstrating areas of strength in the subtests, they had other plans for Will.

Will's recruiter arranged for him to spend time attending Pasadena City College to receive his high school diploma for proper enlistment classification, which would of course also be to the military's benefit.

Within a few weeks, Will completed all of his high school units at an accelerated pace while staying in an old, run-down motel within walking distance of the college. Then he was off to Fort Knox, Kentucky, for basic training.

Right off the bat, his drill sergeant, Mr. Smith, didn't like him. He called him every name in the book and purposely made his life miserable. Mr. Smith's new goal was to transform this good-looking guy from California into a respectable, combat-ready soldier, and he wasn't going to give up. His tactics were, of course, to intimidate and demean Will, but little did Mr. Smith know that he had his work cut out for him.

Will never polished his boots well enough, never made his bed correctly, and never did anything right in his sergeant's eyes. Will thought he had it rough in Natruna, but he didn't have a clue.

Between all of the exercising and limitations on food intake, Will was starving. He decided to sneak to the fort exchange and he purchased peanut butter, jelly, and bread. He hid it in his barracks, inside of a box hidden inside of a utility closet. He would actually hide inside of the smelly closet to gorge on his peanut butter and jelly sandwiches while his mates were soundly asleep. He felt no guilt what-so-ever...only pleasure.

Unfortunately, Mr. Smith discovered his stash during a barracks search, and kicked his ass. The possession/consumption of food, except during designated meal hours and in designated areas, is a punishable offense.

Will's life quickly became even tougher. Food was just too important to him, and it wasn't long before he continued hiding food and eating it in his barracks; he just became smarter in where he hid it.

While Will was preparing for his obstacle course, his drill sergeant approached him with a second pair of boots in hand. From the look on Mr. Smith's face, Will quickly knew that it wasn't going to be good news.

Mr. Smith said, "Gomez, who the hell do you think you are? This is shit work, and you know it. Now, ya gonna carry these damned boots with you during your obstacle course tests, you understand me?"

Will replied, "Yes, sir."

He proceeded to remove his boots, when his Sergeant got in his face and asked him, "You brain stupid, California boy?" Mr. Smith, a bulldozer of a man, black, muscular, and intimidating, continued, "Don't take those off, dumb ass. Carry these sons of bitches with you too!"

Will asked, "How?"

Mr. Smith, with his nose touching Will's nose, yelled into his face while spitting, "Well, I don't care how, you dumb fuck, just carry them with you the entire time, and don't drop them, or your good-looking California ass will be headed home!"

Will wasn't about to argue with him. While working hard to contain his temper, he took a deep breath and answered, "Yes, sir!"

Without any time to spare, he wrapped the heavy, size-twelve boots around his neck, allowing them to dangle next to his broad chest, and he navigated ropes, walls, hurdles, zigzags, tunnels, low rails, fences, cargo net climbs, cargo net descents, and parallel bars—along with his thirty-pound backpack. He wasn't about to fail this test.

He finished the course but had hard, reddish lumps and swelling all over his chest. After a few uncomfortable days, the huge bruises darkened to blue and purple and then to a pretty green color, and then ugly brown and yellow. Finally, after over a month, his gorgeous chest was back to its normal color.

The military offered Will many adventures. There were a small group of hearty black men from New York who pushed their weight around and bullied others. Once, while standing in the chow line, they were on their way to cut to the front of the line as they'd done so many times before. This didn't sit well with Will at all, especially since his stomach was so empty. He stepped in front of one of the guys, instructing him to get to the back of the line. Will didn't think that this tall, dark, Mr. T–looking man with a gold front tooth would do anything, out of fear of military punishment. That wasn't the case. It was only a matter of seconds, and without any debates or discussions, an enormous fist headed directly for Will's face.

Will was out for some time and woke up dazed and defeated. He was especially pissed that he missed that meal.

During Will's six weeks of training, he had stronger abs from all of the sit-ups, his arms were more muscular, his core became rock solid, he mastered push-ups and his legs became massively strong from all of the running. He learned how disgusting men could be while on latrine duty, and he became an efficient dishwasher while on KP duty. And he only liked rules less.

After basic training, he was stationed to Fort Campbell, Kentucky, for permanent clerk duty.

Yeah, his Military Occupational Specialty, or MOS as they called it was "legal clerk."

He asked to be a military policeman, but they turned him down, saying that his scores were too high for that. He needed to pursue law ... law! Will Gomez going into law, ha!

After ten months of being away from his home, Will Gomez returned home during leave from the army. He was happy to be home.

He had a grand time partying while back home. Everyone seemed to miss him, and he felt better returning home after time away, almost like all the things that he had done wrong were behind him. He had a new life that no one knew about. He liked his privacy.

After returning to his legal clerk duty in Kentucky, Will had a craving and needed to be closer to home. He was eventually granted a stateside swap to Fort Ord in Monterey with another soldier that had the same MOS.

Will was ecstatic to be back in California.

Will settled into his new surroundings and tried to make

the best out of his circumstances, but he could never get used to following rules. Any chance that he had, he was cruising the almost four hundred miles down the one familiar highway which met the other familiar highway, headed back to the desert that he knew like the back of his hand.

He had bought a royal-blue '68 Camaro and enjoyed every second that he knew he was free from the strict policies and procedures.

Being in the military made him feel more and more like a caged animal that couldn't breathe. The air around him became thicker and heavier.

The thing about Will was that he was kind, sweet, and endearing to almost all who knew him. People just shook their heads in amazement at how he repeatedly did the stupidest things and always, always got caught.

There were many times when he arrived back after a leave a day or two late and got away with it. His captain was fond of him and hesitantly covered up his absence one way or another. He would lecture Will and warn him, explaining to Will that if caught, they both would be in big trouble. Will would charmingly apologize for his behavior and make it up to the captain somehow. He was good at taking care of people, watching their backs, and was always thoughtful and helpful. People respected him for it and looked up to him, even his captain.

While Will was enjoying his popularity and good times on leave, unbeknownst to him, his entire battalion was sent to Panama for jungle training. Will was nowhere to be found, and a warrant was issued for his arrest.

It was only the thirty-first day of his leave; he was one day late. He had done this before, but when he arrived back to his barracks, he was greeted by an unfamiliar, stern, somewhat scary military policeman who arrested him on the spot and officially listed him as a deserter.

Will was handcuffed and sent to the stockade.

You would think that after being locked up for a month, dry shaving and sharing a toilet with other men along with said charges, Will would be a changed man, but he wasn't. Maybe he had a better understanding of rules and how not to break them.

Will had an admiration for what the US military did for his country and had the utmost respect for the army, but he could never feel that he belonged or was a part of the greater picture. He felt again as an outsider who couldn't take credit for his service. Additionally, he felt that it was a waste of taxpayers' money, and he felt that the money could have been better spent elsewhere.

After Will's time was up, his captain returned and asked him what he wanted to do. Will pleaded that they issue him a Chapter 10 discharge immediately. The captain and a few others pulled it off and granted him his wishes for the service that he had done, and he was relieved of his duties to the army.

Will was disappointed in himself but felt that he had no other choice. At the same time, he was feeling the air move into his lungs more and more easily. He gathered his belongings and aimed for the highway. He couldn't drive fast enough. He didn't know what he was going to do and really didn't care. He was free again.

After getting as far away from the base as possible on the gas that he had, he had to pull over to fuel up again. One more tank and he would make it home and then take it from there.

There was a slight issue with this plan; he didn't have a dime to his name and it was 1979, gas rationing was in effect, it was an odd day and he had an even license plate.

He knew pulling up to that Chevron gas station that he

was going to have to put the pedal to metal and pray that he wouldn't get caught after filling his tank. He had to move quickly. But there was a bigger issue at hand.

If your license plate ended in odd numbers, you could fill up on that particular day. His didn't. He didn't figure this situation into his plan, but he felt he had to add it in last minute if he wanted to get home.

Will unfortunately had zero patience, which seemed to be one of his many liabilities. He had to get farther away and felt that he had to make a hard decision, so he took a small pocketknife out of his duffel bag and eyed a brand-new sliver Mercedes Benz sitting pretty in an empty parking lot. He scoped the area and then went for it.

He squatted down in the dark, strange town, with only the faint shine from a distant, high, yellow streetlight to shed guidance as he loosened the screws from the license plate. He replaced this license plate for his and tossed his inside of his trunk

So far so good. Now to get gas and get out of there!

Mission accomplished.

He was a rebel without a cause on the road again, with the wind in his hair and no direction, nothing to drive him, and nothing to motivate him, except maybe freedom. Even he didn't understand what his future held or if he would ever figure it out.

After a short time staying with friends and avoiding his parents, he and his sister Sylvia moved into a small apartment there in Natruna, and things were going okay. His parents wouldn't have anything to do with him, but that didn't surprise him. They were still raging from him leaving the army.

Will never smoked and never tattooed or marked his body with piercings. He didn't do any drugs and was really only a "beer guy." He was different from most of his friends and *never* gave in to peer pressure. As a matter a fact, he was anti–peer pressure. But that didn't matter to his parents. It was everything else that he did.

Money was tight, and it was taking longer than usual to get back on his feet. They didn't have much furniture, but they seemed to have many guests. Sylvia took the matter into her own hands.

Will arrived home after a hard day's work to find all new furniture in their apartment. Sylvia and few of her friends went shopping at their local furniture warehouse. The storage warehouse was owned by their very own apartment management. And they weren't selling any of the furniture; it was only being stored when Sylvia and a few of her friends decided to take it.

One of her friends knew that the side warehouse door was unlocked and that no one was around. They backed up the truck and loaded the bed with as much as it could handle, and their empty apartment was then furnished. It was extremely easy.

Will didn't agree with what they had done. The only thing that he said before resigning to his bedroom was, "Sis, you'd better not get caught, and you guys had better not get my ass into trouble."

Will had been doing some construction work and it had begun to slow down. Sylvia began dating a much older man named Tyson and soon moved in with him.

Will couldn't afford rent anymore and pretty much was hitting bottom. For some reason, his friends were generous with offering him drugs and alcohol but not money to help out with his living requirements. They just wanted someone to party with. It was not a good time to be introduced to acid for the first time.

Will came up with some cockamamie plan to buy these double-stamped purple sheets of acid for $100. He could turn around and sell each hit for $2.50, earning $250.00.

He didn't have the money to invest but felt confident that he could make the profit and pay back a loan and make some much-needed money.

Not thinking straight, he made one of his stupidest and most regretful mistakes.

Will snuck through his parents' bathroom window while they were at work and stole a bank check from his mother. He forged her name, cashed it at the liquor store without a problem, and was off to make his investment. He planned on paying his parents back.

It didn't take but a few days until all of the double-stamped purple sheets of acid were gone. The problem with Will's plan was that he didn't sell one of them. He gave some away and did some. He lost track of them, of time, of life, not realizing that nearly six months had passed since he'd gotten out of the army and that he was no better off.

A week after he stole the check from his parents, his mother called and asked him to come to their house. She was friendly and welcoming. He felt relieved that he was invited to return home for a visit. He felt that there might be light at the end of the dark place he was in. Maybe his parents were going to invite him to come and live back home and not be angry at him anymore. He felt a sigh of relief.

He arrived to find his mother in the kitchen cooking and his father in the kitchen, sitting at the bar sipping on a Miller Lite. They both froze as he walked into the kitchen. Audrey's face turned pale as she observed Will's state. He had lost so much weight. His once full face now showed off his bony cheekbones. He was pale and bug-eyed.

This broke Audrey's heart for about ten seconds until the anger quickly entangled her deepest being, and she began yelling at the top of her lungs at him. "How could you have stolen from your parents? How could you be such an embarrassment to us! How could you throw your life away and hurt us the way you are? Get out, and don't ever come back!"

He opened his mouth to retaliate and told them his feelings about all of the ways they had always failed him as his parents and how inadequate they were.

At that point, his father stepped in, shoulders up and broad, with his face in Will's face and his chest puffed out. He proceeded to tell his messed-up grown son that Will would not speak to his mother that way. Before Will could respond to that comment, a cast-iron pan hit him upside his head, causing him to become distraught and confused about everything that surrounded him.

It took him a few minutes to come out of it and somewhat back to reality. Once he was alert enough to examine the situation, he was gravely remorseful for all of the horrible things he had done and said. He put his head down, shook it side to side, and then turned around and walked out of the home that he had grown up in.

He sadly got into his car, wondering to himself, *How did I get here, to this place? This isn't me, is it?* His body felt sore from all of the acid, his soul felt empty, and he really wasn't sure how to get well again.

CHAPTER 22

MAGGIE WAS PREOCCUPIED with Brad (The visiting construction worker her uncle introduced her to) and barely graduated from high school. It was the very next day after receiving her diploma that she packed up all of her belongings and headed for Vegas with her new boyfriend. It was a sad day for the family. Her father, Bill, refused to be there and to say good-bye. He disapproved greatly. Carha practiced for weeks on a song especially created for her big sister.

With the suitcase sitting beside Mag, she and the rest of the family all listened attentively as Carha sat on the floor in the back bedroom playing her organ.

She sang with all of her heart a rendition of "Red River Valley." She replaced and added words "Maggie Ann" throughout the song. Enormous tears rolled down Carha's freckled checks as she strongly soldiered forward.

Then after hugs and plenty of crying, they all followed Maggie and Brad down their concrete front steps, continuing down and over the cracked, holey walkway that had worsened over the years, to the familiar Flower Street.

Brad tossed Maggie's floral-printed suitcase into the

backseat, and they drove away in his blue Mustang. He couldn't have comprehended what he was taking from their family on that day.

The girls began to transition into young women, which was not just causing turmoil within themselves, but their father struggled to what seemed like a point of insanity.

Dana and Anna seemed to be going into different directions. Dana's grades began to drop; she began hanging around a different group of girls, harder girls. She and Anna seemed to butt heads more than usual and didn't even talk to one another most of time.

Bill appeared as if he were always angry and upset about something but wouldn't say. He began keeping to himself more and more. He and Patria hardly talked to each other. He wasn't really speaking with anyone, for that matter.

There was definitely a quiet tension replacing the once happy and loving mood of their home.

Bill seemed to be hardest on Dana, correcting her English and grammar every time that she turned around. Anna kept quiet, especially during dinners. The Stones continued having their nightly dinner rituals but they had become awkward and uncomfortable. Patria didn't talk much, either, and Bill acted as if he were disappointed with his family and even gave them angry looks.

Carha and Billy had been playing outside after school until just before dark, as they did almost every night, when they heard yelling from inside of Dana's bedroom (which used to be Maggie's). There was more commotion than they had ever heard before.

The door was closed, and they could hear loud voices and crying from the other side door. They tried to open the door but were cut short by their mother's hand. She said, "Everything is going to be okay. Go play in the living room."

They didn't move.

The door soon opened enough for them to view their sister Dana lying on her side on the floor in the middle of the room, slobbering, crying, and talking incoherently. Her long brown hair mopped the wooden floor, back and forth, her bell-bottoms tainted with dirt.

Bill and Patria stood over her, outwardly wounded and repeatedly scolding her for drinking.

Anna stood in the doorway of the back room, head down, hurt and speechless. This saddened the kids as they watched. They felt sad for their parents. They felt their pain and also felt confused, disappointed and hurt. Their parents appeared surprised and confused at her behavior, maybe even afraid. They probably felt alone and defeated with themselves, too.

Bill progressively became heated. He and Patria began arguing and yelling at one another from opposing directions, with Dana lying between them. Patria was defending and protecting Dana's behavior, making excuses. "She was just experimenting. She is sorry. She won't do it again." This seemed to only make Bill angrier.

Dana eventually ended up in bed, with Patria taking care of her while she puked her guts up into a bucket. Bill ended up outside, and the house seemed to continue evolving with some evil entity.

Carha and little Billy relied on one another. They held hands and stood leaning against the wall in the home's main passageway not knowing what to say or what to do. They didn't understand why these things were happening and just knew that they both were feeling the same way about it. At least they had each other. They didn't talk to anyone else about it. It was embarrassing, and they didn't want people to judge them. They wanted to be normal like everyone else.

Maggie was secretly pregnant when she moved away, and within five months, she gave birth to a healthy baby girl she named Rebecca. Less than two months later, Maggie came home without Brad, but not with approval from her father. He would have nothing to do with the baby and became angrier with Patria for allowing Maggie to return home.

The arguments progressed to full-blown explosive fighting like never before. He called Rebecca a "chink," and it was clear that he was increasingly losing it.

Maggie knew that she was causing too many problems being there and was not comfortable. She wasn't sure what to do. She soon turned to an old friend, someone who had always been there for her. His name was Phillip Walker.

Phillip drove a motorcycle and was easygoing and polite. He'd had a huge crush on Maggie for years. He was more than happy to rent a small apartment for all three of them and quickly took to Rebecca. Phillip was almost five years older than Maggie, but he had a stable job and was completely dedicated to Maggie's every want and need.

On the morning that Maggie was packing and preparing to move out of her family home once again, she witnessed something she thought that she never would. She had just gotten out of the shower and went to check on the baby, who was sleeping in her bassinet in the dining room. The house was empty except for Maggie, her father, and Rebecca. Maggie walked around the corner to find her dad cradling baby Rebecca in his arms. He was talking to her, asking her in baby talk, "Are you Grandpa's girl?" He told her how beautiful she was. He was oblivious to Maggie standing there or that there was even a world that existed outside of that moment.

Maggie didn't say a word; she quietly stepped backward and went into Dana's room.

A few weeks later, it was dark when Carha heard yelling coming from the kitchen. Her parents were fighting again.

Bill was walking quickly, almost running toward the back fence. Patria was standing at the back door screaming at him, "Go, and don't you ever come back!"

Carha wrapped her arm around her mother's leg and repeated exactly what she had just yelled out, "Yes, you go, and don't you ever come back!"

It only took a split second for her father to turn around and head back toward the back door while glaring directly at Carha.

Carha knew she shouldn't have said those words as soon as they spouted out of her mouth. But it was too late. She knew what she had to do: run—and run fast!

Her heart was pounding, her vision was blurry, and she knew that she couldn't make it all the way into her room. She could hear his hard, fast footsteps almost on her heels. She swooped behind Dana's door and barely had time to catch her breath before the familiar hand came at her, hooking her skinny arm and pulling her out from behind the white door.

He kneeled down, looked her directly into her small, beady eyes, and sternly said, "You will never speak to me that way, you understand me? I am your father."

With that, he pulled her farther away from the door and toward the full-size bed covered in a brown-and-blue groovy comforter. He bent her over and kept her in place with one hand while using the other one to remove his leather belt. He whipped her three times hard. He gave one last look into her eyes and turned to leave. She could have melted away from this life from the guilt that she felt. She knew that she deserved the belt. Her words weren't hers that night. She didn't want him to leave. She wanted everything to be as it was. That's what she'd meant to say.

She was so sorry, but she didn't tell him. She couldn't say anything. She was too ashamed.

It was like time stood still during those days. The unhappiness and silence was overwhelming. Bill and Patria continued drinking alcohol and becoming more and more detached with each drink.

CHAPTER 23

I T SEEMS THAT after Patria grew up around a drunk and the unhappiness that followed it all, the last thing she would ever do is bring it into her own home and around her own family. Wouldn't she want to protect her family? She knew first-hand what is was like.

As with most drunks, her own father, Fred wasn't a happy drunk, and most of his anger was aimed toward Ethel. During those days he was mean to her for the majority of the time and really seemed to not like her at all. He always had a temper, but as the kids got older and he was drinking more, he became even more intense.

Often, Fred kicked Ethel when she didn't clean well enough and hit her right in her face. He frequently yelled at her, "Go wash your Goddamma teeth!"

The more intoxicated he became, the more pissed off he grew. Sometimes a seemingly minor thing triggered a big reaction. He eventually began directing his anger toward the children, perhaps hoping for more of a challenge. Ethel placed herself in between Fred and the kids, insisting that he take his anger out on her instead of them. It sometimes worked. At times, the kids even witnessed him slamming her thin, small-framed body straight into the hard floor.

He was the boss, and she had no control over anything. He told her what to do and when to do it. As the kids became older, stronger, and wiser, they became less tolerant of his outbursts. What they had always known to be a normal part of their childhood had become unacceptable, and this began to only complicate matters.

Patria recalled one time when her dad was yelling at her mom when she'd finally had enough and decided to stand up to him. Ethel was crying after being struck in her back for whatever reason. Young Patria reached over to the woodpile that sat next to the cookstove and grabbed a big piece of wood. She held it up high in the air, shaking the piece of wood, looking directly into his crazy eyes as she sternly told her father, "If you hit her one more time, I will hit you, and I mean it!"

He appeared stunned that she did that. She had never stood up to him in her entire life. He squished his face and tightened his lips, shook his head, and then staggered away.

Patria hightailed it out of there. She ran down to the river, found the biggest crawdad hole that she could find, and crawled inside of it. It became cold and dark, and her clothing became moist before she decided to return home. She didn't know what to expect, but thankfully, Fred was passed out on the couch, a very familiar sight.

Patria didn't realize or even recognize that the family was being abused. She had lived with it for so many years. She thought that it was just the way things were and that there was nothing that could be done about it. She tried hard to be a good girl and to not get into trouble—or at least to not get caught.

As crazy as it sounds, she didn't want to upset her father. If she made him angry, or if he was in a bad mood and beat her mother, she couldn't help asking herself, if she was the cause of everything bad happening...was she the reason that her mother was hurt? Was it something she had done? She spent a lot of time asking herself these questions, especially since Wylie wasn't around anymore. Wylie had always made her feel better and explained things to her. It was difficult not having her close.

She used to tell Patria, "It isn't anyone's fault but our hard-ass, no-good, son-of-a-bitch daddy's!" She wished she could be stronger like *her big sister.*

Maybe Patria thought that the hitting, beating, and pushing, and name-calling were perfectly normal ways to be treated, but if that were the case, why didn't she talk about it to anyone? Maybe she learned to distrust people in general. She began to feel a lot of anger toward other people and even herself, even becoming distant from friends. Maybe she felt resentment that no one cared enough about them to confront the situation.

Sometimes she was present but not emotionally there. She became easily upset, angry, and confused after each bout of violence. She felt guilty and embarrassed.

The boys took it even harder. They were more afraid of their father than the girls, because his forceful hand never took pity on them. They were humiliated, put down, and made to feel weak. They were gentle and kind souls, not weak, just scared and bullied.

Patria was never asked by anyone if there was abuse in their home. Had she been asked, she might have confided in someone. She never volunteered the information for fear of her father and for the possibility of being the cause of her family breaking up.

At times, her father could be laughing, complimentary, and fun. It was confusing. She didn't want to lose that, but the longer the abuse took place, the more emotionally confused she felt.

Ethel believed that she did everything wrong, that she was not worth much. She just took it all. After her father leaving her, Roy's beatings, and Fred's years of abuse, she concluded that it was her fault.

The couch had been Fred's usual place for sleep for as long as Patria could remember. Ethel shared the bedroom with the kids. A curtain hanging from the ceiling separated her from the children. Not only did Fred and Ethel not sleep together, but they weren't affectionate, either; they never hugged or kissed. They weren't physically warm to the children, either. They never told them that they loved them, but the kids knew that they did as much as they were capable.

Peggy Johnson moved up the street from the Traughters. She had

Ethel believing that she was her long-lost sister. Ethel didn't lie, and she didn't believe that others lied, either. Peggy looked like she was Native American and even showed proof that she was of Cherokee descent. And she too was from Kansas ... or so she claimed.

Peggy's husband, Dean, worked the night shift at the cotton mill. He was short and resembled a bulldog. On top of his unattractiveness, he was a cantankerous old man. They never had any children, and Patria always felt this to be a good thing.

Many nights, Fred disappeared for hours, and the kids grew suspicious to his whereabouts. They followed him one night, and their suspicions were confirmed. He was at Peggy's while her husband was not. They despised this woman. However, they also knew that their mother was fully aware of what Fred and Peggy were up to. They didn't ever discuss it with their mother.

On the other hand, Peggy Johnson made the best sandwiches that Patria had ever tasted; this made their relationship somewhat of a sham. Peggy frequently visited their home, acting like everything was normal and as if she were a loyal neighbor. Patria usually hung around just in case she received an invitation to Peggy's house for one of the delicious sandwiches. And sure enough, many times, Peggy kindly looked down to young Patria and inquired, "Patria, would you like to come home with me, and I will make you one of those sandwiches that you love so much?" Patria's mouth would water with just the thought. She smiled as she pretended to be surprised. Off she would go up the trail to Peggy's.

The sandwiches weren't just meat, bread, and cheese; they had lettuce, tomato, onions, and her favorite, pickles. They were the best that she had ever had.

Patria knew that Peggy wasn't any kin to her or her family. She felt that Peggy was just a drunken, lying whore who made the most delicious sandwiches. And most of the time, Patria was hungry.

As grown adults with their own children, didn't Bill and Patria think about how alcohol ruins lives? Couldn't they go back in time and remember what it was like? Wonder how Bill felt about his and

Patria's drinking habits. Did he think of his own family? Of how his own father drank alcohol and became detached from his mother and children?

Thankfully, Bill's mother Dora never drank a drop of alcohol in her life.

One time, she went to the store to cash out some flat cans for the receipt. While she was checking out, she repeatedly explained to the clerk that she didn't drink the beer and didn't even drink at all. Young Billy felt that she went on and on, confusing the poor clerk, who really didn't care. Billy was embarrassed.

How can one become so dependent upon alcohol? Always an excuse. It just tastes good…but that is bullshit. Bill drank beer after beer at his workbench. It kept him secluded and in his own world, not theirs. Like an emotionless shield or protective coating from the real world. Was his life that bad? Was his family that bad? Did he not love them?

He worked on things only to not complete anything. He kept his ice chest nearby for easy access. He didn't socialize anymore and hardly laughed.

Patria kept her alcohol hidden throughout the house. Her favorite hiding spot was the laundry basket. She began splitting her drinks between beer and wine. She hid her drinking, yet her behavior was a telltale sign. Her body became more relaxed; the expression on her face drooped. Her bottom lip hung lower, and she wasn't afraid to say what she was thinking, even if she shouldn't have said it. It felt as if she didn't care about anything anymore, even the kids. She began to stumble, even during the day, and had her crying bouts earlier in the day.

Patria had a familiar dream. There was Ardon and Arne together standing in front of the hot water heater, a familiar sight. There they stood, plain as day. Arne smiled showing off his pearly whites and grinning ear to ear. And handsome

Ardon, his beautiful hair slicked back perfectly in place, also smiling and relaxed. Arne preached, "Patria, I know you are in pain, but please know that we are not gone. We are here with you every time that you think of us, every time that you need us, we are with you. You will see. Someday, you will know what we say is true. Be happy Patria, it will be okay. It will all be okay". They both looked so handsome, healthy and strong. They seemed so at peace...so happy...so calm.

Patria opened her eyes to look around her bedroom for her brothers but they weren't there. Her heart wasn't as heavy at that moment, but the pain hit her again like a rush of thorns to her insides. Penetrating them like needles. She wanted to go with them. To be with them and to be as happy and at peace as they felt to be. She knew them to be. Could she ever be as happy as she once was? Why was she so blue and dissatisfied? Why couldn't she be grateful of her life even if Arne and Ardon were gone? She still had her health, family and so much to look forward to. It really sucked.

The kids didn't want to bring anyone over at all. They learned their lesson at least once, and that's all it took.

One early afternoon, Carha arrived home with Tammy, which she instantly regretted. Patria was wasted. She was sitting at the kitchen table and telling Tammy how special she was. She said, "You think that you're so special because you go to church. You probably think that you might even have wings that can fly you to heaven. Yeah, you think that you are better than us, but you're not." She began flapping her arms as if they were wings and started crying as she commonly did when she drank. She confided in ten-year-old Tammy how she was a sinner and was going to hell as she swayed her shameless, beautiful body side to side as if she were slow dancing to music.

Alcohol consumption slowly turned their lovely, perfect, healthy mother into a weak, tactless, embarrassing woman. It turned their father into a withdrawn, uneven man whom they couldn't know. It turned their parents' relationship to silent destruction and their family into oncoming dysfunction. How could two intelligent people with common sense and so much love in their hearts let this happen?

CHAPTER 24

BILL SPENT ALMOST every night sleeping outside, and when he didn't, he slept on the couch.

Dana and Anna didn't really want to spend time with him. They were busy with their friends and chasing boys. Carha and Billy still craved their father's attention, especially since their mother had withdrawn so much.

One night, Carha went outside to hang out with her father. He had his sleeping bag on top of the picnic table as he often did. She cuddled next to him and began asking him a thousand questions about life. She savored his every word. They started their natural discussion of stars and planets. She asked questions she already knew the answer to but just wanted him to reiterate it once again.

She knew it was getting late, and with the invitation of her dad, she ran in to ask her mom if she could sleep outside with Dad. Carha ran eagerly back outside, ready to continue their conversion. The stars were shining brightly, which was magnificent. The crickets were busy at work, and the air was crisp. She could still smell the salt that lingered on the tree limbs and the musty, comforting smell of Natruna.

She was fully enjoying this bonding time with her father, one on one and without distractions.

It was getting later and getting colder. She was lying on her right side and he on his left. He reeked of alcohol, but she was accustomed to the smell from his breath. Talk was slowing and coming to an end, and she knew that he was close to falling into a deep sleep when he suddenly, in a burst of energy, said, "Good night."

She replied, "Good night." But with those words, she felt something wrong, even before anything happened. His mouth came to hers. His arm wrapped around her shoulder as he pulled her tightly into his mouth. He began to move his mouth side to side onto hers; his tongue reached into her mouth. He stopped only to kiss her chin and then her cheek, moving his head every which way. He proceeded down her neck and then back up toward her mouth. His whiskers and cold skin to her face was shockingly disturbing and made her feel sick to her stomach. She didn't move. She was deadened with shock and fear. He continued and continued for what seemed like eternity. She tried to move away from him numerous times, but he just pulled her in tighter and kissed her even more aggressively. Then all of a sudden, it stopped, and he began snoring.

His face was so close to hers that his breath was blowing on her small, innocent, bewildered face. She was only ten, and he was her hero. How could he have done this to her? Words could not describe how this changed her forever.

Respect, really? Respect your father. You are conditioned your whole life to respect your father, and this is what he does.

Her life was turning upside down, but it just turned over to the point of no full recovery. "You bastard", she thought. There was no excuse.

She listened to his snoring, his arm still wrapped around her, until she finally got up the courage to slide down from beneath his encasement and find her footing upon hitting the ground. She put foot in front of foot and arrived at the back door.

She could hardly open the door handle. She was shaking uncontrollably.

The only thing she could think of was how much she wanted her mom, how much she needed her. She went straight into her parents' room and climbed directly in between her mom and her baby brother. She curled into a ball, trying to fight her shaking.

Her mom softly whispered, "Are you okay? Why are you shaking?"

Carha swallowed hard and replied, "I just got cold."

Then they fell asleep.

That was it. It was warm there and comforting. She could smell the secureness of her mom and knew that she wouldn't let anything else happen to her ever, no matter what. She was her protector.

The next afternoon, the sun was shining its rays into the living room, and they were glowing from the brown shag rug, light beams hitting family picture frames from all directions.

Carha remembered because that was all that she could look at. She couldn't look into their faces and tell them the answers to the questions they were asking. It felt too bad.

Patria and her friend Tina sat her down on the couch. They stood in front of her, heads bent, looking down. It was just them in the house. It suddenly crossed Carha's mind that everyone was gone. *Why and how?* She asked herself.

While examining Carha's answers, her mother said point-blank, "Carha, you're not in trouble, but I need to know if your dad has ever kissed you like a dad shouldn't kiss a daughter."

Carha felt as though she was busted for something that was supposed to be a secret—a secret she had planned to keep forever.

Her eyes became bigger than they probably had ever become, and her legs began bouncing nervously in and out, up and down. She began playing with her hands and fingers in attempts to magically conjure the right words to make this whole thing go away.

They weren't budging. Patria gently sat down next to Carha and reassuringly placed one hand on her right thigh. She lovingly rubbed it and attentively looked at her daughter. She whispered, "It's okay. You didn't do anything wrong." She patiently waited, but Carha still couldn't speak. Patria then said something that changed the way Carha was feeling. She said, "He did the same thing to your sister."

Carha's mouth turned as far downward as it could possibly and unpleasantly turn. She couldn't hold back the tears; she couldn't speak. She could only nod shamefully, saying, "Yes, yes."

She didn't want to admit it, because she knew deep inside that to admit it was to ensure that there wasn't any hope at all that things would go back to how they once were. It wasn't that long ago. A year. How could things change within one year as they had?

She later learned that it was almost a year prior when Bill had escorted Dana to her bedroom door, right after Maggie moved out, to say good night. It was then that he leaned up against the doorjamb to hold his drunken self up as he pulled Dana's head into his face and kissed her hard and long, so long that she couldn't breathe.

Dana confided to her mother a few days later. Her mom was supportive and told Dana that she believed her and that she was sorry that it happened, she continued to explain that what he had done was very wrong. That same day, Patria confronted Bill while he was working in the garage. Bill denied it and called Dana a liar. He said that she was making things up to turn them against one another, because she was doing bad things with boys. Bill was so convincing that Patria felt that if he did do it, he didn't remember due to being too drunk. Maybe he was so bombed that he thought that it was his wife and not his young daughter.

Over the next several months, Bill increasingly became meaner toward Dana. He gave her dirty looks. He corrected her every word and made her feel incompetent, insecure, and dumb. It was about that time that Dana was lying in the middle of her room drunk, with her two parents yelling over her. This was the moment when reality and truth hit Patria like a lightning bolt.

She knew she had to come up with a plan. What was she to do? She had five children, no job, nowhere to go … What was she to do?

A year later and the very same night that Carha admitted to her father's inappropriate behavior, the entire family, with the exception of Maggie, sat around the dinner table for the very last time.

However, that night was different indeed. Bill had insane fire in his eyes. He sat at the head of the table where he always sat and began reciting quotes from Dana's and Anna's diaries. He just repeated them over and over— quotes about boys and how they had crushes on them, how they felt about them. Then he solemnly announced, "There will be a death in this house very soon."

As soon as he left for graveyard shift at the plant, Dana, Anna, Carha, and Billy were instructed by their mother to quickly pack one bag of belongings each and meet at the front door. She calmly whispered, "Hurry, kids!"

They did as they were instructed and soon were crossing the dark street to the Kinnys', who were out of town for a few days.

Their home smelled musky and old. It was unfamiliar yet consoling. The Kinnys were such a nice older couple and always seemed stable and normal. Carha felt comfort in this, and even if it was just for a short time, being there in their home and among their belongings gave her hope that maybe someday they could be normal again too.

They all hunkered down low onto the foreign white carpet while their mother frequently peeked out of the curtains toward their home. She kept whispering to the children, "Shh, shh, be quiet, and keep your voices down."

What was going on? Carha told her mother what had happened and now they were in this strange house hiding. What was their father planning on doing? What were they doing? Where were they going? There weren't any answers. Hours passed, and they moved into Mr. and Mrs. Kinny's bedroom. Was it because it was farther toward the back of the house, farther away from their house? Carha wasn't told. The house was kept dark, and they had to whisper. They remained low to the ground and close together.

They snuck ice cream from the freezer, ice cream they had never had. It tasted okay but at the same time wrong. Their mom was on the phone, whispering to someone, but the kids didn't know who it was. They finally fell asleep on the carpet, without covers, without pillows, away from their home, away from their beds and their things. They were exhausted and too tired to think about it anymore. It was too strange, all of it, and nothing made sense.

CHAPTER 25

WILL STILL WASN'T completely honest and out of trouble, but he hadn't done acid or any drug, for that matter, for a long time. That was in his past. His bad ways crept up on him like a black fog. He tried, but something bad occasionally happened that caused negative reactions. Maybe it had to do with boredom, drinking too much, or just stupidity. For the most part, he was being good and focusing on random construction work around Natruna.

Once Will was next to the Pioneer Market, hanging out with a few friends, drinking a beer after work, when an older woman drove up to them and yelled out her window, "Hoodlums! Leave town!"

It made him feel bad, but he wasn't about to leave his hometown. Not now.

Will and a few of his friends decided to break into the golf course and steal some hard liquor to party with one night. Will seemed to be supporting all of his party buddies and getting further behind on rent and bills. He tried not to let that trouble him too much and just ducked as often as possible when he saw Mrs. Franks coming his way for collection of his past-due rent.

The cops had a sneaking suspicion about the person responsible for the break-in. Plus, there was a mouth among the five men involved that wouldn't stay shut.

Will spent about four days in jail for that one and was then released to complete community service. He had to pay back the money for the booze that they'd consumed. Then he had to paint all of the community buildings in town under the direction of Ted Horta, whom he loathed. Ted was in charge of the community service program at that time. Who would have put that devil-worshipping man in charge of anything? Ted made him pick up trash and found any possible degrading job that he could for Will. Will did it without any disrespect, since he didn't care to spend any more time in jail.

Will moved into an apartment and started seriously trying to get his life together and get a good-paying job. That jail time did him in. He was tired of his foolishness.

He heard that a small local construction company was actively hiring but also knew that getting a job in Natruna would be challenging. The interview went pretty well, although it was a rough beginning since, at the time, he didn't exactly look the part of the tough construction kind of man. Luckily, the owner of the company, Lee, was desperate for help and liked Will's honesty and polite disposition. Sure, he had his concerns knowing that Will had been in some trouble in the past, but thankfully, Lee gave Will a chance.

He instructed Will to come back the following morning at 6:00 a.m. sharp and be ready to work his ass off to prove that Lee didn't make a mistake in hiring him.

Will, nervous as heck, showed up forty-five minutes early and anxiously waited for Lee. It was a scorching 112 degrees that day, and they were working a cement job. Will knew he had his work cut out for him.

Once at the job site, Will and Lee got out of the truck, and Lee introduced Will to the site supervisor, Roger Hardy, but this tough guy took one look at Will and told his boss, "No fuckin' way!" Between Will's long, shiny black hair, black comb in his back pants pocket, and a gold hoop earring with a dangling cross from his right ear, Roger wouldn't even give him the respect of a handshake.

Roger didn't even try to hide how he felt about Will. He argued about it to his boss and in front of the other guys. He said that there weren't no girls allowed on his crew!

Lee knew that he couldn't talk Roger into giving this pretty boy a chance, and he definitely couldn't afford to lose his lead on this crew. If he lost Roger, he lost the entire crew.

Will just put his head down and headed back to the truck while Lee and Roger discussed it loudly for a few minutes more. Will really needed this job, and there was a shortage of work in Natruna. He thought to himself, *I'm screwed.*

Lee jumped in the truck and didn't even look at Will. He just huffed and cursed under his breath. Will assumed that they were headed back to the office and that he was out of luck, but Lee surprised him when he turned toward the plant.

The two pulled up to a bunch of men working on the roofs of some of the plant's buildings. This time it was with Roger's younger brother's crew, and Budd was in complete charge.

This time, Lee looked over to Will, shook his head, and instructed him to keep his ass in the truck.

Lee and Budd had a discussion which Will couldn't hear and really didn't want to hear. It was obvious that Lee was pleading with Budd to give this young guy a chance, and after some debate, he did.

Lee waved his hand to Will, gesturing for him to get out of the truck. Will did as he was instructed to do as he smoothed his long hair back out of his face. Budd just shook his head and said out loud, "You have got to be *shittin'*!"

They were all much older tough guys and had worked together for years and didn't like the idea of this good-looking younger guy showing up to join their clan at all.

Will knew the only way that he was going to get a paycheck was to work as hard as he possibly could and take one minute at a time.

The entire group of tough guys ignored Will. No one even told him what to do in the beginning. He just started working until finally they began to bark orders at him while calling him names. He kept smiling, kept responding politely, and moved as quickly as he could.

The friends shared sunflower seeds and wouldn't offer any to Will. Will thought to himself that the salt on the sunflower seeds would taste so good in the heat, and he was sweating like crazy. At night, his legs cramped, but he refused to buy his own sunflower seeds; he wanted theirs.

He hated going back every day and hated them, but he needed the money. He became cross but refused to quit this too. He had nothing, and he had no choice. His parents wouldn't help him in the least bit, and he didn't blame them.

His hands bled. He was given all of the hardest grunt work—cleaning gutters, sweeping, hammering nails one by one, and carrying the heaviest tools and equipment for the others. You name it, he did it.

He kept busting his ass and working through breaks day after day and taking their bull. He knew very well how to do this after growing up working on the ranch in Idaho every summer for as long as he could remember. His uncle Hugh pushed him to no end, and he liked it after a long, hard day. He liked knowing what his body and mind could accomplish if he just worked. He wasn't afraid of work and associated it with the good times on the ranch with the most special, loving people he knew.

His grandparents, aunt, and uncle loved him unconditionally, and he always knew that, he also knew however that he had to work hard while there if he wanted the reward of praise, and good fresh farm food around the picnic table, and that unforgettable look he got from his uncle when he put in a hard day of labor. Moving pipes from field to field, replacing pipes, broken fences, moving cattle, stacking hay bales, and feeling his body throb and ache after a day on the ranch made him feel more alive than he ever did anywhere else.

This was no match ...

Finally, after a few months of proving to the whole bunch of assholes that he could outwork all of them and take all of their harassment, he won them over.

It began with Budd, and then the rest of them followed suit, and when they finally offered Will sunflower seeds, it was sweet justice. His paychecks were nice too.

Will met a young kid named Geno. Well, he was seventeen years old, new in town, and had a beard—not just a small one but a full-blown beard. He had curly dirty blond hair, lots of it-a medium build and the glassiest lit blue eyes that didn't look real. They looked like porcelain dolls' eyes that Will's grandmother owned. One day, Geno just showed up at Will's house and introduced himself. They hit it off instantly and became the best of friends. Geno had a witty—maybe even warped—sense of humor for a seventeen-year-old. He was a little odd but sharp.

Geno didn't like his new school whatsoever and wanted

to get on with his life and find a job. At the beginning of his senior year, he ended up passing his GED and working for the local hardware store.

Eventually, Geno Munz joined their team and worked just as hard as Will, this impressed the heck out of Will and reaffirmed his respect for Geno even more.

On the next project, they joined Roger and the other team. Will was pretty hesitant about that reunion, but on the first day, Roger walked right up to him with a cigarette dangling from the corner of his mouth and one tucked above his ear and offered his hand out to shake. Will reached his hand out to shake it and felt pretty proud. He also felt a bit intimidated. These two brothers weren't the tallest, but they had muscles like none of Will's friends. Budd had served three years in the army and was a tough dude.

Roger then asked Will while looking him directly in his eyes, "So, tell me, pretty boy, why the fuck do you wear that shit in your ear?"

Stunned, Will didn't reply. He just nodded his head and raised his eyebrows and shrugged his shoulders. He gave a big smile and laughed nervously, but Roger didn't smile.

That night Will removed his earring and never put in back in again.

Will continued bonding with this group of guys, which included their wives, girlfriends, and even kids. They all spent time together after work, hanging out at the pool, enjoying one another's company, and having the bond of growing up in Natruna. They also spent almost every weekend together swimming, talking, and drinking beer.

Will's bank account was growing along with his confidence and happiness.

That following summer, the gang was all sitting around on their cars, just chilling behind the fence at the Vale

Springs pool like they usually did—same spot, same group, just talking—when they heard the roar of one of their buddies' car coming their way.

Their friends were having good times playing around on those desolate desert roads, doing doughnuts around the bunch, yelling out the window, and laughing their butts off.

There were four young roughneck good guys just out having a good time.

Adam was driving his trophy white '67 Cougar with black top that he worked on daily. It was his pride and joy. Jack was showing off his bright smile while toasting his can of Coors Light out the window and to the air at the guys, saying, "This one's for you!"

"What a day!" Will thought to himself. Life was really coming together.

He didn't have a steady girlfriend but dated plenty and when he wanted to. He enjoyed the freedom of being able to do whatever he wanted when he wanted.

Barry and Kent were laughing from the backseat, trying to get the others to race them.

Will and his friends just blew them off and told them they were just chilling out.

"Yeah," Kent yelled, "You're just chickenshits!" Kent was only twenty-five years old and just had his second boy with his Natruna sweetheart. He wasn't about to settle anytime soon.

The guys drove away just as fast as they arrived. They were crazy! There were dust clouds shooting straight up from every inch of road they drove. Will and his friends just watched in amazement as the hot rod drove away.

They heard the engine as it hit the main highway stop sign, where the fork intercepted and you could go either left to Pioneer or right to Village Gully.

They heard the slow, low roaring of the car and then

the gradually louder roaring of it as it sped toward Village Gully.

The guys looked at each other and thought, *Man! Those guys are wild!*

They continued to watch the dust cloud and then heard the most horrifying bomb of metal hitting metal. It was the most disconcerting, indescribable sound that they had ever heard.

Will, Roger, Budd, and Geno quickly jumped into their cars and headed toward the site, almost a mile from the stop sign, and there it was—the most unbelievable and nightmarish scene that would be entrenched inside their minds always.

The beautiful white Cougar was crushed, dented, and bent, lying on its side right in the middle of the road, smoking and steaming, still making what sounded like cries and moans—if a car could cry.

Approximately forty feet away was an old blue van on its side with an old, gray-headed, bloody man crawling out of the top of it.

Barry was lying distorted in the middle of the highway, dead. The car must have rolled over him, because he was smashed. Adam's body lifeless was crushed between the steering wheel and seat. The roof had caved in, smashing his head down. Jack was lying halfway out of the passenger's seat like a limp doll, blood dripping from his head and face. Kent was trapped in the backseat. They could barely see his legs but could hear him gurgling or maybe trying to ask for help. There wasn't any way for them to get him out.

It was a shocking, surreal picture. It seemed to be in slow motion, and no one knew what to do.

They helped the old man out and down and sat him down on the side of the road. He was dazed and confused and bloody. He couldn't talk. He just looked like he was in shock.

A car came passing through, and Will yelled for them to go get help. It took an hour before help came. Meanwhile, the four young men didn't know what to do other than to direct traffic, since the accident was in the middle of the highway and bodies were everywhere. Barry was still in the middle of the road, dead. They didn't move him. They just looked, watched, and then tried not to look, spacing out. It was like a bad dream. It was weird. One minute, they were all laughing and having fun, and within minutes, their hot-rodding friends were all dead.

Most of the guys were married or had girlfriends and some had kids. They had lives and families. People loved them, and they were gone within minutes. How could that be?

The older man stated that they swerved and hit him.

It was life changing for a lot of people, and for Will, after seeing that, it confirmed his belief that life was short and to enjoy it while you could. Live life to the fullest, because you can be taken out of the game in an instant. He also firmly believed in reincarnation and felt that he would meet up with those souls again eventually, but he was still brokenhearted and felt the loss, just as everyone did in Natruna.

CHAPTER 26

THE FAIRWAY APARTMENTS were for those with little or no income. They were small, all the same, and nicely displayed alongside the only main highway running through Natruna.

The Stone family was quickly placed in emergency housing there and had a corner unit, a two-bedroom apartment situated second to the last row. There were no trees, and there was no landscaping, no park or playground, no toys, no yard ... just nothing but a few scattered, dried-up weeds behind the plain white apartments.

At the early age of fifteen, Anna moved in with her boyfriend's family. They became her new family. The Ronas were well known and liked in the community. Mr. Rona worked at the plant, and Mrs. Rona worked at the credit union. They were sympathetic to the situation and really cared about Anna.

Anna was torn between her mother and father. She couldn't figure it out. Her way to deal with the circumstances was to move away from it, ignore it as much as she could, and focus on school, sports, and her new love, Ryan.

Ryan was popular and a beast of a guy. He was athletic, worked at the local grocery store, and had a car. It was young love and an opportunity for her to stay away from her now divided family. She pretended that her life's difficulties were not happening.

Dana was hardly ever home. Maggie hardly visited. It was Patria, Carha, and little Billy living in the generic, low-income apartments.

The apartment had a tiny eat-in kitchen and was not even a quarter of the space that their home had. The living room was too small for a normal-sized couch, so they sat in an old love seat draped by a colorful brown-and-yellow sheet. The one bathroom had a toilet and a bath/shower. There weren't even cupboards in it for storing toiletries. The two bedrooms, toward the back of the apartment, were crammed with clothing and personal belongings.

The walls were thin, and they could hear the neighbors' conversations and even what they did in the privacy of their bedrooms late at night.

Billy and Carha shared a room, along with Dana's clothes. Their mother had the other one. The apartment was cramped, solemn, and cold.

The kids ached for their home and old lives. They thought of it regularly and felt depressed much of the time. They kept hoping that they would return home again and everything would be the way it had been.

They had to ride the school bus, which was humiliating. They had to stand at the bus stop where everyone could see. The other kids all knew that the Stones were now living in these project apartments, separated from their dad. They definitely were going to struggle to fit in now.

Their father, Bill, didn't visit them; it was as if he had dropped off the face of the earth. Their mother was withdrawn and grave. She didn't smile or laugh anymore.

Once again, it seemed that Carha and Billy only had one another. They lived away from their friends now. They didn't want to get to know the other kids in the projects. The two of them listened to records in their bedroom, visited, played cards, went for walks, and were alone in their misery.

Only a few months had passed when Maggie came over bringing Ted Horta to give Patria some company. She thought that it would cheer her up and that she wouldn't feel so lonely.

Ted had long, black, wild wavy hair, a long beard, and the evilest eyes. He didn't keep jobs, drove his brother's van, and still lived at home in his early forties.

It was fun in the beginning for Maggie to party with her mother, but the fun soon ended when she saw that her mom was drinking too much and not taking care of her kids. By then, it was too late.

Carha and Billy hated this man hanging around, always kissing their mom. He was fat, rude, and disgusting. He was loud and said curse words that they had never heard before.

Patria seemed to be intoxicated from the time she woke up until she passed out at night. There were strangers hanging around their apartment, entering their bedroom unannounced, and people using their belongings, their bathroom, and invading any privacy that they had.

Their mother was no longer their mother. Their apartment became cluttered and unkempt. This large, vulgar man with tattoos all over his body became a too-familiar sight, and to top it off, their father was still out of their lives.

The kids began to mimic their surroundings, sneaking beer, and even smoking cigarette butts behind the apartment. Nobody that they used to know came around.

It wasn't long before Patria, Dana, Carha, and Billy

began trying to blend in with the Horta family.

Now their reputations were really going to go to shit, the Horta's were not good influences for the Stone children, and they were fully aware of this.

Ted's dad, Big Ted, as everyone called him, was obese, balding, and had an array of acne scars on his face. He was always out of breath when he moved, and he spoke Spanish half of the time.

The Hortas were always cooking and always eating. Their entire dirty home smelled of lard, and it felt like lard dirtied their surroundings. Their house was a thirty-five-year-old ranch-style home with four bedrooms, two bathrooms, a living room, and a kitchen area with a little room for a small dining table.

The television was always turned up extremely loud, which was disturbing in itself. Big Ted just sat around all day, ate, and watched TV. Everyone seemed to kiss his butt, since he had all of the money since the railroad lawsuit years earlier and it was his house.

His wife and the mother of his three grown boys, Carma, had early Alzheimer's when the Stone children first met her. It was troubling, as well. She walked around with her right hand out in front of her, shaking it, and she repeated incomprehensible Spanish words over and over again. She was a very short woman, hunched over as she constantly paced the house. From looking at the pictures on their walls, she once was a pretty woman. She now had to be diapered, could barely feed herself, and always seemed to have food crumbs around her mouth. Her shirts were always dirty with food stains. She required endless supervision. It sounded like she used to be a very kind person and tried to do a good job in raising her sons.

Rusty, the oldest son, was thirty-six years old and living in the home with his two teenage girls. His wife was still residing in the mental institution. The daughters were wild and unruly. He lived off of state welfare and was a slobbery alcoholic.

The first time that Carha and Billy visited their home, the girls, Robin and Amber, were in the garage, when Carma came out and startled the Stone kids. They hadn't been around anyone in that state. The two girls began to tease her and call her names. One of the girls pushed her, causing her to trip and fall back. Her glasses broke. They both quickly helped her up and tried to shrug it off like it was an accident. After strongly sensing that the Stones disapproved of their actions, they threatened to beat them up if they told anyone.

For the most part, the kids adapted to the situation at the Hortas'. There was always something going on. It seemed to always be in a state of pandemonium and was never boring. Their house was loud and active. It was quite a change from the past year, and even though it was an unhealthy one, they still welcomed it.

The divorce proceedings began, and it was a mess. It was Patria, Ted, Dana, Carha, and little Billy on one side of the hallway, and across the hallway and down toward the double doors sat Bill, Maggie, and Anna.

It seemed like there was a war occurring, and the once close, loving family was at odds.

Ted and Patria had discussed for months in front of the kids how awful a person Bill was.

Patria was so mad about what Bill had done that it seemed to explode after she left him. Now she had Ted, who acted super tough, as though he would protect her from her perverted ex-husband.

At one point during the proceedings, Dana and Anna called each other names. One would yell, "Traitor!" and the other one would yell, "You are!" One time, Dana walked up to Anna and spit in her face.

Bill was in the same blue suit he had married Patria in.

Carha and Billy sat next to each other feeling mixed emotions—confusion, sadness, and anger toward their father ... and guilt too.

They felt guilt that they were with their mother, guilt that they were with Ted, and guilt that maybe in some way this could have been their fault.

One day, they were all together, they weren't happy but they were together, under one roof. Then the next day, Carha was questioned about what happened that night, then they were gone, separated...they fell apart. Not just the marriage, but everything. Her whole family. It destroyed everything. Carha felt that it was her fault for a long time, but didn't ever tell anyone. She thought that if she did, then they would know that it was her fault. She didn't tell anyone what had happened, how she confessed to her mother and Tina that day, or how it was her responsibility that her mom took them away from their dad, from their home.

Carha was the first to be called into a conference room with a long, brown oak table and chairs all around it. There was only one picture on the wall of an older man with white hair, intense eyes that seemed to stare at her, and a white beard. He was dressed in a dark suit, hands crossed in his lap.

The chairs were all empty except for the one the nice woman asked Carha to sit in at the very end of the rectangular table. Then the middle-aged man with curly brown hair finally sat down across from her.

A man entered the room wearing a suit, and he didn't say a word; he just sat away from them and wrote on a writing pad.

The woman had friendly eyes, yet she seemed serious.

Carha could smell the breeze of flowery perfume she

was wearing. She thought to herself that this woman probably lived in a beautiful home with nice things. She imagined her bedroom with flowery prints scattered throughout it and a vanity with all sorts of perfume bottles, hair brushes, and makeup on it.

This brought feelings of separation from these people. They were foreigners and couldn't understand all that was going on. How could they? They were too different.

This made her feel angry when they began to ask her questions about the private things that her father had done to her. She wasn't going to volunteer any information to them no matter what they said. *They* were the bad people, not her. They were judging her, she was sure of it. She felt like she was ugly for what her dad did to her. She was ugly with freckles all over herself. He didn't care about her and thought she was ugly too. That's why he'd done it. He made her feel so unhappy. It was what he did that caused all of this. He had to have hated her.

Now these people wanted her to admit to having anything to do with all of the mess. Why? To make her feel worse. They were cruel to her. They kept asking her over and over again, "What did he do to you that he shouldn't have done?"

Now the man was speaking too. They kept saying, "You need to tell us. You have to tell the truth. Tell us."

Finally, after what seemed like forever, Carha shouted, "Yes, he did! Yes, he did! He kissed me for a long time! He kissed my neck, he kissed my throat, he touched me, he rubbed me through my clothes. He did! He did! Are you happy now?"

She cried, feeling more ashamed, more embarrassed, and uglier. They made her admit to causing all of the mess. She hated them.

The same woman called Billy in to question him. It was

all a blur from there.

Patria and Bill were given joint custody but the children would live with Patria. Bill was given unsupervised visitation every other weekend in his home.

The children were never explained how this happened. They didn't understand, especially Carha. After what he did and how hard it was for her to tell the truth about what he did to those strangers, why would she and her little brother have to go to his house? It was confusing on top of everything else that felt like a whirlwind. Carha thought that they must have thought that she was a liar. Which made her even feel worse about it all. Not only did she cause the divorce, but she was a liar on top of it. She wasn't in the court room for most of the trial and was in the dark about what was said, or happened. Much later, her mother only stated that horrible lies were told about Patria during that trial and that is why possibly he was awarded joint custody. As far as why they were allowed to be with him without supervision, this was never explained.

It's not that Carha didn't love her father. It was probably even more confusing and caused her to feel even more guilt. She did love him and she still looked up to him. She didn't hate him, even if she tried, she couldn't ever hate him. This made her feel that maybe something was wrong with her, like she was warped in some way for not despising him, she couldn't control how she felt though. What made everything more difficult was that her mother and Ted said horrible things about him. They wouldn't come right out and say specifics but Carha knew what they really were saying. They were talking about her and each and every time those comments were made, it made her feel even more to blame.

Bill was ordered to move out of the house on Flower Street and let Patria move in with the kids. Of course, Ted

Horta moved in- into the home that was their family home...The Stones. The home that their father bought...the home that their father worked so hard for. It was disgusting and unbelievable.

One day, their father left out that back door, down the walkway, and through the back gates to his truck, suitcase in his hand, leaving his home, his family, and his things, their things.

It was unreal.

CHAPTER 27

PATRIA AND TED drank a lot. Their fights seemed to escalate and be happening more and more often. During the fights, things were broken. The house seemed to suffer along with the children.

Half of sixth grade wasn't too bad, but the other half was a blur for Carha.

She didn't like when her teacher came up to her, whispering in her ear, secretly passing the hall pass to her, and telling her it was time for her meeting.

Carha would desolately walk toward the office doors, take a left into the brown hallway, and then go down a few steps until she opened the wooden door to the left.

It was a small office with white walls and one desk, placed in front of the big window. Out the window, Carha could see kids walking by, happy, laughing, and talking to one another.

This desk was older but was covered with beautiful knickknacks, green plants, and flowers. It felt cheerful, which was a nice blessing.

Behind the desk sat a lovely young woman with big, long, ash-colored hair with big curls, but only to the ends.

She always wore fancy, earth-toned clothes. She never talked of herself or her problems.

Carha thought that she was pretty, nice, and kind. Her name was Cara, which made Carha feel that they had a special bond. Carha felt better about who she was after she talked to Cara. She felt understood and accepted. She felt better for short periods of time but sad about her life, about the divorce, and about her family being a disaster. It would have been easier if it had always been a disaster. Then she wouldn't have felt that she had lost something once so wonderful.

Carha visited her counselor a few times a week, and she dreaded the visits because, after the meetings, her eyes would be red and puffy from crying. She felt that everyone knew that she had to see a counselor and was called out because she was different from all of her classmates. She returned self-conscious of her red, swollen eyes too. But she found some peace during those sessions, as long as they lasted, and Carha wanted to someday be just like her counselor and help kids like herself.

The fights between Ted and Patria seem to intensify with each passing day. Big sunglasses to hide her mother's black eyes became the new fad.

Visits from friends were a thing of the past.

Why couldn't Patria understand and anticipate what her own children could have been going through? Not being comfortable having friends come to your own home because it wasn't normal. It was embarrassing. They were embarrassing. Everything was embarrassing and humiliating. How could their mother put them in that situation when it didn't have to be like it was for her growing up? She had choices, right?

When Patria was in grade school, she continued to attend school, but only to maintain her friendships and because she was also ashamed of her home and embarrassed of her drunken father.

The small groups of girls that Patria hung out with were tight and closely bonded. Recess and lunch, in particular, were the reasons for her existence during those years. The girls' restroom was their meeting hot spot. It was full of echoing laughter and high, excited voices whispering secrets. They played jacks from the sound of one bell to the sound of the next, waiting as long as they possibly could before leaving their hideaway. The cold white floors and cemented bare walls were larger and felt more secure and more alive than the home in which she lived.

Occasionally, Patria visited her friends in their homes, and she was amazed with all of the modern conveniences. How different they were than the world in which she lived. They had nice furniture, inside plumbing, running warm water, stoves, refrigerators, and the smell of good food radiating from the kitchen. That smell alone was enough to satisfy her cravings at times. She just sat in her girlfriend's bedroom while listening to the clinking of silverware hitting plates as they ate, talked, and laughed as families did. They must have not been aware of her hunger; she learned to hide it well. Why they didn't invite her to eat with them was unknown to her and of course, she didn't ask.

She had a list of rehearsed excuses at a young age to why the girls couldn't come to her house, but soon, they were not necessary to recite; the girls didn't ask after a while.

The same thing gradually began to happen with the Stone children and their friends. At first they made excuses on why they couldn't have company and over time their friends stopped asking. Did they know that the Stones were making excuses or were they not allowed to visit with them anymore?

In the beginning, it was when the kids returned home after being away for a while that they would notice things broken around the house. The house seemed to be slowly dying along with their previous lives.

Church was the saving grace for Carha and Billy. They

looked forward to Wednesday evenings and Sundays. The longer that they were out, the better. The church was their safe place and a place where all the adults appeared stable and sober. They all had friendly faces. They talked civilly to one another and laughed often. It was all comforting.

When Patria was growing up, it also helped alleviate some of her and her sibling's boredom and gave them some sense of direction and accountability. When they were teenagers, they began running around the neighborhood, and unfortunately trouble began to follow them.

Patria would encourage the kids to attend church and understood the safeness, security and comfort that church and God gave to her children and to her own self at many times while a young girl.

The Traughter kids needed more help than their parents could offer them while they were teenagers. They were mischievous and up to no good for most of the time.

For a time, they would sneak into the hobos' camps and destroy them. Even the girls were involved in the destruction. It wasn't that they didn't like them; or they didn't know that it was wrong; they seemed to be getting meaner and meaner by the day.

When they were finally caught, Fred whipped each one of them with a belt and Ethel felt the only thing that would straighten them out was God.

That is when the Traughter kids were highly stimulated to attend the Nazarene Church with Ethel every Sunday. They had to be ready by 9:00 a.m. sharp. The preacher of the church or one of its members faithfully came to pick them up. They all eventually loved going to church and it was helping in keeping them on the right track. The quartet came every Sunday. They all sang hymns and talked in tongues, which was entertaining to the kids. It was interesting and gave them something to look forward to.

If the kids got out of hand, Ethel reminded them, "Remember what you learned in church on Sunday."

For Carha and Billy, God also gave them incredible strength through difficult times. The two children participated in the Christmas plays and choir. The stage seemed to be magical. The kids could be someone else up there, and all eyes admired them. All of the men, women, and children clapped for them, smiling grandly and showing their approval for what Carha and Billy were doing for God. It felt good, fitting and healing.

Everybody congregated at the two wooden front doors, carrying bibles in their hands.

Sometimes, it was overwhelming to be with so many strangers and caused Carha to feel insecure. Whenever she felt that way, she would have to look around for Curt and Beverly. Once she could see them, and one of them would make that brief reassuring eye contact with her, she felt better. How did they know that she needed that? It felt like they were always keeping their eye out for just that right second when Carha would need that reassurance. They were gifts from God.

The Robbinses became their second parents. They were still foreign, their smells and touch distant and strange, but the kids knew that they loved and cared about them, and their family too. The Robbinses were a little reserved and concerned about the influence on their two precious daughters, but they didn't mind taking Carha and Billy to church with them.

The Beel family had a similar effect on the Patria and her siblings while growing up. They became tremendously close and comforting.

Joel Beel went through grade school with Patria. Laramy, who talked funny and had only one ear, was good friends with Ardon and Arne, and Gwyneth was close to both Patria and Wylie.

They played like kids did, which included girls against boys and boys against girls. The girls spent hours building the best rock playhouses. The boys always seemed to get angry with them for some stupid reason and tear them down, but this never prevented the girls from rebuilding their playhouses.

The Beels included the kids on many of their family's outings, but Patria's favorite outing was going to "the Banks." They all piled into the Beels' small car, never complaining, only giggling and enjoying the closeness and excitement of it all. The Banks, as they all called it, was located next to the railroad. It stood firm, steep, and strong. They grabbed their flattened cardboard boxes, eagerly walked their way to the very top, stood in line in between the other anxious children, and then zoomed when it was their turn. Their hearts raced as they sat on the cardboard, and then off they went, down the steep bank, their behinds smoothly sweeping the smooth sandstone, hair and spit flying in the air, and the hugest smiles on their faces.

Mr. and Mrs. Beel waited patiently at the bottom and seemed to enjoy watching as much as the kids enjoyed sliding down over and over again.

CHAPTER 28

BACK IN THE Stone's household and to present day, Dana was never home anymore and the house was the saddest that it had ever been and felt empty. She was doing bad things, and the kids knew it. They were aware that it had something to do with Ted's older brother, Rusty, alcohol, and drugs. They were somewhat blinded due to dealing with their lives, addressing Dana's life seemed to be too much to handle, plus what could they do about it?

Sometimes it seems that people have to go in survival mode just to survive day-to-day. It is the only way that they can deal with life. That was how they all seemed to feel during those days. Almost like living in a fog.

Anna was living with their dad, Bill, and engaged to Ryan. She had her own life and didn't mingle elsewhere. She was trying to avoid the pain of it all like the plague. You couldn't blame her.

Maggie had married Phillip, and they were raising Rebecca and doing the best that they could. By this time, Maggie had washed her hands of her mother and the choices she was making.

Bill had Carha and Billy on every other weekend and moved into a house a few streets over, within walking distance of their house.

It was small, older, and a bit bare. It was depressing there. Their father was sad. The kids felt that sadness saturate their beings. He really tried to act happy, but he was just going through the motions. He seemed tired of the fighting and defending his rights for his children. He was trying to keep his family together, but he was fighting an uphill battle at the time.

He constantly denied what he had done to the girls, so much so that they began to believe that he truly didn't remember. Maybe he was too drunk. They never for a second doubted what they remembered happened. How could they? It is not something that could be made up or something that any young girl who cherishes their father so much would ever fathom could happen. They wished they could forget too.

Will rented a large nice white van to ensure everyone would be comfortable. He even arrived an half an hour early and waited. No one showed up on time. He had his doubts and began thinking that due to his reputation, turning his life around wouldn't be so easy, but finally Mr. Hemet showed up with his boys.

It was a track meet scheduled that early afternoon and a few hours' drive. Will volunteered, hoping that it would be showing service to the community.

Will was expecting more passengers, but no more arrived except for Mr. Hemet's four sons.

It meant a lot to Will that Mr. Hemet entrusted him with his sons, although Will was fully aware that Mrs. Hemet wouldn't have been so supportive…had she known.

The trip to the track meet went well, and Will felt that he was on the right path.

Will spent most weekends out at the pool, and on yet another hot, sunny day in the desert, the gang was all enjoying seeking shelter under the large salt cedar trees that covered the picnic tables encircling the Vale Springs pool. It had been an exhausting week at the construction site, and they definitely needed some R & R.

Geno was making his bad jokes and thinking that everyone got them when usually no one ever got them except for Will. Nonetheless, everyone liked Geno, despite his young age, he became part of the group.

Food was on the barbecue, and the music was radiating from the jukebox. The sound of kids came to them like being transmitted via a speaker phone. The screaming and splashing could be heard all the way to their picnic area as intensely as if they were footsteps from their ears.

The smells were always the same there: the combination of salt from above their heads to the salt twirling from the pool, they were all familiar and tranquil fragrances that they utterly relished.

All was going great without any drama, when Greg Wells showed up from out of town to visit his children, Jacky and Mike.

Greg was also a Natrunan, but he had moved away a year earlier. He adored his kids, and although there was never any money in his pocket, he always tried his best to be present as much as possible for his family. He was even close to his ex-wife and her new husband. He was doing much better and had a pretty good job four hours away. A car was something he was still saving for, so he hitchhiked to his hometown that day.

He immediately got a ride from a middle-aged, overweight guy who seemed a bit nerdy. He worked for some sales company and drove a pretty nice car, so Greg felt pretty fortunate to have a comfortable ride on that awfully scorching day.

Once they surprised everyone at the barbecue and excitedly said their hellos, the odd guy out in his extra-large, red-and-white Hawaiian button-up shirt was about to leave when Greg invited him to join them for some food. He felt that is was the least that he could do. He instantly accepted, and the party continued.

The sun was still up and raging its madness. Most of the guys went for a swim to cool off and then rejoined the others around the tables.

Budd noticed that Greg's daughter was all of a sudden gone from the end of the table where she had been sitting all day, and her snow cone was melting. They were all pretty protective and were sort of like uncles to the kids.

Jacky was a beautiful, very sweet eleven-year-old. She had copious amounts of long golden hair and long legs. For eleven, she was already tall for her age, and she stood out. She had blue eyes and dark skin, just stunning.

Budd asked Greg, "Hey, dude, where's Jacky? Her snow cone is melting."

"She was right there a few minutes ago," he replied.

Greg asked his ex-wife, and she didn't know. Within a few minutes, Will noticed that the stranger who'd given Greg a ride was also missing.

They quickly spread out and began looking around the pool and area. Geno came running and yelling, "His car's gone! The creep's car is gone!"

They regrouped and decided to go different directions to look for this man's car.

There were probably five cars going in different directions.

Will, a guy named Glenn who had lived in Natruna for his entire life, and Roger went in one car and were headed to Village Gully, but for some strange reason, Glenn said,

"Hey, dudes, we need to go to Stele Range." Why he came up with that, no one could understand, but they had to go with his gut. They spun around and headed in the other direction to the range. As they neared Stele Range, they spotted the car's shiny blue roof. The car was parked down the dirt road, totally secluded.

They parked their car close to the highway and began running down the road.

Upon coming up on the car, they could see the two of them naked in the backseat of the car, the stranger and Jacky. This big, fat, sweaty man was on top of this young, innocent little girl, who wasn't making a sound.

Roger flung the passenger-side door open and yanked the pervert out of the car. Glenn reached in and pulled Jacky's limp body from the backseat. She was breathing, moaning, and slobbering drunk. He had literally made her drink whiskey and at times even poured it into her mouth, ordering her to drink and threatening to kill her and the rest of her family if she didn't comply.

Glenn wrapped her up in a towel and began running back toward his car with her in his arms, yelling, "I am going to get help! Do not let that son of a bitch go!"

It must have been challenging, running barefoot on the hot sand, but he was flying, not knowing what condition Jacky was actually in.

Roger and Will heard the car drive away, and it was just them and the rapist.

They made him get on his knees behind his car and look down so they couldn't see his face.

Roger looked at Will and said, "Let's kill him."

Will took a breath, looked at the ground, and had a flash of Jacky earlier that day playing with her little brother, laughing and smiling her innocent, beautiful smile.

He had visions of her as a baby, as a toddler dancing in

Greg and Clair's living room, and then just the year before when he'd seen her and her friends snickering and playing on their bicycles in the front yard, and he thought about how amazing and joyful she was. He knew that she would never be the same.

This brought anger and rage to him and he seriously contemplated killing this man. Not really having trust in the court system, he thought to himself that taking this creep from this world would prevent this from happening to any other young girl.

Will looked around at the vast mountains, the miles of un-walked land, and thought about it.

Will didn't reply. He was thinking. They should kill him, he knew they should.

CHAPTER 29

IT WAS A dreary night. The desert air was moist, and the dampness of the sagebrush engulfed all of Natruna's air, almost like a new light or cleansing. It was anything but revitalizing.

It dropped down to a nippy fifty degrees. They had celebrated Carha's birthday the day before, which was a day erased from her memory. However, the night was not and could never be. The night was as remembered as an engraving in stone.

The stars were bright and moving along to their midnight dance along with the crickets.

Carha and Billy were awakened on that Friday evening by two policemen who knocked on the front door. They showed their IDs to these two young children after properly introducing themselves but never stated the actual reason for their visit. They asked a few questions while the four walked onto the porch and looked toward the sky and discussed the crisp desert air.

The small yellow porch light shone downward, almost like mood lighting, creating graceful shadows in the front yard.

"Is there anyone else in your home with you?"

"No," Carha replied.

"Do you know where everyone has gone?"

"No," Carha shyly responded.

The pauses in the conversation were almost natural. The two kids didn't question why they were there. They felt sort of comforted and reassured having these men of uniform on their porch.

Before long, Maggie was turning up Flower Street in Phillip's truck, closely tailing a sheriff's car that was silently flashing its colorful lights. The scene seemed to move calmly in slow motion.

Maggie pulled up in front of the mailbox and got out of the truck, approaching Carha and Billy with a solemn, worried look on her face. She had black mascara lines running vertically down her face.

Upon closer inspection, she seemed disheveled and stressed.

Maggie began, "Kids, there has been an accident, and we need to go to the hospital." She then instructed the two to go get dressed.

Their new cop friends looked at the two while nodding, reassuring them, "Yes, do as your sister instructed you to do."

After the kids changed and headed out the front door, they found Anna there. She was standing on the freshly raked and watered-down yard with a young, gangly, dark-headed, clean-shaven deputy. Her head was tilted upward, her eyes weary, and her shaky mouth moved, but her words couldn't be heard. She had her hands in front of her, rolling while continually caressing her right and left fingers against one another and then twisting and turning her palms opposite of each other. Her petite body quivered.

Carha looked at their shoes and heavy boots and

thought to herself, *How can they not feel badly about making those indentations in the recently groomed yard that Mom worked so hard on?*

Anna, Carha, and eight-year-old Billy all piled into Phillip's truck, and they were off and on their way to Maggie's apartment to make some calls and get some of her things together as she explained what she knew to her siblings.

The kids waited and paced the apartment while Maggie called their father to explain. He was working the night shift at the plant. All of a sudden, Maggie seemed to become more anxious with every passing moment and hurried the kids back out to the truck to head to Ridgefield Hospital.

The thirty-minute drive to the hospital was divided by minutes of nonstop verbiage pertaining to what might have happened, how it happened, and what was happening right then. Then there were minutes of nothing except worried, agitated energies taking up too much of the vehicle's oxygen.

The mountain peaks didn't change from one rocky peak to another as they usually did; they seemed to connect in synchronization while Carha fought hard to keep alert and awake during such a crisis. Her head was flooded with her confused thoughts.

It was after midnight by the time they arrived at the hospital. The family held hands as they walked across the parking lot and through the giant glass doors while making eye contact with one another for support and to gather strength needed to face what was ahead.

The waiting room was decorated in dark brown and light browns, all in befuddling shapes.

The siblings sat still without any further information, without interaction from a soul, just united together with every agonizing minute.

"What's going on? Come on, tell us. This is too much!" Anna and Maggie took turns twisting and turning from one side to another on the firm cushioned chairs while huffing and whispering aloud their frustrations, exhausted but with adrenaline flowing through their young veins at the same time. Not a healthy combination.

Finally, a nurse's silhouette calmly walked toward the group, which was anxiously waiting in the dim, eerie hospital waiting room.

"Only a few bruises," she reassured. "She's pretty banged up, but it looks like she will be okay. You all can't go back there just yet, so sit tight. The doctor will be out shortly to talk to y'all."

Finally, air came into their lungs. Thank God. They all let out sighs of relief and praised the Lord.

A few more hours sluggishly passed by, they were feeling pretty beat up, using one another as pillows while attempting to find relief for their tired, burning eyes. They all kept awake while restlessly working on finding comfortable positions, which were nonexistent.

Finally, a different, much younger-looking nurse approached them and whispered directly to Maggie. "Hi, I'm Ms. Hillary. Sorry that this is taking so long, but I wanted to let you know that everything is okay. It shouldn't be much longer."

Maggie looked up at her, nodded her head, and quietly responded, "Thank you."

It was almost morning; the sun was beginning to pierce the large windows like little sharp toothpicks stabbing their eyes.

Becoming frustrated with the medical staff, Anna asked Maggie, "Why is it taking so long? Shouldn't we know by now? This is mad!"

Maggie nodded her head in agreement.

It was almost 7:00 a.m. when a man also dressed all in white walked directly toward the family. His eyes were squinted and red, and his face serious as he introduced himself.

"Hello, I'm Dr. Jonas. It's a bit worse than what we had thought; there is a possibility that she may have suffered a spinal injury. She is in critical condition at this time. I am sorry."

"What? No, that's not what you all said. No, this can't be ... she just has cuts and bruises. Do you have the right woman? Maybe you all are confused. That's okay. It must get confusing between patients back there," Carha's conscience rebutted.

This middle-aged asshole of a doctor instructed them to follow him.

They followed one another in a single line. They heard a man screaming from behind one of the many enormous blue curtains which hung from the metal rings attached to the ceiling. Everything was white and hazy.

As they moved through the vacant, unnerving passageway, they couldn't help but to try to perversely peek at those sick behind the curtains. There were only cracks revealing partial faces, partial bedside tables, tubes dangling to the floors, yellow basins, and blue blankets elevated at the ends of their beds by their feet underneath, as white uniforms moved swiftly in and out.

It seemed quiet until they heard the moaning and crying of that man again. This time, his voice was irritatingly recognizable. He must be severely hurt, yet there wasn't any pity felt for this man, only the guilt of what the children were actually thinking and wishing.

Their hearts were beating so fast that they felt as though they were going to explode from their chests. The longer they walked, the harder it was to breathe.

The doctor stopped in front of the corner room, which was protected by frosted glass windows and heavy drapes on the other side of them to provide for privacy. He then waved his hands, gesturing for them to enter.

There she was underneath the machines, tubes, and bandages. It was her, wasn't it? Only parts of her were identifiable.

She had a plastic breathing tube coming from the mouth. There was a large, square machine standing next to her making a soft, rhythmic noise as she took breaths—to give her breaths, the doctor explained. Small lights flashed, and numbers were displayed on the machine each time she breathed.

The doctor explained that it was called an "endo-something" tube, or ET tube for short. He said that the tube went down her throat, between the vocal cords, and into the large airway of the lungs. The breathing tube was connected to a hose. Those hose connected to a ventilator, which was the machine helping her breathe.

She wouldn't open her eyes. It felt like she wasn't even there, even though she was. The kids begin to cry, each one.

The doctor said that she wasn't in any pain. They were giving her strong pain medication to help her. He must have known that knowing this would ease their pain some.

The kids walked closer, standing and holding on to the side rails. Occasionally, they took turns gently touching her while reassuring her, "We're here, Mom. We love you." They really wanted to scream in her ear, "*Wake up!*"

There were tubes everywhere, and there was hardly any room to safely stand.

There were only few unwrapped, available parts of her body that could be touched. There were obvious cuts, bruising, and swelling. Her eyes were so swollen that there were dark purple marks lining her eyelids. That was difficult for them.

The doctor said, "Okay, children, you will need to leave now and let her rest." Maybe the doctor wasn't that bad.

One of the detectives they had met earlier was waiting in the hallway. He murmured, "I'm sorry to interrupt. I understand that you all are all very scared and upset right now, but if I could have a few minutes of your time, please."

He proceeded to explain that they still couldn't locate their sister Dana. Maggie told the police earlier that no one knew where she was, but they suspected that she was with Ted's older brother, Rusty. The redness and anger written all over this policeman's face told the children that this situation was as serious as the accident.

He wrote notes on his small pad of paper and shook his head. "I see, I see," he repeated. "It appears that Ted was driving his brother Rusty's van. Luckily, a driver passing by discovered the crash site, which was almost an hour northeast of Natruna, heading toward Devil's Valley. Why they were out that far is puzzling. It took almost another two hours for the ambulance to arrive. Between the drive to a telephone and then for the ambulance to get there ... The paramedic found your mother lying on a large boulder. She landed on her back. She was unconscious. She is fortunate to be alive, we all agree." He shook is his head again. "They were apparently drinking. I will be around if you should need me, and please call this number if your sister shows up." He handed a small card to Maggie.

They froze in silence, in unity. What would they do now?

At that very moment, a man with dark, shiny hair all slicked back with grease and wearing dark clothes walked toward them. He had a sad but calming manner about him. He introduced himself as Adam Vanderwerken, the hospital's clergyman.

He apologized for what they were going through. After slowly saying a few more words, he looked down at the floor and paused for what seemed to be minutes. Then he repeated the process. He didn't seem to have a lot to say. What already seemed like a dark and somber time now felt even worse.

This minister asked if they would join him in the chapel for prayer. There was nothing else that they could do. They agreed and stood in a circle behind the wooden pews with their hands joined, repeating after him as many of the words that they could remember. If they repeated the prayer and really meant it, God would have to hear them.

Hours passed, and Dana was still nowhere to be found. This compounded their worry. Bill joined the search, trying to locate her without any luck. He finally joined the kids at the hospital. By this time, it was almost noon. His eyes were bloodshot and puffy, and his skin pale, but he was as quiet and composed as always.

Dana finally arrived to the hospital, wasted and reeking of alcohol. She had been with Rusty that night, hiding out at a friend's house. They couldn't imagine what was going through their dad's head.

Rusty went inside of the hospital to see his brother but entered through the back door. He must have known it was safer.

Ted had already been discharged from the hospital, suffering from only a minor leg injury—that was it. He knew to stay away from Patria and her family at that point.

Bill just paced the waiting room, staying to himself but near enough to have his eyes on his family.

Dr. Jonas and the younger nurse informed everyone

that Patria needed to be airlifted to Kern Medical Center in Bakersfield immediately, where they had a team of specialists there to help her. He advised the children to visit their mother and to say their good-byes. "There isn't time to waste," he added.

The children asked their dad to join them, but he refused. He said that he didn't want to upset her.

The intensive care unit wasn't any less terrifying than the ER. Patria was in the same exact state as she was earlier that morning—same tubes, same bruises, same bandages, and same cataleptic sleep.

Bill phoned his sister Natalie to inform her of what happened. He asked if the kids could stay with her and Uncle Chuck. "Of course," she quickly responded.

They swiftly headed back to Natruna to gather their belongings, just to immediately turn back around, drive past Ridgefield, and then continue for another four and a half hours to get to their aunt and uncle's.

Natalie was the acting liaison for the family and hospital. She and her family took charge with loving care over the Stone children.

Patria arrived safely at the hospital in Bakersfield. Natalie and Maggie were there upon her arrival but weren't allowed to see her. The rest of the kids were resting at Natalie's.

It wasn't until that evening that the two physicians came into a new waiting room to discuss Patria's condition with the Natalie and Maggie.

"She has broken several of her vertebrae and is still in critical condition. We have to do surgery now, or she will die. She will never walk again ... if she makes it through the surgery." They seemed genuinely saddened by the situation. The physicians added, "Only time will tell."

CHAPTER 30

WILL STOOD OVER the pedophile freak and contemplated what he should do next.

Roger looked around and at the lowlife.

The pig began to plea, "Please don't kill me!" He began to cry and beg that they let him get his clothes on. His skin was reddening, hot and wet from perspiration.

Roger's and Will's breathing became faster, their hearts beating faster and faster.

Roger told him to shut the fuck up and then kicked him in the thigh, hard. The guy moaned. Will pushed him and told him to shut up. The lowlife cried and begged for his life, which sickened Roger and Will.

All they could see was Jacky ... and it made them see red.

They beat him badly.

When the cops showed up, he was dirty, muddy, and bloody, crying to the cops that the two guys beat him up repeatedly.

The cops ignored his cries. The cops dragged his naked body to their car and read him his Miranda rights. After they placed him in the backseat, he kept repeating, "I want those two arrested for what they did to me!"

His eyes were swollen and already changing color, his lip fat and bleeding, and dirt stuck to his dreadful face. The officer calmly and professionally stated, "In the United States, civilians are empowered to stop perpetrators in the act of a serious crime and use reasonable force to hold them until an officer of the law arrives on the scene, and you, sir, were trying to flee the scene. These two gentlemen were doing their lawful duty."

No one had questioned Roger or Will up to that point.

Jacky's parents protected and shielded her for many months that followed. The group never asked how she was doing. No one talked about it. It was too difficult, and because it wasn't brought up, no one felt it appropriate to discuss.

Will, Roger, and Glenn all went to court to testify several times, and then it was quiet. Jacky's mom told them that the court case was over now and thanked them for what they did. That was it. They were never told what happened to the rapist, and they never asked, but always secretly believed they had made a mistake by letting him live.

Jacky was never the same after that. She was too silent.

Life continued in Natruna …

Months later, Will, Roger, Budd, and another man named Steve were all working a roofing job out at West Point inside of the plant. They had worked many roofing jobs in the past and had the process down. Will thought it was cool and adventurous doing roofing because of the risk involved. The heights were atrocious inside of the plants. And the big buckets of hot tar heated to 525 degrees added to the danger. It seemed like they all felt a bit of a rush, but they also practiced safety. They wore their harnesses and didn't take their jobs lightly.

This particular roof was of sloped, corrugated metal, which made it particularly dangerous. It was on a very large storage shed that sheltered chemicals. It was almost February, but it seemed to be warmer, which was nice for the small crew. They had been working the job for several weeks and were pretty much in the groove of things.

That day they were hauling ass and were proud of themselves. They were the team to beat, and they knew it. They had just finished their lunches, and after spending so much time together, they knew just about everything there was to know about one another. It had been about three or four years by this time, and they had each other's backs.

They loved to give each other shit and joke around. It was a lot of fun for them, and they were extremely close. They had been through some pretty serious situations, which bonded them even more.

For Will, these friends had become his family. They were all quite a bit older and took Will under their wings. They cared for him and accepted him for all of his faults, and as he used to say, "I really dug it."

They were finishing up that day, each were harnessed to rope, which was properly secured by the two anchoring points at the end.

Budd was making his way to the other side of the ventilation unit and decided to unhook his harness to get around in; he planned on reharnessing once on the other side of it. In doing so, he lost his footing, and his feet slipped backward. He tried to catch his balance, and Will could see him working on it. He could also see the fear in Budd's eyes as he continued slipping backward.

It happened too fast to do anything.

Budd fell twenty-five feet backward into a large dumpster, hitting the back of his head on the edge of the dumpster. The guys got off the roof as fast as they could to help him. He was unconscious, bleeding from his head, and making abnormal sounds.

They pulled him out and tried to help him. They called the plant medics, who began resuscitation measures.

The ambulance took forever, as they always seemed to in these situations.

The crew arrived, turned on the sirens, and sped away, with Roger, his brother, following distraughtly behind.

Within the hour, Will, Geno, Glenn, Steve, Budd's wife, and a bunch of others arrived at the hospital.

Budd was pronounced dead shortly after they arrived. He was thirty years old, was married, and had a young son.

Will could not believe it. Within seconds, he was gone. If he only would have had his harness in place and if only the dumpster wasn't there. Will went through a time in a dreamlike state of disbelief and pain.

Roger never recovered from the loss of his brother and began drinking even more than usual. He drowned his pain in alcohol. He couldn't function. It was really on that day that Roger died too. The person he had been, had left the earth.

He never worked the same; he didn't take care of himself. His appearance changed. It became harder and harder for his friends to grieve the loss of Budd when they were also grieving and worrying about Roger.

He drank and drank until his death eleven years later.

A few months after Budd died, Will struggled to keep on the right track. He quit his job doing construction. It seemed to remind him of Budd and Roger too much, and the calm in him slowly disappeared.

You would think that he would never drive fast or recklessly after what he'd witnessed, but it was the opposite for Will. In his mind, it was be crazy and free, because it could be over at any time, and it doesn't matter.

That year, Will spent four and a half months in the county jail, thinking about his feelings. They arrested him for the failure to appear for speeding tickets—not just one but seventeen of them. He actually had thirty of them altogether, but the jail time was for the seventeen.

After the first couple, he began throwing them in his glove compartment, crinkling them up after that, and throwing them in with the others. He gave up after a few.

The jail was hours from his hometown, and no one, not one person, visited him while he was there. Not one letter, not one phone call, nothing.

After being released, he hung out wherever he could get some sleep. He had lost his apartment and anything and everything he had. His parents still didn't want anything to do with him, and he didn't talk much to his sisters anymore.

He resumed his friendship with Geno, and that was comforting.

While Will was away, Geno had met a girl in Hickersville and couldn't get his mind off of her. His obsession quickly involved Will, and any chance they got, they were exploring new friendships in another town.

Trips to Hickersville became costly. After losing his license and car, Will wasn't going to be driving for a while, so at times, they hitched rides. Sometimes they didn't have any money for a room or a place to stay. They were long nights.

Once they broke into a vacant double-wide mobile home and wrapped themselves in carpet to sleep, but they favored breaking into motel rooms more. They did whatever it took to fit their lifestyles: partying, girls, and more partying.

On one of those trips, Will met Dion and quickly fell for her. She was one girl that he didn't want to be a one-night stand. She was living with friends, an emancipated minor, and she was very popular. Will had never known anyone so young that lived out on his or her own like that.

Dion's mother died of cancer, and her father shot himself. She was pretty messed up, but she also showed unbelievable strength, which was an attraction for Will.

She was different from girls in Natruna, and she fell head over heels for Will. She was a thin girl, really a bit plain looking, fair skinned, with reedy blonde hair, dark eyes, and a nice smile.

It didn't take Will long to come to the conclusion that he wanted to take care of her and to get his life in order. He got a job as a contractor at the plant, which he felt grateful for to be given another chance. They eventually rented a house in Village Gully, and moved in together. It wasn't long before Dion was pregnant. It wasn't planned. She was on birth control, but it happened. Unfortunately, at the time she became pregnant, they both felt that it was all a mistake. It happened too fast, but it was too late.

They began living separate lives in the same house. Will was hardly home, and Dion was involved with her studies and friends at school. She was still finishing her high school diploma, and it was almost near graduation.

Graduation in June, baby in January... that was doable.

Will came home one day to find Dion studying with some geek named Peter. He wore high waters and thick glasses. Will wasn't jealous, but he didn't want to be overly friendly to some guy hanging out in his home with his pregnant girlfriend.

Later Will and Peter became best of friends, but on that day, neither of them knew it. Seems the way that life is, you never know why someone is put in your path and you in theirs.

Finally Will's healthier choices and hard work paid off and he got a permanent job at the chemical plant! He ended up being on the same shift as Bill Stone-this was prior to the car accident. He was immediately taken aback by this man's gentleness and short stature. Maggie used to tell stories of how her father was this intimidating man. Will quickly learned that his childhood friend had hugely inflated reality.

He took to Mr. Stone and began to look forward to their daily walks and talks while departing from the plant after the swing shift. Will felt Bill to be soft-spoken and very laid back. Not only did he like this man, he also felt sorry for him and his family situation.

Little did Will know how close and connected that he would one day be to Bill Stone and the Stone family, up to Bill's final breath.

CHAPTER 31

A FEW DAYS following the accident, Bill had to take care of things on the home front in order to prepare for his children's eventual return home. He notified his boss that he would need some time off from work. He decided that the best place for the kids would be in their own home, the only one they knew. He also would return to his home for as long as needed.

Walking through the home to assess what needed to be done was another painful experience. Things were different. There were new things, moved things, and what was once a nice home was now falling apart.

It felt diseased, unhealthy, and plagued.

For one, the heavy front door looked as though it had been kicked in. The dead bolt had been forced through the concrete wall. It appeared to have taken a huge part of the wall along with it, according to the patch job. It couldn't even close right.

There were a few broken windows in the living room, where taped cardboard was now covering over them. The carpet even seemed to have aged with the stress. The heater wasn't heating. The house was cold in more ways than one.

The bedroom that he once shared with his wife had Ted's things strung all over it—his clothes, knickknacks, pictures, shoes, a watch, and some other jewelry, a variety of feather roach clips, a repulsive worn leather jacket draped over a chair. There were also empty beer bottles strewn throughout the house.

On top of it all, in his garage, he found motors, car parts, and tools that he knew didn't belong to Patria.

Anger boiled up inside him, rage and helplessness for what had become of his home and his life.

He sat by himself in the old green lawn chair next to his old workbench in the backyard, recollecting the past.

When he first saw Patria as a young, beautiful woman at Sidney and Wylie's ... her gorgeous smile and laugh in reaction to his dumb jokes. The way that she looked at him with so much love and admiration. The first time he met baby Maggie and how much she cherished and needed him. The first time that he and Patria made love. Their first small home together and how happy they were. Moving to Natruna, all piled in the station wagon, and the excitement of it all. Having their babies and the pride they felt together in what they created.

How did we get here? And now she might die. My kids ... our lives ... their future ... my dear wife. What we have been through. How could this happen? This can't be happening, Bill contemplated.

He remembered his own childhood and parent's relationship. As far as Billy could remember, his parents got along well. He did recall one argument. It was after World War II broke out, and Erland told Dora that he wanted to go fight. Dora told him, "There is no way you are leaving this family to fight any war!" Dora was furious at him. Billy remembered vividly hearing his dad's only reply to the one-way argument, which was, "I'm dying, anyway."

Billy's painful childhood memories come flooding back like knives jabbing his heart and awakening it like it hadn't felt since he was an eleven year old young boy. He didn't want to remember, he didn't want to think of it. He had buried it, he had drowned it in his alcoholism, his hidden illness, condition…yet here it comes likes a splinter festering inside of him, inside of his soul. If he feels it, it may infect him like the plaque. But this time, this moment, he can't keep it inside, it refuses.

It was like a foggy, surreal recorder in Billy's head which he hadn't played since the Air Force or at least when it tried to play, he purposely hit the "stop" button.

The day when he and Natalie were the first to arrive home…it was extremely hot day that day and maybe a little humid which was unusual. He was probably only around nine years old. The two young siblings were almost to their property, jabbering away like they did, when they heard the sound of a gunshot. It came from inside the house. They began to run, almost racing one another subconsciously. Upon entering the house, it was eerily quiet. Billy noticed a burnt, smoky smell as he flew through the door. It slowed him down, almost to a tiptoe.

There were two different doors which entered into the kitchen, one from the backdoor and one from the living room. Billy ran through the backdoor, while Natalie ran through the one from the living room.

Natalie was the first to see her father lying on the floor, looking first to see the bottom of his boots, then his legs, and in one single picture … the gun a few inches from her dad's hand, his fingers still twitching, thick bright red blood flowing from the side of his head and face, the pillow beside his head slowly swallowing in some of the blood. She covered her eyes with her hands and froze in time.

Billy entered through the door with the view of the top of his dad's head.

He was confused. His first thought was that the doctor must have placed red Jell-O all over his dad's head. Then he thought that he had cracked a bowl of Jell-O on his head. But he didn't recognize the bowl. It was not like one he had seen before. This one was white, no gray. It looked strange like an animal's bone. He couldn't understand. Then he asked himself, "Why is part of his head separate then the other part? Why is his head broken and the insides of his head on the floor?" He became angry and thought that they doctor did something to him. There was so much blood over his head and face and flowing over the floor. It was even bubbling up in different places. It was thick and had white stuff all in it. "Mother won't be able to clean that up." He thought. Then he saw the gun. It was smoking and his father's hand was sometimes jerking up next to the gun. He stood frozen and couldn't move. He just stared at his father, examining the entire picture and trying to make sense of it all. He knew what happened deep down but couldn't grasp that his father put the gun to his head and pulled the trigger. Why would he do that? He taught his kids gun safety and knew that he couldn't do that. To have the children find him that way…to even chance that they could find him. Why? Did he have a time of mental incapacitation? Who would do that to their kids?

Natalie looked up to see her little brother's white face. She ran to him, hopping over her father's arm and the gun. She slipped on the blood. Billie watched as if it were in slow motion as Natalie pushed herself up from the floor, her hand now drenched in warm blood, leaving her small hand print stamped next to her father's head and matter.

It felt like the world went silent and came to a complete stop.

Natalie needn't study her father for life. She knew the very instant that she saw him lying there that he was dead. It wasn't the traumatic injury as much as the feeling of nothing. There wasn't anything inside of him. His energy left his body. She knew that.

Billie couldn't hear anything except grunting, distressed quick breaths in and out of his sister as well as his own heart beating so hard and loud in his chest that it felt like it had climbed into his throat cutting off his air.

Billie looked foggily at the blood over her sister's dress and thought that she may get into trouble.

He was numb and very hot. His skin felt like it was on fire and he couldn't breathe again.

The picture began to blur and blur, mutating into a thick white fog. His lips began to tingle and he felt like his legs couldn't hold his body up any more.

At that time, Natalie yanked him by his hand, twirling him around and pulling him towards and out the front door.

The air felt a little bit better.

Natalie made Billie sit down on the steps next to her. She wrapped herself all the way around her little brother's body and squeezed hard. They shook together. She rubbed his back, his arms as she told him that it was going to be alright. "It will be alright Billie, I have you," She repeated over and over.

Billie could only quiver. His thoughts and feelings were too much to make out. He felt like it was too much to try at that point.

He and Natalie were the only ones home that day. The two siblings waited outside in the blistering heat until their mother and baby sister finally arrived... what seemed hours later. They just sat there on the steps, their sweaty legs touching, their bodies shaking next to one another, and their tears flowing, synchronized in disparity.

The blood dried on Natalie's hand and dress created a horrific nauseating smell that was difficult to ever expunge from their senses.

Natalie always felt that she should have been the one to enter through that doorway, not Billy. She felt that she should have protected her little brother.

That afternoon, the doctor, Dora, and Toby placed Erland's body on a bed, where they washed and prepared him.

The following day, Dora told Billy to take Suzanna to the front yard and stay there until she told them otherwise. He heard voices and commotion coming from the backyard. He left Suzanna, curiosity getting the best of him, and went to look. They were washing out the blood-soaked mattress with the hose. The bright red blood just kept coming out from it until it was finally pink; it soaked deep into the ground of their yard.

The mattress stayed out there, leaning against the side of the house to dry for what seemed like weeks. Billy tried not to look at it or think of it, but he couldn't help it. When they eventually brought it back into the house, they placed that same mattress exactly where it was originally. Billy and Toby slept on it for the remaining years while still living there.

When questioned about that day, Billy said, "I wasn't mad at him. I wasn't mad at all."

A few days after his dad's death, when their bus driver was dropping them off at their stop, he pointed up towards the house and made an announcement to all of the kids remaining on the bus, "That's where Old Man Stone killed himself." This made Billy angry at the bus driver. He felt that it wasn't necessary for him to announce that; it was private and personal. It hurt to hear it and to know that it was true. His father was gone and took his own life at the young age of forty-four. Billy would never see him again.

Billy's mother, Dora, never spoke of it. She couldn't put words to her grief, so they tried to move on in bitter silence. His suicide demanded an explanation ... a simple truth. If little Billy would have had some kind of explanation, he wouldn't have filled the void he felt with his own interpretation, which naturally gravitated toward blame and guilt. He didn't have a choice to fully understand and to free himself of the dreaded assumptions that resided deep in his bone marrow.

At such a young age, Billy didn't actually know that his father was dead and not coming back. Every day, every week, every month, and every year thereafter, Billy's understanding of his father's suicide changed with his evolving maturity. He had new questions about his father but never asked. It wasn't an open forum.

Then he sobbed and sobbed for it all…he cried for the loss of his father years earlier for the first time in a long time, for the loss of his family, of his home and for the probable loss of his wife and he cried for hours.

Bill left and went to his rental, grabbed a suitcase, and

headed toward his family.

Hours passed, and time stood still. Why was it taking so long? When would it be over? All of the family anxiously waited. Bill had made it back to the hospital and also waited with his family for what took hours. Finally, a doctor came out shouting, "Stone family!" as if they had won a prize. The physician's eyes searched through the filled waiting room.

Natalie looked up, raised her arm in the air. "Over here!"

The doctor quickly walked over to them and sat down in the chair. Everyone gathered around to hear.

The doctor explained, "Okay, we placed a Harrington rod down her back to replace and support her vertebrae. It was even worse than we had expected. She completely severed her T12, meaning she will not walk again and never be able to move anything from her waist down. She also had subtle fractures to the surrounding thoracic vertebrae."

He paused, ran his hand through his hair, took a breath, and continued, "She seems to want to stop breathing, almost like her will to fight just isn't there. These injuries shouldn't be affecting her breathing ability, yet she has stopped breathing many times. It is perplexing. We have had to perform CPR on her twice now." He glanced behind him at the obedient nurse. She appeared to disapprove of his statement.

Why would she not fight, and how did he know that she wasn't? He wasn't God.

"She has lost a lot of blood since the accident, and we've already began transfusing blood, but the blood bank is short," the doctor reported.

"Can we see her?" Maggie asked.

The doctor answered, "As soon as she is out of recovery and is more stable. Hang in there." He waved his hand as he shuffled from the waiting room, his long white coat floating behind.

They volunteered to donate blood, but only Bill was a match.

He donated as much as he possibly could give to her. After having the A-negative pint of blood extracted from his worn-out body, he fainted over and over again when trying to get up from the table. It took hours, patience from the nurses, and five large glasses of orange juice to finally bring him around, but he had no regrets.

Bill once again returned home to Flower Street and prepare for the kids return home. While driving, he had time to think.

He took anything and everything that belonged to Ted Horta and threw it all to the end of the driveway. He didn't box anything up; he didn't wrap anything to protect it. He didn't even place items or clothing in bags or suitcases. It all went in one big pile smack-dab on top of good-old Natruna soil. Then he gave Ted a ring and told him to come and get his damned stuff or it was going to the dump.

That afternoon, Ted did as he was told. He and Rusty quickly loaded his belongings and drove away without a word.

Patria wasn't doing well. Bill was advised by his sister to return to Bakersfield as quickly as possible. Patria's heart stopped several times. They'd had to shock her, and they tried every medication they could think of to assist with the circulation to her heart and organs. It didn't look good.

Only the adults were allowed into the intensive care unit to see Patria; Carha and Billy weren't permitted to see her, due to their age.

Bill went into the unit but stayed outside her room. Maggie, Chuck, Natalie, Dana, and Anna all went in to find her looking worse than before.

There wasn't any color to her face. She was swollen and still had tubes coming out in every direction. Machines were loud and distracting. She was unresponsive no matter what they said to her. The doctors reassured the family that she could still hear them and that they should talk to her.

They stood around her bed, softly expressing their love for her. They all took turns saying something. Anna could hardly speak. Her words were stuck inside of her.

When it was Dana's turn, she cried, "Mom, I'm so sorry for the pain that I've caused you. Please don't leave us. We need you. Please, Mom … I'm sorry. Please, Mom. I'll be better." She repeated this over and over until Natalie had to embrace to calm her, saying to her, "It's okay, Dana. She's not mad at you. She loves you. It's okay."

The Stone children couldn't have imagined what was ahead of them…the dysfunction that they had endured up to this point was only the beginning but again, through all of the hardships, there were also blessings and blessings sometimes came from the most unexpected people, places and things.

Through it all, came love and bonds that were rooted so deeply that they could never be broken. Some families never have the ability to experience such unwavering and unconditional love.

And through it all, they laughed, played, enjoyed the good things in life and were grateful, for the most part.

No regrets, only lessons learned to guide and lead them on their lives paths.

ACKNOWLEDGEMENTS

Naomi, Chris and Sara from *The Artful Editor*.

My tolerant and generous co-editors —Bob, Fallon and Sarai.

All those who guided me, listened to me and gave me helpful advice while on my journey.

About The Author

Caroline Snow was born and raised in the California desert. She has been a registered nurse for twenty years and practices the mind, body, and spirit approach to health care. She believes in reaching inwardly to find resolutions, creativity, and peace. She has been a lifelong writer and currently lives in Northern California with her husband and Goldendoodle, Roo. She loves life thoroughly and tries to read, write, enjoy the outdoors, stay healthy, travel, eat amazing food, and spend time with her family as much as possible. *Flowers of Dysfunction, Part One* is her first literary fiction novel and the first in a series of three.

By *Caroline Snow*

* Flowers of Dysfunction, Part One

* Flowers of Dysfunction, Part Two (not yet published) - follows Carha's life from adolescence through early adulthood.

* Flowers of Dysfunction, Part Three (not yet published) - follows Carha's life from early adulthood to middle age.